THE BOY IN THE WOODS

THE BOY IN THE WOODS

Carter Wilson

This first world edition published 2014
in Great Britain and the USA by
SEVERN HOUSE PUBLISHERS LTD of
19 Cedar Road, Sutton, Surrey, England, SM2 5DA.

British Library Cataloguing in Publication Data

Wilson, Carter, author.
  The boy in the woods.
  1. Authors–Fiction. 2. Suspense fiction.
  I. Title
  813.6-dc23

ISBN-13: 978-0-7278-8385-8 (cased)

All Severn House titles are printed on acid-free paper.

Severn House Publishers support the Forest Stewardship Council™ [FSC™],
the leading international forest certification organisation. All our titles that
are printed on FSC certified paper carry the FSC logo.

MIX
Paper from
responsible sources
FSC
www.fsc.org   FSC® C013056

Typeset by Palimpsest Book Production Ltd.,
Falkirk, Stirlingshire, Scotland.
Printed and bound in Great Britain by
TJ International, Padstow, Cornwall.

To Ili and Sawyer
You can't read this until you're eighteen

'The woods are a lonely place. That's why I always put the bodies there. Even dead trees need company.'

Samuel Lowry,
convicted serial killer

Turn the page for a preview of Tommy Devereaux's
upcoming novel

THE BLOOD OF THE YOUNG

ONE

I t was 1981 and we were twenty minutes away from the rest of our lives. Except for one of us.

Spencer was fourteen. He was the oldest, so we followed him everywhere. I was eight months behind him and Drew lagged two weeks on me. The three of us spent every day together in the summer. I suppose you could say we were best friends. At that age, there's a fine line between being best friends and simply having nothing better to do.

My name is Bobby. Never been a Robert or a Bob.

The summer air that day was heavy for Oregon. Mosquitoes like werewolves. We were sitting on the floor of a small crook of woods a half-mile from anything. Nothing too interesting about the woods except that was where we happened to be, which was good enough for us.

We went often to the woods.

'We could go to McKinney's and try to swipe a *Hustler*,' Drew said. It was rare he made a suggestion.

The day yawned.

'Nah.' Spencer poked at the dirt with a stick. 'That stuff just pisses me off.'

'What does?'

'Porn mags.'

'Why do they piss you off?' I asked.

'Cause I'm tired of beating off.'

I knew exactly what he meant but didn't want to say so.

'I wish I had a stack of *Hustler*s to the ceiling of my room,' Drew said. 'I never get tired of beating off.'

'That's because you're a creep,' Spencer said. He scrunched up his face. 'I just get . . . I don't know how to describe it.'

I knew how. Maybe that's why I became a writer.

'Frustrated,' I said.

'Yes.' He pointed the stick at me. The small gesture made me proud. 'Frustrated. Exactly. Sick of drooling over chicks I can't have.'

'Get used to it.'

'Blow me.' This was Spencer's preferred phrase of dismissal. 'I'm the only one who's felt a chick up.'

Heather Winalda. We had all heard the story. I wanted to say she let anyone feel her up, but since she'd never let me feel her up I kept my mouth shut. Someone once told me she showed herself to Mike McCarty in the girls' room. I didn't believe it, but I had the image in my mind for months.

I wasn't a bad-looking kid, but I wasn't a good-looking one either. I stood in the shadows of mediocrity, cloaked in a general awkwardness and eaten alive by hormones like they were nits.

Sunlight tore through a crack in the dense foliage above us. About noon, I guessed.

'Burger King?' I suggested. A squirrel edged up to our pile of bikes in the dirt and sniffed at a tire. Drew threw a small rock at it that went far right. Squirrel didn't seem to notice.

'Works for me.'

'I need some money.'

'Jesus, Bobby. You always need money.'

'We all need money,' I said. 'I just don't happen to have any.'

'I got ya,' Drew said, patting his front pocket.

'Thanks.' Drew could afford it. He got ten bucks a week from his parents just for being a fuck-all.

My Walkman bulged in the front pocket of my shorts. I wore the bulky headphones like most kids wore baseball hats: all the time. I took the Walkman out, flipped the cassette, and pressed play. David Lee Roth started to tell me a thing or two about beautiful girls while Eddie, harmonizing behind the vocals, let his rear-loaded Charvel speak for itself. All other sounds fell away like dominoes around me, and I just watched that squirrel explore our bikes as I lost myself in the music.

After a few more seconds, something spooked the squirrel and it ran up the nearest tree. I looked over at the thin path snaking past our bikes and saw movement. Someone was coming.

I saw the boy first.

Younger than us. Several years. Black hair, cut by someone who didn't like paying barbers. Goofy grin on his face, arms dangling. I knew him.

His name was Brian. He lived four houses down from me and I

always heard he was a little soft in the head. He had never shown me anything to disprove the rumors. Brian was about ten, more or less.

I didn't know the girl walking behind Brian. She was a head taller than him, and when Brian shuffled to the side, I could see all of her at once. Long red hair swished side to side as she made her way toward us. She wore a tank top and shorts, both of which she was on the cusp of outgrowing. She looked at us and smiled. My insides stirred.

I turned my music off.

'Goddamn,' Drew said. Something must've stirred in him, too.

'Hi, guys,' Brian said, his small voice creaking.

'Hi, yourself,' Spencer called out. He stood. 'Who are you?'

'The kid lives near me,' I muttered. 'I don't know who the girl is.'

She came within ten feet of us and stopped. Brian clamored right up to me like a puppy.

'This some kind of secret place or something?' she asked.

'Nothing secret about it.' I watched Spencer's gaze take her in as she put a hand on her hip.

She nodded at Brian. 'I found him wandering alone.'

'He's always alone,' I said. 'I see him around our block all the time.'

Her eyes widened a fraction as she studied Brian. 'Thought I'd help him find his home.'

'His home is right back there,' I said, pointing in the direction from which they'd come. 'Same as mine.'

'Told you,' Brian said. He looked at me. His skin blended almost perfectly into the nougat white of his faded t-shirt. 'She said we should go for a walk.'

'What's your name?' Spencer asked her.

'Elizabeth. You?'

'Spencer.' He pointed at us. 'Bobby and Drew. You live around here?'

She nodded. 'New to the area. Dad got transferred. Came from Portland.'

'You at the high school?'

'Just started.' Her gaze flitted between all of us. 'I'm going to be a junior.'

We were all starting our freshman year.

She looked around. 'This where you guys come to smoke pot or something?'

The question seemed so . . . adult. I didn't know anyone who smoked pot.

'No,' Spencer said. 'It's just a place.'

'What do you do here?'

'Not much.' Spencer took a step toward her. He cocked his head as if listening to the wind. 'What do you think we should do here?'

'Are you taking suggestions?'

Spencer shrugged. 'Best idea so far was Drew's. Said we should go steal some *Hustlers*.'

The woods seemed to still. Brian smiled at me in a dopey way.

'What's a *Hustler*?' he whispered.

'Never mind,' I said. I shot a glance at Drew, who was staring at Elizabeth. Spencer took another step toward her.

'What did you do for fun in Portland?' he asked.

'This and that.' She took a step closer and the three of us were now in a loose circle surrounding her. She had the kind of blue eyes only redheads get to have, the color of aged denim. A thin line of sweat stained her tank top, highlighting the curve of her breasts.

Brian wandered over to a nearby tree and stared up into it.

'Where were you taking him?' I asked her. 'For real.'

'Told you. Helping him find his way home.'

'You found a kid wandering near his house and told him to go for a walk with you, then you took him into the woods? Kinda weird, don't you think?'

Her mouth broke into a thin smile. 'You sure are curious about things.'

I turned to Brian. 'I'll take you home, Brian.' I started walking toward him. 'Before your parents are missing you.' Which was bullshit. I don't think his parents would even have noticed if he was gone the whole day.

'Maybe he doesn't want to go home,' Elizabeth said.

Brian turned to me and nodded. 'I think I do want to go home.' Another nod. 'Actually.'

I put the Walkman back in my front pocket, pulled the headphones down around my neck, and then grabbed Brian's hand, which was soft and clammy. He seemed a hell of a lot more than four years younger than me.

'C'mon, Brian.'

As we got close to Elizabeth I smelled her for the first time. The woods carried her scent, which was delicious and exotic in this small clearing that was used to having only boys occupy it. She wore perfume, but it wasn't flowers I smelled. She smelled like excitement. Excitement and anticipation. I wanted to push my nose against her soft neck and breathe her in, as if by doing so I could transfer her excitement to me.

Elizabeth sidestepped toward us, smiling at me. Was she trying to block my way?

'It's OK,' Spencer said. 'Let them go. I'm sure we can find something fun to do.'

She grinned. 'Yeah? Like what?'

I could almost hear Drew panting.

Spencer spit into the dirt. 'Somethin' better than looking at *Hustlers*.'

I had never heard Spencer talk like that to a girl before. I can't say I was excited, but I sure as hell wasn't bored.

'Nah,' she said. 'You boys are too big.'

Spencer laughed, but not with humor. Nervousness. 'Too big? Too big for what?'

'For what I had in mind.' She nodded at Brian. The ten-year-old beamed. 'That's what I wanted him for.'

Spencer took his gaze away from her and looked at me. I stared back.

Was she talking about fucking the kid?

It was an impossible possibility.

Then she asked, 'Brian, you ever seen a naked girl before?'

'My mom,' he said, without the slightest hesitation.

'What about a younger girl? Like me.'

'No.' He squeezed my hand a little tighter. 'No.'

She stepped forward and came within three feet of us. Then she took off her tank top. No pause. Just took it off like she was alone in her own bedroom.

'Holy shit,' I heard Drew say.

I didn't look at Spencer's face because I couldn't stop staring at her.

'You can touch them,' she said. 'If you want.'

I felt my hands shaking as I slowly lifted them out to her, Frankenstein-like.

'No, not you.' She nodded at Brian. 'Him.'

Brian looked up at me. He was confused, but he wasn't scared.

I didn't speak, but in my look I told him everything he needed to know. Holy shit, kid. Do you realize what's going on? You're the chosen one. You might not appreciate this now. But in a few years you'll realize the significance of what's happening here. You'll be a king.

Brian nodded, not at her, but at me. In that moment I knew the kid wasn't retarded. Barely even goofy. He was just a kid, and he was about to take a big step into becoming a man.

Brian stepped forward and reached out with his right hand. His thin fingertips brushed against her puffy, going-to-be-a-junior nipples. She looked down at him and smiled.

'Good,' she said.

He began to withdraw his hand but she snatched it.

'Over here,' she said, pulling him from my grip. As I let go of him I felt a wave of jealousy wash over me. She led him to a small clearing near where our bikes slept in the dirt. As she passed Spencer, she turned to him and said, 'You can watch if you want.'

Nothing made sense. But in that moment, for a fourteen-year-old boy, it didn't have to.

The towering maples and oaks seemed to close tighter above us, locking us in. The girl told Brian to lie down in the dirt, near a pile of large rocks we occasionally used as a make-shift fire pit when we would come here at night. Brian obeyed. She stood over him and slowly lowered herself on to his crotch, her shorts against his jeans. The only piece of clothing missing between them was her shirt, so I wasn't sure what her next move was going to be. It was obvious Brian wasn't going to make any move at all. He looked up at her with wide eyes and pursed lips. My guess was he forgot to breathe.

I shot a glance at Drew. His gaze was glued to her as if watching the bottom of the ninth in game seven of a Mariners World Series. Then I glanced at Spencer. Spencer looked pissed.

'The hell you doing?' Spencer asked her. He rubbed his chest in a bothered sort of way.

She caressed her breasts with her fingertips and tilted her head back. Eyes closed. Face toward the towering trees. 'Engaging my desires,' she said.

I will always remember that. *Engaging my desires.*

She opened her eyes and looked down at Brian. 'Close your eyes, sweetie.'

Brian closed his eyes.

He kept his smile.

'Why him?' Spencer asked. 'Why not me?'

'I told you, baby. You're just too big.'

'Too big? I'd be gentle.' Spencer's voice took a hardened edge. It was all there in the tone. Frustration.

Pants still on, Elizabeth rocked back and forth on Brian.

Brian remained still as a mummy.

'Oh, baby . . .' she said. Turning toward Spencer. 'Maybe I'll do you after I do him.'

Spencer's lip pulled into a thin snarl. 'How about you do me first?'

She rotated her hips in small, tight circles. 'Like I said, I prefer 'em small.'

Brian's eyes were still closed.

I felt my excitement turning into a whole body tremor. 'Why?' I whispered. 'Why the kid?'

Elizabeth didn't answer at first. She kept pressing her pelvis against the crotch of Brian's faded, tight jeans. From where I stood I could only see her from behind, the curve of her naked waist. The strong, white shoulders. Red hair spilling down her back like water. She was fifteen feet from me but she existed in another world.

She stopped moving and turned her head toward Spencer, who stood a few feet to my right. In that moment I could finally see her face.

She had changed. The girl was no longer smiling. She was no longer anything. There was no warmth or depth to her at all.

Elizabeth was no longer human. I can't explain it any better than that.

'Because the little ones can't fight back,' she said.

Then she picked up a softball-sized rock from the fire pit, held it high over her head for less than a second, and smashed it into Brian's skull.

PART I

ONE

Denver, Colorado
Present day

Tommy Devereaux stared out from the twenty-fourth floor of the downtown Hyatt, soaking in the expanse of the Rocky Mountains, laid out before him like a painting. The Peaks Lounge was one of his usual late-afternoon writing spots. The drinks and the Wi-Fi signal were both strong, and that's about all any writer needed. More than anything, though, the lounge always had a good buzz of energy, which he preferred around him when he was working. Ironically, a room full of people talking and laughing helped him to focus. And, when he needed the help, Tommy could look into the crowd and pluck out the perfect description for a character he was writing. Characters were everywhere; all you had to do was look.

'Excuse me,' a voice said behind him.

Tommy turned and saw a middle-aged woman with dyed hair, an excess amount of makeup, and a figure that was just entering the giving-up phase of life. Pity, Tommy thought on first glance. Something about her suggested she could have been so much prettier. The woman held a book in her left hand.

A character.

'I am *so sorry* to bother you, Mr Devereaux,' she said. Tommy heard Minnesota in her voice. 'I heard you sometimes come here. I . . . I just love *all* of your books. I've read each and every one.'

'Thank you,' Tommy said.

'Can I get you to sign this, please?'

'Of course.' Tommy took the book from her hands. It was an old hardback of *The Blood We Know*. Ten years ago, that book had allowed Tommy to quit his day job as an executive in a small but profitable real-estate company. The first day he had woken up as a full-time writer and no office to go to was one of the best days in his life.

'Do you want me to sign this to anyone?'

'To Maggie would be great. Thank you so much.'

As he wrote he waited for her question. If they asked a question – and they almost always did – they waited until he was busy doing the signing.

'I was just wondering . . .' she said. She seemed to search for the right phrasing. 'How . . . how come your villains are always women?'

Third most popular question, behind *Where do you get your ideas from?* and *Will you ever let your children read your books?*

Tommy looked up at her, noticing her blue eyes. He thought she had probably been a beautiful young woman, and wondered at what age she had gone from beautiful to Maggie.

'They're not always women,' he replied. 'Sometimes they're merely girls.' He winked, letting her know that was as much of an answer as she was going to get. The truth behind the question was much too personal to discuss with the likes of Maggie. Or anyone.

Maggie smiled and nodded at him, as if he had given her all the insight into his literary soul she needed.

'Well . . . thank you, Mr Devereaux. And . . . that is, if you don't mind me saying, not *all* women are bad.'

'Of course not, Maggie. But they make much more interesting killers, don't you think?'

She nodded and smiled. 'Yes, I suppose they do. Well, then. Goodbye.'

'Goodbye, Maggie.'

She turned and started to shuffle away before she paused and turned back to him.

'Sorry, just wondering. You working on something new, Mr Devereaux?'

'Always, Maggie.'

'Can you tell me what it's called? Or is it a secret?'

If she had read all his books, why hadn't she read the first-chapter teaser of his latest work in the back of *The Blood of the Willing*?

'It's called *The Blood of the Young*.'

'What's it about?'

'You'll have to buy it to find out,' he said. 'But I will tell you it has the scariest killer yet.'

Maggie smiled. 'Oh, my. I'll make sure to buy it.' She blinked in a kind way, but to Tommy it seemed forced, as if she was trying to bring warmth into cold eyes. 'Well. Goodbye again.'

Maggie left the lounge just as a margarita materialized in front of him.

'You ever get tired of the fans?' Erin asked. She'd been serving him margaritas for years, and that was just how he liked it. Routine comforted him, even though he hated to think of himself as a routine sort of man. Still, Tommy wondered if he'd keep coming to the Hyatt if Erin wasn't here to hand him his drink.

'Never. My career wouldn't exist without them.'

'How about the ones who are fantasizing about you while you're signing their books?'

Tommy looked back to the lounge entrance. 'Who? The one who was just here?'

'Oh, please. She looked ready to devour you while you were signing her book.'

'Come on.' He felt his cheeks threatening to blush.

'A bestselling author who looks like you? I'm just sayin'.' Erin didn't pause to let him react. 'So, you writing or procrastinating today?'

Tommy was happy for the change of subject. Erin always flirted, and while he had to admit it wasn't unwelcome, he never flirted back. 'Haven't decided yet,' he said. He looked out the window and saw mountain-sized thunderheads rolling in over the Rockies, an explosion in slow motion. The late-September sky was a gunmetal blue. 'Thought I'd be here at least to watch the storm.'

'Best seat in the house. Enjoy.'

Erin left and Tommy looked at his watch. Becky would be here any minute. It was their late-afternoon routine, at least on the weekdays. *Routine.*

His wife would read while her husband wrote, and there was some kind of yin and yang to the whole process. Tommy took a sip of his margarita and opened up his laptop. The screen came to life where he left it: his latest book. *The Blood of the Young* was scheduled for publication by Christmas, but Tommy was fairly certain that wasn't going to happen. He'd already missed three deadlines, the first three of his career.

'Hey, babe,' said the voice in his ear. Tommy smiled as Becky leaned in and kissed his cheek.

'Hey, yourself.'

She sat next to him and smoothed her skirt over the top of her thighs. 'Can I tell you again how much I love these afternoon breaks? Evie has been a terror today. Melinda can deal with both of them until we get home.'

Melinda was their nanny. Sometimes Tommy wondered if Becky could remember the days when they struggled to make mortgage payments and ate ramen for dinner, while their baby boy (with colic, no less) cried endlessly with no nanny around to help. That was over a decade ago, of course. You can get used to lots of things after a decade, Tommy thought. Especially wealth.

She nodded at the computer. 'How's it going?'

'It's not going anywhere at the moment.'

'Are you stressing?'

Tommy shook his head and stared at the glowing screen. 'As Douglas Adams said, "*I love deadlines. I love the whooshing sound they make as they pass by.*"'

'Seriously, Tommy.'

'I'll have it done soon. I just need to figure out the ending.'

She touched his knee. 'Sure you don't want me to read it?'

Truth was, he couldn't wait for her to read it. But he never showed anyone – not his wife, agent, or editor – anything more than the first few chapters of a work in progress. Not until it was done.

Especially *The Blood of the Young*.

It was a special book. Worth missing three deadlines over.

The tip of Becky's shoe poked him softly in the shin. 'Well, Mr Bestseller, you let me know what I can do to help.'

He looked at her and she arched one eyebrow.

'You're sexy,' Tommy said.

'Damn right I am. You're lucky to have me.'

'Don't I know it.'

Thirteen years, Tommy thought. Thirteen years and he still wanted her day in and day out. Seemed she felt the same way.

'What's that?' she asked.

'What?'

Becky leaned over and picked up an envelope from the floor. She began to pull out the contents before stopping herself. Instead, she handed it to her husband. 'This yours?'

'I don't know,' he said, taking the envelope from her.

He removed the sheet of paper from within and began to read.
'Baby?' she asked.
Seconds or hours passed.
'Baby? What is it?'
Tommy said nothing.

TWO

He read the sentence only three times, then just stared
blankly at the words because he didn't want to look up at
his wife.

You didn't even change my name.

When Tommy was twenty-two, he'd crashed his aging Toyota Camry
into the back of a pickup. It had been raining that day and his
balding tires couldn't grip the road when the truck in front of him
slammed on its brakes. He'd been going nearly sixty miles an hour.
There came a point in that instant before the collision when Tommy
had accepted his fate. Car won't steer. Going to hit a huge piece of
metal in front of me. Don't know what's going to happen to my
body. Nothing I can do about it.

On that day, he had accepted a situation he could not control.
Somehow, deep inside himself, he knew he'd be OK. Because
Tommy Devereaux was always OK, no matter what happened.

This moment was nothing like that. Thirty years of silence just
exploded in his face.

Tommy ignored his wife's question and snapped his head toward
the front of the lounge.

Where did she go?
Maggie.
Only Maggie wasn't Maggie.
Maggie was *Elizabeth.*
Dyed hair or maybe a wig. Excessive makeup. Maybe some
padding underneath her clothes to look heavier than she actually
was. But the eyes. The blue-jean eyes were the same. He should

have known. Despite the decades, he should have recognized her, because Elizabeth was the reason why Tommy was who he was. He saw her every day in his mind.

'Tommy? What is it?'

Becky's voice was far away, calling him from outside the dream he was in.

Tommy stood and walked to the window, gripping the note in his hand.

He looked twenty-four stories down to the streets. Looking for the blonde.

There were too many people. Besides, what would he do if he saw her?

'OK, now you're freaking me out.'

This time his wife's voice was louder. Closer. He had to say something.

'Nothing.'

He was a *New York Times* bestselling author and *nothing* was the best word he could come up with.

'Nothing my ass. You read that note like it was your own obituary. What did it say?'

'It was . . .'

Come on, Tommy. What are you going to say? If you decide to lie, the lies all begin with this moment. Everything changes now, and you have about three seconds to decide what to do.

'A woman came up to me to get my autograph, right before you got here. I guess she left this note behind.'

'*What did the note say?*'

'In so many words, she said the world would be better off if I wasn't part of it.'

As he sat back down, Tommy realized it was the wrong answer. He could've just shown her the note. Told her he didn't understand what it meant. But then she would have wondered why he reacted so strongly to a note he claimed not to understand. It didn't matter now anyway. He was committed to the lie.

Concern washed over her face, making Tommy feel instantly guilty. 'Let me see,' she said, holding out her hand.

'No. There's no point.'

Erin approached with a drink in her hand. It was Becky's cosmopolitan that she never had to order.

'Afternoon, Mrs Devereaux.'

Tommy hoped Erin would distract Becky, but Becky dismissed her with a meager *thank you* and turned her attention back to her husband.

She examined him. 'Why would she want your autograph if she hates you?'

'To get close enough to leave me the note, I guess.'

Death threats weren't new. Neither were they common, but given the wide distribution of Tommy's books, he would always have his critics. Some of those critics were crazy. It was just the odds.

'No one's ever done that in person before,' Becky said. 'You should call the police.'

'No.'

'*Tommy.*'

'I said no. I just want to get back to enjoying my evening.'

'Well, I'm a little freaked out.'

'Don't be.'

Tommy felt Becky staring at him as he focused on his laptop screen.

'Why won't you let me read it?' she asked.

'Because you don't need to.'

She let that sit for a minute.

'You would tell me if there was something else, wouldn't you?'

Tommy looked up and tried his best to keep his expression blank. 'Something else like what?'

'I just don't like having secrets between us.' There was the beginning of a look in her eyes. A look he never wanted to see again.

Both of them knew what she was referring to when she used the word *secret*. There had been another secret. Once. Tommy had come clean about it, and it had nearly destroyed their marriage.

Two years ago, Tommy had an affair.

The guilt had been too much to keep the secret inside him any longer. When he told her about it, they were in bed, getting ready to go to sleep. The TV was on, and two detectives bantered playfully with a suspect in an interrogation room, warming themselves up for the kill. The moment seized Tommy, and he grabbed the remote, pressed mute (but not off), and just started talking.

He remembered her face as he told her. He said it matter-of-factly, because he didn't know how to soften the crushing words.

Becky, I slept with someone else.

He remembered feeling the vomit well inside his throat as he spoke, the pain in the stomach, and knowing it was nothing compared to what she was feeling.

Who was it? she asked. It was the first thing she said after minutes of silence. *Who the fuck was it?*

This was the part where he kept lying, because the truth involved someone Becky knew. Someone who didn't deserve to be hurt, and someone who was no longer a threat to Becky. Tommy lied to protect this woman, but he told the truth about his infidelity because Becky needed to know he had wronged her. If they were going to rebuild, they could never do it without her knowing he had cheated on her.

It was in Dallas. On the book tour. It was only one night, and I don't even know who she is. She never contacted me again. I don't even know her name. It was meaningless, but I completely abused your trust and faith in me.

Becky was crushed. Truly, deeply, soul-shreddingly crushed. The look on her face was the same as if he looked her deeply in her eyes while he slowly shoved a knife into her stomach. Wide-eyed. Fearful. Intense pain. Intense confusion. *Why would you do this? Who are you?*

The moment he told her he had wanted to take it back, say he was only playing a very cruel joke on her, because the look on her face put Tommy into a freefall, a plummet off a skyscraper, arms and legs flailing, as if somehow the movement would keep him from slamming into the concrete a hundred stories below. There was helplessness in that look. He was going to lose her, and there was nothing he could do about it.

That same look that threatened to creep over her face now. *I don't like having secrets between us.*

Yet they had rebuilt their love, because at the heart of their marriage was the fact that they truly and deeply loved each other. Over the past two years, through many tearful nights and much couples therapy, Becky had learned to trust Tommy again. Yet it had taken that event for Tommy truly to realize the importance of family above all else. He vowed never to do anything to hurt Becky or the kids again. He could not live without them. He *would* not live without them.

At least, in the future. There was still one secret he kept from her. One from his distant past.

And it was a big one.

THREE

Tommy's pulse raced as he stared blankly at the laptop screen. Calm yourself. Breathe slowly.

He hit a few random keys to make Becky think he was writing. But he couldn't concentrate. All he could do was think of Maggie's – *Elizabeth's* – face.

Their conversation had only lasted seconds. She had seemed so *normal*, except for the chill that seemed to come from behind her gaze.

But it was her. The woman who used to be a girl with long red hair that spilled down her back like water.

You didn't even change my name.

No, he hadn't. He figured Elizabeth was a common enough name, and since she'd been out of his life for over thirty years he felt safe using her name in the book.

Or did he want her to find him?

She was, after all, the reason for Tommy's success. What had happened that day in the woods was the reason Tommy wrote. It was how he escaped the past. The words allowed him an outlet, all cloaked under the simple heading of *fiction*. *The Blood of the Young* was almost completely fiction. All except for the opening chapter. The one chapter Elizabeth had read. Now she was back.

Why?

His phone chirped.

Dominic. His agent.

Take the call, he told himself. Get back to normal, even if it's for just a few seconds. He answered.

'Shouldn't you be home with the wife and kids?' Tommy asked.

'Hello to you too, Tommy. And for your information, I *am* home. I'm just ignoring them so I can talk to my biggest client.'

'Well, doesn't that make me feel special?'

Who is it? Becky mouthed. She never asked who was on the phone.

'Dom,' he whispered to her.

This answer seemed acceptable to her and she went back to her book.

'Tommy,' Dom said. 'I have my finger in the dike here. You missed a third deadline yesterday. What the hell?'

'It's not done yet, Dom. I told you.'

'You're a rainmaker, friend, but even that will get you only so far. You have a contract.'

'It's my best book yet.'

'That's what you keep telling me. But how the hell would I know? You haven't let anyone read anything but the first chapter. Nice and creepy, admittedly.'

'I'm close. I just have to figure out the ending.'

There was silence on the other end, but not for long.

'You don't know the *fucking ending*? You don't know the one thing your readers want the most from you? Why didn't you tell me this?'

'I just did.'

'You just ruined my night.'

'You should have called me in the morning. I could have ruined your whole day.'

More silence. Labored breathing.

'When?' Dominic asked.

'Three weeks.'

'How firm?'

'Completely. Three weeks and I promise you it will be done.'

At least that's what I thought before a few minutes ago, Tommy thought.

'OK, that's what I'll tell them. Don't fuck me on this.'

'Dom, you paid off your house thanks to me. I'll fuck you any way I want to.'

Becky raised her gaze to him. Tommy shrugged.

'Touché,' Dom said before disconnecting the call.

'What did he want?' Becky asked.

'Wanted to know when the draft will be ready.' Tommy looked out the window as he spoke. He wanted to look at his wife, but he was too afraid of what his face would show.

His phone chirped again. Tommy finally glanced at his wife.

'Another call?' she said. '*Now* who is it?'

Tommy looked at his phone.

PRIVATE CALLER

'I don't know,' he said.

'Ignore it, then.'

Tommy normally would have. But this day was now far from normal, and Tommy answered.

'Hello?'

'Hello, Tommy.'

Maggie's voice. It was deeper and without the soft Minnesota accent, but he knew it was her. Maggie.

Elizabeth.

Tommy stood and walked away from his wife. He didn't turn around to see her expression, but he could feel her gaze burning into his back.

'How did you get this number?'

'That's a pretty clichéd question coming from a writer. That's really the first thing you want to ask me?'

He bowed his head into the phone and lowered his voice. 'Is it really you?'

'Of course it is. You didn't recognize me.'

'That was a disguise.'

'You're a genius.'

She sounded younger than Maggie. In the darker parts of Tommy's brain, she even sounded sexy.

'How do I know it's you?'

A pause.

'Do you want me to tell you where the body is buried?'

It could still be a joke. Or someone with some information but not all of it. Hoping to blackmail a rich novelist.

'Yes,' he said. 'I do.'

'Very well. Rade Baristow is buried four feet beneath the dead elm tree, thirty paces west of the clearing in the woods behind the Jackson Creek subdivision in Lind Falls, Oregon.'

A small hand squeezed Tommy's heart. 'More,' he said. 'Tell me more.'

'Buried with him is a steak knife,' she said. 'On the blade of that knife is the blood of—'

Tommy pressed the disconnect button on his cell phone. He didn't know why, and wasn't even sure he had wanted to. But his finger had done it just the same, as if beyond his brain's control.

His fingers raked through his long dark hair, squeezing and pulling until it hurt.

He turned and looked at Becky. He was certain she hadn't heard anything, but that didn't comfort him much. The last thing Tommy wanted to do was walk back over to his wife.

Dear Jesus. If ever I need a blank expression, it's now.

His legs felt stiff as he walked back to the table.

'Who was that?' she asked.

'No one.'

'Clearly it was someone. Phones don't ring by themselves.'

'It was a solicitor. I was surprised they had this number.'

She stared at him. Assessing.

'What were they selling?'

It wasn't in her nature to probe like this. *She's spooked.*

Tommy knew he could play this one of two ways. Deepen the lie and hope it all went away, or cut her off until he could think of a better story. He decided on the latter.

'You don't believe me?'

'I didn't say that.'

'Why do you care who it was, then?'

'Because,' she said, sitting up in her chair, 'you seemed freaked out and you walked away from the table. So I'm thinking they must be selling some pretty crazy shit for you to have that kind of reaction. I'm a little curious.'

The worst part of all of this was he *wanted* to tell Becky. More than anything he wanted her to know. What a relief that would be. To share the pain he'd felt for so long. To let Becky into the darkest part of his life, so that she could bring some light with her. But he couldn't. No one could know, because if she knew, Tommy would lose her. He had almost lost her once, and he didn't want to risk that ever again. The darkness had to remain his and his alone.

'It wasn't a solicitor,' he finally said. 'But, it's like the note. You don't need to know.'

Becky's right eye twitched. Not a good sign.

'That's an arrogant thing to say. Have I ever held back something from you?'

'If you did a good job of it, I suppose I wouldn't know, would I?'

More twitching.

'Damnit, stop trying to humor your way out of this conversation like you always do.'

'Becky, listen to me for a second. Let me ask you honestly, do you tell me everything that you do during your day? Do you not hold any secrets from me?'

'I tell you everything that's important.'

'How do you decide what's important?'

She squeezed her right fist until her knuckle was nearly as pale as the diamond on her wedding ring.

'I . . . just . . . *know.*'

'OK, then. Give me a little credit.'

'You used that credit up two years ago.'

Ouch.

'In this case, I just know that I don't want to tell you about the note or the phone call.'

'Are they from the same person?'

'I don't want to discuss it.'

'Are you . . . are you in some kind of trouble?'

'No,' he lied. He said it fast enough for it to sound convincing. Or so he hoped.

Becky closed her eyes and her mouth turned into a small, tight frown. She took a breath and made it two words into her next question.

'Are you . . .'

She didn't finish.

He saw the pain in her face and he forced himself to keep eye contact.

'No, Becky. Nothing like that. I promise.'

She was questioning his fidelity. The truth was much darker than that.

FOUR

Tommy squeezed the leather steering wheel, wanting to feel it crumple under his grip. He and Becky each drove their own cars home, and Tommy was thankful for the ten minutes of silence. He changed lanes and wove in and out of traffic, then sped through a yellow light that had turned red just as he entered the intersection. A fatal wreck might just be the distraction I need, he thought.

Tommy tried to process what was happening, assessing the situation objectively while not really believing any of it was real. She wants revenge, he thought. That's it. She's been following my career and she read the teaser chapter of *The Blood of the Young*. She's afraid I'm going to reveal who she is.

But that's crazy. I have no idea who she is. I don't even know her last name, or where she's even been in the last thirty years.

Tommy pressed down on the accelerator and swerved around a Honda, earning him a honk from its driver. Finally, he entered his subdivision – *Cherry Creek North Estates* – and swerved his Audi on to the winding, crushed-stone driveway of their house. He looked up at the massive *casa de Devereaux* as he always did: like it couldn't actually be theirs.

The *house* was over six thousand finished square feet, and they used barely half of it. When the book money went from serious to laughable, Tommy had bought it. Now and then, he yearned for the poorer times, when it was a splurge to get a babysitter and go to the movies.

Tommy got out of his car and stepped into the night. His shoes crunched against the pea gravel path as he walked toward his front door.

The phone vibrated in his pocket. He took it out.

PRIVATE CALLER

'No,' he mumbled. His thumb found the power button and he shut the phone off without answering.

He put the key into the front door and turned, but nothing happened. The front door was already unlocked. Not unheard of, but not the norm. Melinda – their nanny – was diligent about locks.

He opened the door and slowly stepped inside his house.

'Hello?'

His voice echoed in the cavernous entryway. More lights off than on. No sound of a television. No fighting. No laughter. Nothing.

A glance at the security system showed it was deactivated.

Lights glowed down the hallway. Tommy walked down the corridor and entered the kitchen, finding it similarly empty. If the kids had eaten, there was no sign of it. Maybe Melinda had already cleaned up.

The silence was stifling.

Tommy placed his messenger bag on the counter and checked the time on the microwave. Seven fifteen.

Too early for bedtime. Kids must be upstairs.

He heard the front door open at the same moment he saw the note on the refrigerator.

A wave of nausea rolled through Tommy's stomach, like he was freefalling in a nose-diving airplane. He thought of ten-year-old Rade Baristow (known as 'Brian' in the fictionalized version), the boy who hadn't done anything wrong except talk to a pretty stranger on an empty summer day. Rade, whose skull opened like an eggshell under the weight of a rock.

Then Tommy thought of Chance, his own ten-year-old boy.

He squinted at the Post-it note on the stainless-steel surface, not really wanting to read it. Not really. Because Tommy knew there could be nothing good written on it.

I got your kids! Can't wait to teach them everything I know!

Those were the words that appeared in Tommy's mind. Elizabeth had come back into his life, and the idea that she could have access to Tommy's own children horrified him in a way he never thought possible. He felt the power drain from his legs and his brain begin to cloud, threatening to shut off completely.

He forced himself closer to the refrigerator, not wanting to read but having to.

Then he saw the familiar handwriting.

Took the kids to MaGee's. Back no later than 8. I promise!
Melinda

Tommy closed his eyes and exhaled.

'Where is everyone?'

Tommy jumped at the voice. He snapped his head toward Becky, who had just walked in the kitchen.

'Um . . .' He held up the note, which stuck to his index finger. 'Melinda took them to MaGee's for dinner.'

'You're a little on edge,' she said. 'I don't think I like secretive Tommy.'

Tommy thought of more lies but held back. It didn't matter. Becky knew he was hiding something, and denying it served no purpose. What *did* matter was they were now alone. It would give Becky time to pry a little deeper, which was exactly what he didn't want.

'I need to work,' he said.

'What, now? You never work this late.'

'I do when I have to. And the book isn't going to finish itself.' He walked over and kissed her on the forehead, which suddenly felt like the wrong thing to do. Confirming this, Becky pulled away.

'What about dinner?'

'I'll grab something later.'

'Fine.'

'I won't be too long. I promise.'

She paused for a moment before turning and walking out of the kitchen, and Tommy understood why. That pause was an opportunity for him to change his mind. To sit and have dinner with her. Assuage her fears.

Tommy said nothing. He let her go.

This wasn't the time, even if by avoiding her he was making the inevitable confrontation worse.

He walked into his office and shut the door.

The smell of books brought him comfort, a sense of place. His office housed nearly three thousand books – some rare, most not. They stood like sentries on their shelves, floor to ceiling, covering three walls. Tommy breathed them in as he settled behind his hulking cherry desk. He pulled his laptop from his messenger bag and plugged it into his monitor.

The glowing screen showed the same nothingness he'd been staring at on the laptop screen just one hour ago. A page half-filled with words.

As the wireless network established a connection, his e-mail icon appeared.

Three new messages.

Two were spam.

His gaze went to the third one. The one from someone named *deusexmachina1135@hotspot.com*.

The one with the subject line reading *THE BOY IN THE WOODS*.

FIVE

Do you still think about it? About what it felt like carrying
that little body to the hole we dug? About the blood you got
on your jeans, and the knife we used to cut ourselves? Do
you think about how you were the only one who refused me
afterwards? How you wanted to hit me, but my Watcher
stopped you? Do you wonder who he was and what happened
to him?

Of course you do, Tommy. You think of all these things
every day. That's why you write, isn't it? And your killers are
always women. I'm not going to call that a coincidence.

You have always needed me.

And now I need you.

Contact Mark – he's easy to find. Go to him.

ommy stared at the plain black lettering on the monitor, the
cursor blinking away time.

We had no choice, Tommy thought. Your *Watcher*? Is that
what you call him? Tommy remembered the man who had come
out from behind a tree that day, the man with the ski mask and the
shotgun. The man who had said very little, but what he did say was
the reason Tommy and the others hadn't all run to the police. He
was the reason Tommy lived for years with his shameful secret.
This *Watcher* was Elizabeth's partner, but Tommy didn't include
that detail in his teaser chapter. In fact, he wasn't in Tommy's book
at all, because after the teaser chapter Tommy told an entirely
different – and fictional – account of that day.

Elizabeth disappeared after Rade's murder, but Tommy had always
wondered if this . . . Watcher . . . was someone from Lind Falls. A
neighbor, even. Whoever he was, he'd gotten off on the murder as
much as Elizabeth had.

Tommy forced down the urge to vomit.

Contact Mark. Go to him.

Mark. In *The Blood of the Young*, the boy Tommy knew as Mark was renamed 'Spencer'. His friend Jason had been renamed 'Drew'. In that opening chapter, the name changes were the only thing altered from reality. And Elizabeth now wanted Tommy to seek Mark out. Clearly, she had already found him (*he's easy to find*). But now she wanted Tommy to find him as well. Why?

He turned his gaze from the screen to the rows of books in the shelves, the millions of words. How many others had died because Tommy, Mark, and Jason were too scared to talk? How many more bodies were there in those woods?

Somehow she'd gotten his private address – not the one designated for fan mail.

That thought stopped him. Tommy's assistant, Sofia, went through the fan mail account. What if Elizabeth had written there as well?

But three words mollified him, if only a little.

I need you.

That's what she had written, hadn't she? He looked back on the screen and assured himself. If she needed him, then she wouldn't do anything to jeopardize Tommy's ability to keep their secret hidden. Not yet, at least.

Whatever she was doing, she was making sure it was for his eyes only. For now.

Having a hunch, Tommy replied with a blank e-mail.

Moments later the bounce-back message arrived.

MESSAGE UNDELIVERABLE

Communication was only to be one-way. Elizabeth wanted control.

Tommy put his face in his hands and peered through his fingers out at the wall of books on the far side of the study. His gaze caught his Stephen King collection. All hardbacks. All signed.

He stared at one volume in particular.

Misery.

The irony didn't elude him, but his mind wasn't quite ready to assess objectively the whole life-imitating-art aspect of what was happening. Besides, in that book, the author was just trying to mind his own business. It wasn't like he had a history with his tormentor. A history of violent crime. A *collusion*.

Tommy stood and stared out the office's solitary, massive window into his backyard. October was three days away and the days were tightening. Despite the heat that lingered during the late-summer days, the cold of fall would be upon them soon enough. Darkness draped over the pool and the rolling lawn, punctuated only by small circles of light thrown off by the solar lamps lining the pathways. His eyes searched for movement. For anything out of the ordinary. Monsters in the dark, demons in the blue grass. Finding nothing, he lowered the shade.

A rap at the office door.

'Yes?'

'Can I come in, Daddy?'

'Of course, darlin'.'

The door opened and Evie walked in, her long hair kinked and knotted.

'I didn't know you guys were home,' Tommy said. 'How was MaGee's?'

'Good. I had mac and cheese. Chance had a burger.'

'Was it yummy?'

'Uh huh.' She was wearing *Wizards of Waverly Place* pajamas.

Tommy sat back in his chair and put his arms out. 'Come give me a hug.'

Evie walked over and climbed into his lap, then buried herself deep in his arms. Tommy swiveled the chair and leaned back, soaking her in, her little arms wrapped around him, depending on him to hold and protect her. Shield her. In these moments, when he held his little girl tightly and didn't want to let go, he would realize it was more her shielding him than the other way around. Tommy's kids were his connection to everything good in the world, and he could stay in that place as long as he was with them. If he let go, and if they floated away from him, there would be only the bad things left.

Tommy remembered the morning after he told Becky about his infidelity. He had considered going to a hotel that night. He knew he wouldn't be sleeping anyway, but he really didn't want to stay awake and stare at the ceiling of a lonely hotel room. So that night he had left Becky in their bed – she was still crying but refused any comfort from him – and went to the twin bed of his little girl. Evie had been buried deep beneath a multicolored *Sofia the First* comforter, a small lump of dreams and innocence, her small, deep nighttime breaths slow and steady. Tommy had crawled under the blanket with her, draped his arm around her, and breathed her in as he did now. 'I'm sorry,' he had told her as she slept. 'I'll be a better man for all of you. I promise.' He squeezed her that night as he did now, not letting go, vowing never to let go.

Evie's voice stirred the silence of the office and pulled Tommy from his memory. 'The . . . boy . . . in the . . . woods.'

'*What?*'

'That's what it says there. "The boy in the woods." That's funny. What's the boy doing there?'

Tommy looked at his monitor. He had left Elizabeth's e-mail on the screen. He reached over and turned off the monitor.

'Is that one of your stories?'

'No, darlin'.'

'But why did it say that?'

'It's . . . it's just a note from someone.'

'From who?'

'No one.'

She furrowed her brow. 'It has to be from *someone*, Daddy.'

'It's not polite to read other people's messages. And when did you become so argumentative?'

'What does that mean?'

'It means you keep asking questions when you don't like the answers I give.'

Evie offered an extra squeeze as she mulled that over. Tommy sought to change the subject.

'How was school today?'

'Good.' He watched as she tried to remember the day's events. 'We're learning about time and about money.'

'The only thing you need to know is you'll never have enough of either.'

'Daddy! We have lots of money.'

Tommy had no argument. 'You're right, sweetie. We do. We're very lucky.'

She kissed him on the cheek. 'Are you coming upstairs?'

Tommy stared at the dark computer screen. 'Daddy has to work.'

'You're *always* working.'

'I know. But that's how we get all the money. From hard work.'

Evie furrowed her brow. 'But what about the story?'

Most nights he told Evie and Chance a story, making one up on the spot. Chance sometimes opted out because he insisted he was getting too old for such things, but Evie never missed one.

'Not tonight, OK?'

'But why?'

'Because Daddy can only think of scary stories tonight, and I don't think you want one of those.'

'*Pleeeeasse . . .*'

'I'm sorry, love. Not tonight.' *I have to figure out if my life is over*, he didn't add.

'Will you do an extra long one tomorrow night?'

'Deal.' He squeezed her tightly and considered the horror of being forced away from his family. He didn't want to think about it, but he had to. He had to admit to himself that if Elizabeth wanted to, she could destroy Tommy Devereaux's life. Of course, she would destroy her own life in the process, but Tommy didn't know if she even cared. He had no idea what she wanted, and the inability to deal with the situation was maddening.

Tommy squeezed Evie again and kissed his daughter good night. She scooched off his lap and bounded out of the room, her bare feet slapping against the hardwood floor.

'Love you, Dada,' she called out as she raced toward the stairs.

'Love you, sweetie.' He walked over and closed the office door.

He needed to do something. Anything. Anything that, if even for an instant, gave him some sense of control. Because right now he was tumbling through an open void, and his stomach couldn't adjust to the freefall.

'Mark and Jason. I have to find Mark and Jason.'

SIX

Mark and Jason.

In *The Blood of the Young*, Tommy had changed their names to Spencer and Drew, and the opening chapter of the novel was the exact account of what happened to all of them that day in the woods.

Tommy thought about them often. The faces of his fourteen-year-old friends were frozen in time in his mind. Mark, the de facto leader of the three, the sexually frustrated boy-man who wanted nothing more than to become a full man, but not the way it ended up happening. Jason, the soft giant, who had cried that day.

In the weeks and months after the killing, the boys had disbanded as a group. They hadn't exactly ended their friendships with one another, but they avoided each other, as if any contact might lend credence to what had happened. Or, more truly spoken, the lack of contact maybe let them believe that, perhaps, the killing never actually happened. This was certainly the case for Tommy, who at first burned to tell his parents, his friends, anyone who might help provide relief from the guilt he felt. But fear stopped him. Then, after some time passed (and not as much time as would seem necessary, he always thought), Tommy found his continued silence actually buttressed his fantasy that it was all just a vision, a bad dream. Something he had seen on TV, perhaps.

Tommy assumed the other boys felt the same, because any words he had exchanged with either of them after the killing were always on a different subject. Small talk.

Though he thought of his old friends often, Tommy had never searched them out in the past thirty years. But now everything had changed. It was time to see if ghosts were real.

Tommy pressed speed dial #3 on his phone, then locked the office door.

'Hey, Tommy.'

Sofia's voice was bright and alert.

'Hey there. Catch you at a bad time?'

'I'm always on call – you know that.'

'Good. I need help.'

Sofia was more than just his assistant. She managed his life. Tommy was in continuous wonder at how a thirty-year-old could have both her shit and his shit so together.

'Name it, boss.'

Tommy knew the request was not a typical one. 'How do I find a long lost friend?'

'You could finally join Facebook and search for them.'

'No,' he said. 'I don't want to go through all that. I just want to locate a couple of people.'

A brief silence. 'Do you have any idea where they are?'

'None.'

'High school friends?'

'Yeah. How did you know?'

'Because everyone wants to find high school friends, though I can't imagine why. Shouldn't be too much of a problem – there are websites that can run names. They charge for it.'

'Not a problem.'

'Names?'

'Jason Covington and Mark Singletary. We went to high school together in Lind Falls, Oregon. Back in eighty-one, eighty-two.'

He could hear her typing on her laptop. 'That's the last you know of them?'

'Yes. Jason didn't even finish. He dropped out and his family moved. Not sure where. Maybe Texas?'

'Sure thing. What's the interest? They owe you money?'

How many different females was he going to have to lie to tonight?

'I want to see if they remember something the same way I do.'

It wasn't a complete lie, and Tommy took some solace in that.

'Ooh. Sounds intriguing. When do you want the info by?'

'Any chance tonight?'

'Sure. I'll just put my life on hold for you.'

'Oh, I mean, of course it can wait—'

'Take it easy, Tommy. I was joking. All I was doing here was catching up on my shows. You sound a bit wired tonight.'

Tommy felt his face flush. 'I'm just a little stressed out about my deadline. I think talking to these guys could help me with my ending.'

'Give me an hour.' Then she hung up.

It took less than forty minutes, which was good because Tommy's mind was racing in every direction except a positive one.

'OK, I have what you're looking for. Cost thirty bucks, by the way.'

'Fine, fine. Tell me.'

'Mark Singletary was easy. Didn't even need to pay to find out where he was – Google search was all I needed.'

She let it hang there for a moment, letting Tommy know he could easily have found this information himself. Tommy knew he could have, but he relied on Sofia so much that she effectively was his Google.

'Where is he?'

'He's a State Senator in South Carolina. Up for re-election in November.'

Pretty impressive. 'Republican or Democrat?' he asked.

'Republican.'

'That sounds about right.'

'Lots of articles on him. Found a bio that referenced Lind Falls, and he's the same age as you. Figured he must be the guy.'

'You find a picture?'

'E-mailing you now.'

Seconds later a link arrived in his inbox. Tommy clicked on it. Mark Singletary's campaign site filled the screen in front of him.

Ghosts were real.

It was him. Thirty years older for sure, but it was him. Tommy could hear his voice, clear like water.

Why don't you do me first?

The intensity. The desire to have more. The urges. The wants. They were all in the face on the screen just as they were in the fourteen-year-old boy that day.

'Yes,' Tommy said into the phone, aware of the edge in his voice. 'That's him.'

'Hardcore right-wing,' Sofia said. 'Anti-tax, anti-gay, anti-abortion, the works. Christian conservative. Wife, three kids. Schooled in West Point, a few years of service, then Duke Law. Moved to South Carolina to clerk for a federal judge. Ran for State Senate four years ago and has been there since. His big achievement last year was getting a creationist museum funded with state tax revenue. You know, the kind of museum that shows Adam and Eve riding on dinosaurs.'

'Sounds like you don't approve,' Tommy said, knowing it to be true.

'Whatever. Just glad I don't live in South Carolina.'

Tommy read snippets from Mark's home page, catching words like *FREEDOM* and *FAMILY* and *SERVICE.*

'How do I reach him?'

'Contact info is on his home page.'

'Won't I have to go through his staffers?'

Sofia sighed. 'He's a State Senator, not the President. Besides, you're Tommy-fucking-Devereaux.'

Tommy scrolled to the bottom of the page and found Mark's contact information. Probably some campaign phone number, which meant normal business hours only.

Too late to call tonight.

'So what cost me thirty bucks?' he asked. Tommy heard a yelp from upstairs in the house. A happy shriek from Evie. The sound of family life moving forward without him.

'Finding Jason Covington.'

'More difficult?'

'Took an extra twenty minutes.'

Tommy pictured Silent Jason, the kid who just wanted to please but not lead. He had been a strong kid, but those muscles only went to sports. After that day in the woods, Jason barely spoke to anyone. Six months later his family moved away.

'Where is he?'

'He's in New York.'

'The city?'

'Yes.'

'What's he doing?'

'He's dead. So, not too much.'

Dead?

'But . . . you said he's in New York.'

'He is. That's where he's buried.'

Tommy's mind took a moment to reconcile all his vibrant memories of an old friend with what was now a heap of dust and calcium deposits.

'What happened to him?'

'Suicide,' she said. 'Hanged himself in a studio apartment in the city about twenty years ago.'

'You sure it's him?'

He heard the clicking of a keyboard over the phone line.

'Jason Covington. DOB July seventeen, nineteen sixty-seven, Seattle. Moved to Lind Falls, Oregon in seventy-four, then McKinney, Texas in eighty-two. Was a mechanic there until moving to New York in ninety-one. Killed himself a year later.'

Tommy processed the information for a few seconds, despising the fact that a few seconds was all it took to come to terms with an old friend's death.

'You OK, Tommy?'

Her voice pulled him back. 'Yeah,' he said. 'Yeah, I'm OK.'

'Need anything else, boss?'

'No . . . no. Thanks so much, Sofia. See you tomorrow.'

'Tomorrow's Saturday.'

'Oh, right. Monday, then.'

'Night, boss. Don't work too hard. And . . . sorry about your friend.'

'Thanks, Sofia.'

Tommy put his phone on the desk and thought about the three people who had just come back into his life: Elizabeth, Jason and Mark. The four of them had been all together only once, thirty years ago, and just for a couple of hours. Now it was coming full circle. Elizabeth was back. He would contact Mark in the morning. And Jason was dead, but Tommy didn't think that was the end of that storyline.

Why did Jason kill himself?

Tommy hovered over his desk for a moment before yielding to his chair. Grabbing his mouse, he clicked back to the draft of *The Blood of the Young*. Ninety thousand words and not an end in sight. He scrolled to a page somewhere near the middle and stared at the words.

'Why did you kill yourself, Jason?'

The words before him blended together into nonsense. All of it suddenly seemed like such nonsense.

'*Drew* wouldn't kill himself. Why would *you*?'

It was in that moment Tommy realized his mistake. His mistake was in writing the book as fiction. Only the first chapter contained elements of the truth, and the rest he'd constructed out of his own mind, out of his own desires for a compelling series of events where the heroes were strong and the villain was a monster. But the truth was much murkier than that. The truth contained conflicted heroes who lied to their wives and villains who were just doing what nature built them for.

Tommy's book needed more of the truth. And in finding that truth, maybe Tommy could finally put to rest the ghosts of his past.

SEVEN

S ofia D'Alle parked her blue Prius at the Cherry Creek mall, sliding into a freshly vacated space near the entrance to Crate & Barrel. It was a minor stroke of good luck, but it was good luck nonetheless, and she let such things speak for themselves.

Bad things rarely happened to Sofia.

She had been living in Denver for nearly seven years, working for Tommy the entire time. *That* had been a good luck day – the day she met him. She had just graduated from the University of Denver with a BA in English, wondering what to do next. Graduate degree? Temp work? Move back to Des Moines, where her parents said she could always stay as long as it took 'to find a proper job'. One month post-graduation, she realized she had fallen into that trap that so many college students do. Between student loans and her parents' long-saved money, Sofia's education added up to a tidy eighty grand, and she had spent it studying books. She dreamed of opening an independent bookstore someday, the kind that people like her would stroll into, a place where you could smell the paper and ink, where the patrons would run their fingers along the spines, pick up a title under the 'Sofia Recommends' section, then grab a latte in the Coffee Nook.

Like all dreams, they sounded perfect. But dreams were the fuel of the future, and rarely of the present. A month out of school she needed to find a job, something that would give her money without sucking her in where she would suddenly find herself twenty years later asking where her life had gone. A professor of hers from her college days sat on a charity board with Tommy, and had introduced them. Tommy was looking for a new assistant at the time, his last one having just moved to Rome with her husband. Sofia had never been much of a thriller reader, preferring the classics. But she had taken an immediate liking to Tommy, whose soft charm and relaxed nature belied a story-teller who was devoted to his craft and worked endlessly to satisfy his readers. They tested the waters with each other for a few months before mutually deciding it was a pretty good arrangement.

It was essentially administrative work, but the truth was Sofia

couldn't have been happier. Tommy paid her well, gave her a lot
of room to make decisions, and working for him was more education than she ever had in school. She assisted heavily in his research,
which she found fascinating given Tommy's near-obsession with
female serial killers. She even started writing her own short stories
– something she never thought she'd be good at – and Tommy was
the best critic she could ever have hoped for.

Bad things rarely happened to Sofia, but when she and Tommy
slept together two years ago, she knew nothing good could come
of it. It had happened so quickly, which, she acknowledged, sounded
stupid. It was after a book launch party, they were both a little
drunk, Becky took the kids home early, and a whole list of etceteras
after that. They spent the night at the Ritz in downtown Denver,
and Tommy had told Becky he crashed at the office. Sofia had actually watched him make the call, that first call to the unsuspecting
wife, the first lie. Sofia had still been in bed and Tommy was looking
out the bedroom window in his boxer briefs, his fingers pushing up
through his hair, his body lean and muscular. Sofia didn't regret the
night, but she knew it was a mistake.

They made seven mistakes after that over the next two months,
each time amazing, each aftermath tinged with guilt and growing
feelings for one another. It was more than a fling, they both knew.
There was a relationship that existed which they could not easily
dismiss. She cared for him more than she would probably ever let
him know, and she had told Tommy their affair was his to end. She
wouldn't put up a fight or ask him to leave his wife. She just wanted
to be near him, working with him, learning from him, and she was
happy to do that platonically.

When Tommy decided to tell Becky about the affair, Sofia realized her time with Tommy Devereaux was over. She hadn't expected
him actually to tell her, but she had to admit it made her respect
him. As a woman, she would want to be told, after all. She assumed
when Becky found out, Sofia would be fired, and the next phase of
her life – whatever that meant – would begin. Sofia held some
bitterness about that outcome, and she tried to feel anger for Tommy.
Sometimes it worked. Most times, she just felt sad.

But Tommy never told Becky who the woman was. He said
she was someone Becky didn't know, some fan from a book tour.
It was then Sofia realized Tommy didn't want his assistant to go

away, and theirs was a relationship that could exist without the sex. Even flourish. For the next two years it had, though rare was even the hug between them. Truth was, Sofia and Tommy depended on each other, like old friends who had been through war. They simply needed each other in their lives, though they could exist in silence about things in their past.

Still, there were the mundane tasks of her job. Like Becky asking her to return a wooden bowl to Crate & Barrel. That kind of thing hadn't happened before the affair, and Sofia saw the change in Becky in regard to women in Tommy's life. Becky now exerted control in areas she hadn't before. Tommy said she trusted him, but Sofia knew that kind of thing never went away. Becky would never be the same with regard to her husband.

Sofia was crossing the parking lot when someone walked into her from behind. Sofia stumbled, turned, and saw a woman struggling to keep her balance.

'Oh, I am *so* sorry,' the woman said. 'Sometimes I get lost in my own world and I don't even bother to look where I'm going.'

'You OK?' Sofia asked. She wondered where the woman had come from. Sofia hadn't noticed her at all until the woman walked right smack into her.

'Oh, yes, dear. You're kind to ask. Just embarrassed.'

Sofia guessed her in her fifties, though the use of the word 'dear' made her seem older. Hard to tell her age owing to the extreme amount of makeup and the bad hair-dye job. Sofia bent down to help the woman collect her purse when she noticed a copy of Tommy's last book jutting from it.

'You enjoying the book?' Sofia asked.

'Excuse me, dear?'

'The book. How do you like it?'

'I love it. I'm on my second read.'

'Wow.'

'Have you read it?'

Sofia was the fifth person out of millions to have read it.

'Yeah, I've read it. It's my favorite of his.'

The woman's eyes shone. 'Mine, *too*. Have you read all of his?'

Sofia smiled. 'Actually, I work for him.'

'*You do?*'

'He lives in Denver – did you know that?'

'Oh, I know. But I've only ever seen him at Tattered Cover sign-ings. Never about town. What's it like working for him?'

'It's . . . it's really good.' Sofia picked up the book and flipped through the first few pages. 'Want me to get it signed for you?'

'*Would you?*'

'Be happy to. Give me your address and I'll mail it back to you. I mean, if that's OK. You might have to wait a few days to pick up where you left off.'

'No, that would be just *amazing*.' The woman dug through her purse and pulled out a pen and sales receipt. She scribbled her address on the back.

Sofia took the receipt and wedged it in the pages of the book.

'What a coincidence,' the woman said, beaming. 'I literally run into someone who works for my favorite writer in the whole world.'

It was at that moment Sofia sensed something a bit off about the woman. Maybe it was the way her eyes widened a bit too much as she spoke, or how her lips pulled back just a bit too far over her gums as she smiled. Whatever it was, Sofia was no longer certain that any of this was coincidental.

Sofia took a step back and offered a meek smile. 'It certainly is. Well, I'll take care of this and send it back to you. Goodbye.'

She turned and started to walk away.

'Wait,' the woman called.

Sofia froze and turned her head back. 'Yes?'

'Don't you want to know who to sign it to?' She pointed at the book in Sofia's right hand.

Sofia turned around and exhaled. 'Yes, sorry. Of course. What's your name?'

'Elizabeth,' she said, her voice noticeably sharper. 'My name is Elizabeth.'

'OK, Elizabeth. Thank you.'

Sofia turned once again and walked toward the store, feeling Elizabeth's gaze on her the whole time.

When she reached the front of the store, she opened the door and glanced back to the parking lot. Elizabeth hadn't moved. She remained standing in the middle of the parking lot, her eyes tracked on Sofia, her mouth open in a vacant, wide smile.

Still beaming.

EIGHT

Saturday morning. Tommy stared at the espresso dripping from the silver machine into the small porcelain cup. He didn't even want any, but he hoped keeping his morning routine would alleviate even a small amount of the guilt and the desperation he felt.

It didn't.

Becky stood at the kitchen counter, flipping the pages of the Denver Post. The pages slapped down, one after another, and he could tell she wasn't even reading anything. Just slapping. They were just a few feet away from each other and the silence between them was deafening.

Ever since he first fell in love with her, Tommy had wanted to tell Becky about that day when he was fourteen. About how he was an unwilling accomplice in the cover-up of a little boy's murder. Tommy swore an oath that day he'd never say anything, but his bond to the oath was gone. What kept him quiet was the certainty that, no matter what he said, he had committed a horrible crime by helping to bury Rade. By not saying anything. By letting Rade's parents lose their sleep and sanity to the demons of uncertainty that made them wonder every minute of the day if their little boy was suffering. Such crimes do not expire. Tommy could go to prison. Tommy could miss his kids growing up. He had risked losing his family when he told Becky about the affair. In that case, he would at least have had the kids half of the time. There would be no such arrangement if he went to prison.

For the first half-decade after the murder Tommy remained quiet mostly out of fear and denial. In his early twenties, his silence was fed by guilt and shame. He combated this by beginning to write, writing about women who kill, discovering both a natural talent and a means of therapy at the same time. The writing freed him, and the more he did of it the more he hoped the past would simply become another story. Fiction. Over the years this technique worked; when the riches poured in from his writing, it became much easier to shove the memory further back on the top closet shelf, near the dark corners where dust motes collected into feathery layers.

Every now and then he suddenly yearned to tell Becky. But Tommy was simply too scared ever to speak of it. Prison was a distinctly possible consequence of the truth coming out. Though he had never told anyone about the crime, he had done enough research around his type of scenario to know there were a multitude of crimes associated with his silence, some of them carrying no statute of limitation. With the evidence that was surely still along with the body, there was no way Tommy could convince a jury he wasn't there that day. Which made him guilty. Which meant he could go to prison, even after all this time. It was no more complicated than that.

It killed him to lie to Becky, but he had to. He had already lied too much.

He turned to her.

'Becky . . .'

She didn't look up.

'Mmmmmmm?'

'There's something I need to show you.'

Now she looked up. Her expression was as plastic as a mannequin's, but Tommy saw the storm beneath.

Here goes.

He handed her a note. Not *The Note*, but one typed on similar paper and folded as the original had been. She took it from his hand and kept her gaze on his, questioning. He simply nodded.

Becky read, and then paled. Tommy wondered if he had gone too far.

'Oh my God,' she mumbled.

The pain in her voice sickened him. He immediately wanted to tell her the note was a fake, but he didn't. He couldn't. He didn't look at her as he spoke.

'I know. That's why I didn't want to show you, but I realized I had to.'

She kept staring at the words Tommy had written last night.

I read your first chapter you sick fuck. How much money you hoping to get writing about that shit? You going to buy another manshen writing about child murder? You will burn in a fiery Hell, Mr Deverux. What if that was your boy getting killed? You think it would be funny to write about then? Or your little girl. I know where they go to school. It would be easy. But they shouldn't have to suffer for your sins, those lambs. Its you who needs to feel the pain of punishment.

'It was the person who called me as well,' he said, relieved and revolted about how convincing he knew he sounded. 'A woman. Basically said the same thing as the note.'

'The woman from last night? Who asked for your autograph?'

'Yes.'

She rattled the paper in her fist. 'Tommy, we have to go to the police with this. I mean . . . holy shit. *This is disgusting.*'

'I know. I'm going to give it to the cops. In the meantime, I . . . I was thinking. I don't know. Based on what I know about crazy people – and you know I know a lot – I think this is a pretty empty threat. And, even in the way-off chance it's not, it doesn't make sense to send a note threatening our kids. I think the real threat – if there is one – is to me, not to anyone else.'

'Tommy . . .'

Elizabeth's words flashed in his mind.

Contact Mark. Go to him.

He pushed on. 'So I was thinking about going away for a few days, maybe a week. You know, go hole myself up somewhere and finish my book.'

Becky squeezed her eyes shut for a moment. 'What good would that do? It doesn't feel right that the family isn't together right now.'

He reached out for her hand. 'If someone is out to get me, I'd rather not be near my family. I couldn't take the idea of something happening to any of you. Let me go away for a few days, and, just to be safe, I want to hire some private security for the house.'

'*Private security?* What does that mean?'

It was easier for him to stand on firmer ground with this argument, because his desire for a security detail wasn't just part of some ruse; Tommy truly believed his family was more in danger if he remained around them now.

'Just a couple of guys to sit tight and make sure nothing out of the ordinary happens.'

'The kids will *freak out*.'

'Are you kidding me? Chance will love it.'

He knew there was nothing she could say. If she refused and something happened, she could never live with herself.

Becky's eyes widened, and the crow's feet around their edges stretched smooth as she leaned across the table at him. 'Tommy, what the hell is happening here? You're just supposed to go hide out somewhere while some goons pace back and forth in our house all night? That will keep us safe? And for how long? When will you judge this threat to be over? A threat, by the way, that you just said you don't put much stock in.'

All damn good questions, Tommy thought. Ones he really didn't have good answers for.

'Tommy,' she continued, 'we can't just change our lives because some lunatic wrote a nasty letter.'

'*And* called me on my private line.'

When she spoke next, Tommy heard calm in her voice. There was also fear, but above all there was calm, and Tommy loved her for it. 'Are you really worried about this? You've had your crazies before.'

'I . . . I don't like the feeling of it.'

'I don't know, Tommy. I mean, this is *insane*. It's just a book.'

'That's what Rushdie said.'

He let the moment linger until he felt the timing was right.

'Becky, I've made up my mind. It's what we're going to do. And you can be pissed off and angry at me, but it won't change anything.'

He reached over and took the letter from her hands, then folded it over neatly along its creases.

Becky said nothing, because there was nothing to be said. Tommy knew she was scared, pissed off, and confused. There was too much to be said, so she just kept silent.

'I'm going to the office and arranging for the security. Then I'll book my travel.'

Finally she spoke, her voice hollow.

'Where will you go?'

'I have no idea.'

'When are you leaving?'

'I don't know. Maybe tomorrow.'

She closed her eyes. 'Tommy, tell me this isn't about something else.'

The words forced his gaze to the ground. 'Something else like what?'

'Anything else,' she said. 'Just tell me this isn't about anything else.'

Tommy couldn't look her in the eyes.

'It's not about anything else,' he said, his gaze to the floor.

She nodded, but it wasn't in acceptance. She was dismissing him.

NINE

Tommy was in the office by ten. Being in the office by that time in the morning was rare. Being there on a Saturday was almost unprecedented.

But he needed privacy to call Mark Singletary.

Tommy leased nearly fifteen hundred square feet in an office building in downtown Denver. He rarely wrote here, but it was a good place to escape or catch up with the business side of things. Sofia also had her office here, and there was some open cubicle space when contract workers were needed for help with PR campaigns, website upgrades, or any of the other number of essential business tasks successful authors never thought they would be dealing with. A conference room overlooking the mountains provided the perfect place for Tommy to sip coffee and panic about running out of ideas.

He picked up the phone and called Mark, dialing the number from the website. It being Saturday, Tommy held little hope anyone would pick up.

Yet on the fourth ring, someone did.

'Senator Singletary's campaign office. This is Susan.'

Hearing Mark Singletary called *Senator* jolted Tommy. *You'd think they'd have to say State Senator at least*, he thought.

'Hi, Susan. I'm trying to reach Mark. This is an old friend of his.'

Her voice was clipped. 'I'm sorry, *Senator Singletary* isn't available right now. Would you care to be transferred into his voicemail?'

'I know it's Saturday and all, but I was really hoping to reach him. It's important that I speak to him.'

'Sir, you'll just have to—'

'Can you at least give him a call and tell him Tommy Devereaux wants to say hi?'

That stopped her.

'Tommy Devereaux. The author?'

'That's right. Mark and I went to school together as boys back in Oregon.'

Susan's voice deviated from her previously scripted tone. 'Oh my God, I *love* your books. I read *The Blood of the Many* after a bad breakup and it totally made me want to be the main character . . . what was her name?'

'Gillian.'

'That's right. *Gillian.* The scene where she killed her boyfriend and dumped his body in that filthy river. That was amazing. I think that was the first time I smiled in weeks.'

'I'm glad you found her a sympathetic villain.'

'She was a villain?'

That was a first.

'So, uh, any chance you can give him a quick call?'

'Heck, Mr Devereaux. I'll give you his cell phone number. He's just out golfing this morning. I'm sure he'd love to hear from you.'

It was better luck than Tommy had expected. She gave him the number and Tommy promised her a signed copy of his next book. If he ever finished it, that was. He started to key Mark's number into his phone when Sofia appeared in his office. He hadn't even heard the door open.

He froze, mid-dial. 'What are you doing here?'

'Me? What the hell are *you* doing here? I think the last time you came in on a Saturday was after the last launch party. And that's because you were drunk and slept on the couch here.'

Her words surprised him. It was the truth, but all he could think of in the moment was the launch party two books before that one. The one where he called Becky from the Ritz and told her he had slept on the couch at the office.

Sofia.

There were moments where he found himself holding his breath at the sight of her. Just for a few extra seconds, and it was usually when Sofia was the least put-together, her hair thrown into a loose ponytail, her lips pursed in concentration on something, her smooth cheeks – free from any makeup – just the perfect hue of femininity. This didn't happen often, and Tommy always caught himself, exhaled, then went on with whatever he'd been doing.

He never told Becky it was Sofia, even when she had outright asked him. *Was it Sofia? Was she the one you fucked?* And the answer had been no: a lie, yet another lie, but it was the answer he gave. He told Becky it had been a fan on a book tour, and Becky was always cold now when Tommy traveled, which was far less often than it used to be. Sofia remained in her job and Tommy couldn't think of anyone better for the role. She dealt with things, and she knew Tommy well enough that they often communicated in partial sentences, half-words, and body language. Tommy was able to confide in her, bounce ideas off her, learn her perspectives on things he had never even considered. In a weird, fucked-up way, Sofia was Tommy's best friend, and he wanted her around him. But it was Becky he loved, and he had learned, mostly from his affair, that Becky and his kids were the only things he was not willing to sacrifice. Not for anything. There was a time he hadn't realized this, but not anymore.

'Something's come up. Actually, I could use your help.'

He showed Sofia the letter. He felt just as slimy lying to Sofia as he had to Becky. Sofia's reaction was similar.

'Holy shit, Tommy. This is horrible.'

'I know. I'm leaving tomorrow to go away for a few days, and I want some security for Becky and the kids. Can you arrange that for me?'

'Security? Like what kind?'

'The kind that makes sure nothing bad happens to them.'

She blinked. Once. Twice.

'Where are you going?'

'I don't know. I need to finish my book, and I think this lunatic is more interested in me than my family. So I'm going to keep myself away from her for a few days to make it safer.'

Sofia stood there staring at him, assessing.

'Tommy . . . this is—'

'Crazy, I know. Becky said the same thing. Sofia, please just take care of it, will you? I need it done today, and don't worry about cost.'

Sofia seemed lost in thought, her gaze drifting out the window, unfocused. Then she snapped out of her reverie and looked at her boss.

'Of . . . of course, Tommy. I don't have a clue how to go about it, but I'll figure it out. I . . . I was just thinking about something else.'

'What?' Tommy asked.

'About a weird thing that happened this morning.' Then she told him about the woman in the parking lot. Tommy didn't find it too strange. He had a lot of fans, and many were a little off.

'I think the weirdest thing is my wife asked you to run her errands,' he said. 'I'll talk to her about that.' Becky always assigned a lower status level to Sofia's job description than what her role actually encompassed. Tommy often thought she felt threatened by Sofia.

Sofia took a step forward. 'But you don't think it's a little coincidental that this woman – who happens to be this massive fan of yours – literally runs into me?'

'There's over a million and a half copies of that book out there,' he said. 'It's not like the Magna Carta fell out of her purse.' He nodded to her own purse. 'You have it in there? I'll sign it now.'

She looked at him for a moment, as if waiting for him to change his mind. Then she pulled the book out and handed it to him.

He put it on his desk and grabbed a pen. 'Thought you said she read this a couple of times.'

'That's what she told me.'

He opened the book and felt the spine resist. He had opened a lot of unread books before, and this was exactly how they felt.

'No way,' he said. 'This book is brand new.'

'You see?' Sofia said. 'I told you there was something weird about her.'

Then he knew. Tommy felt his stomach hollow out.

'Who did she want me to sign it to?'

Sofia answered immediately. 'Elizabeth.'

'Elizabeth?'

'That's right.'

Tommy leafed through the pages of the book, looking for another note. He pulled out the receipt and saw an address scribbled on it.

Elizabeth
71481 Rade Cr.
Centennial, CO 80015

Rade's name jumped out at him. So did the house number: 71481. July 14, 1981.

The day of the killing.

'This is her address?'

'It's where she asked me to send the book. *You think she's the one who wrote this note?*' She shook the note in her hand.

Tommy did his best to seem disinterested, but had to lower his head to do so.

'I don't know.' He looked down at the receipt with the bogus address written on it. Elizabeth was sending him another message: *You can't hide from me.* 'Listen, I know I'm asking a lot, but just get some kind of security ASAP for them, OK? Cancel any plans you had today – this is now your priority. I'll make it up to you. I promise.'

'Of course, Tommy.'

Sofia stood there for a moment longer.

'And please shut my door on the way out. I need a little privacy, please.' It was a colder tone than she was used to hearing from him, but Tommy just needed things done now. He didn't have the time or the energy for massaging relationships. Sofia would understand.

'Be safe, OK, Tommy?'

'I will.' He gave her a smile, and she gave him a weak one in return. Two smiles, neither of which conveyed happiness.

She walked out of the office, the door softly clicking shut behind her.

Tommy grabbed his phone and dialed Mark's cell phone.

Mark answered on the second ring.

'Mark, it's Tommy.'

There were a few seconds of silence before Mark Singletary's lead-lined tone rumbled into the phone. Tommy hadn't heard that voice in thirty years.

'Tommy. Hell. I was going to call you today. I know why you're calling.'

'Mark . . .'

'The bitch is back.'

TEN

'She found you, too?' Tommy asked.

'Showed up at a campaign rally last week. Passed me a note. Didn't recognize her at first. But it was the eyes. The eyes brought me back.'

'What did the note say?'

Mark hesitated. '*I still remember what you taste like.*'

'Jesus,' Tommy said.

'Yeah, no kidding. I thought my heart was going to stop. It was all I could do to keep smiling at the people in the crowd. What about you?'

'Pretended to be a fan. Passed me a note. Then harassed my assistant a bit.'

'Your *assistant* knows about this?'

'No. I didn't tell her anything.' Tommy heard voices in the background over the phone. 'Aren't you golfing right now?'

'Just finished,' Mark said. 'I can't be overheard where I'm standing. But don't say anything stupid.'

Tommy wasn't sure what qualified as stupid.

'Do you know about Jason?' Tommy asked.

'No. She talk to him, too?'

'No. He's dead. Fifteen years ago.'

Mark's voice was full of practiced emotion. 'You're kidding me? How?'

'Hanged himself.'

'That's a horrible shame.'

'Exactly.'

'He was a good kid.'

'We were *all* good kids, Mark.' *More or less*, he didn't add. 'She wants me to come to you. Did you know that? She wrote me an e-mail. It said, "Contact Mark – he's easy to find. Go to him."'

A small sigh escaped from the other end of the phone. 'I know. She sent me an e-mail as well. "Bring Tommy here," it said. I tried to reply but got a bounce-back. Why does she want us together?'

'God knows. Some kind of sick reunion fantasy?'

'You have to come here,' Mark said. 'We have to do what she says. No choice here, Tommy.' Tommy could hear the tendrils of desperation in his voice. 'Too much to lose.'

Tommy wanted to disagree, tell Mark he was weak. But he couldn't because he agreed with him.

'I told my wife I was leaving for a few days to work on my book.'

'That's perfect,' Mark said. 'My wife's family owns a gorgeous rental property in downtown Charleston. Place is three hundred years old. I'll make sure we don't have any renters in there, and you come out as soon as you can.'

'Sure thing, Mark. But I want to leave soon. Like, tomorrow.'

'Got it. I'll make sure it's ready.' He rambled off the property's address, which Tommy quickly jotted down. 'Call me after you make your flight reservation, and I can meet you at the house. It'll be good to see you.' He paused, and Tommy could picture his old friend softly shaking his head the way a bad actor would if instructed to think of something nostalgic. 'Goddamn. Tommy Devereaux. Where did all the time go? Life moves by too fast.'

'Faster for some than others,' Tommy replied. *Rade never made it past ten.*

'Amen to that.'

Then Mark was gone. No *goodbye*. No *see ya soon*. Just *amen to that* and then a silent line.

Tommy put the phone on his desk and stared out his office window, wondering if Elizabeth would be following him to South Carolina.

He was hoping she would.

ELEVEN

Sunday morning.

Tommy woke and sucked in traces of the cool October air that had crept in through the bedroom window during the night. He looked over and saw Becky burrowed beneath the covers; she was either trying to stay warm or she was avoiding the day. Maybe both.

The rest of yesterday hadn't gone well. The security firm Sofia had contacted had sent someone over within three hours. Man by the name of Stuart. Despite his non-threatening name, Stuart looked like he could eviscerate someone with his gaze but would prefer to do it with his bare hands instead. He arrived at Tommy's doorstep in a perfectly tailored gray suit and sunglasses so dark they seemed to bend light. He did a full perimeter 'check and diagnostic' before sitting the whole family down to tell them how things were going to be done. Tommy watched Becky turn white, then red, and then redder, before wondering if he should be worried about her blood pressure. Despite the perceived threat looming over all of them, it was clear Becky didn't like having her schedule or freedom of movement fucked with. But, as Tommy knew, there was nothing she could do.

Stuart was very clear he was in charge.

Chance was excited. Evie was anxious. Becky was pissed off. Tommy and Becky barely seemed to share a bed that night, and they had fallen asleep in a screaming silence. He had thought about her question from the day before, about her asking him if this was 'about something else'.

He tried not to let his mind wander to the days after his confession of cheating, but Becky's current iciness toward him reminded him of that time, though now there was just an undefined suspicion rather than knowledge of any betrayal. Tommy's stomach tightened remembering the unanswered phone calls in the days after his confession two years ago, or receiving calls from the kids but not from his wife. Or the heartbreaking confusion in Chance's voice when, by the third day of silence and hotel rooms, Tommy asked his boy to put Mommy on the phone. Chance had only said, 'Mommy doesn't want to talk to you. I don't know why.'

By the fifth day she had agreed to talk to him only in a counseling session, which started their long and painful road back to trust. But once a trust like that is broken, it's never fully restored. It's just glued, and all you can do is hope the glue holds.

Tommy knew he was a fucking idiot to think she would just fully trust him again. People just aren't like that. He couldn't even imagine what he would have done if she had been the one to cheat. Probably not been so forgiving. But she was a better person than he was. She always had been, and being with her made him a better man. He could not lose her. He would not.

Tommy forced himself out of bed and into the bathroom. He looked in the mirror and decided the two-day-old stubble was going to become three. Then he threw on a bathrobe and walked down the hall to the kids' rooms. Evie mimicked her mother – a motionless lump underneath a blanket. Oswald, their fourteen-year-old tabby, was a motionless lump on top of the blanket.

Chance's room was adjacent to Evie's, and Tommy pushed the door open. Chance was up, or at least awake. He was on his back in bed, ear buds nested in his ears, playing his ZoomBox Go. The glow from the game console's screen made Chance look like something from a wax museum.

Chance caught the movement and turned his head. He paused the game and looked over.

'Morning, Dad.'

'Morning, yourself. You don't want to sleep in a little more? It's Sunday.'

'Uh uh. Not tired.'

He got that from his father. Mornings were not to be sacrificed for sleep when anything else could be done.

'You looked good in the game yesterday,' Tommy said. 'Real good.'

'Thanks. We still lost.'

'That you did.'

'You hitting the gym?' Chance asked.

'Not today, buddy.' Sometimes Chance would join him in their home gym, and Tommy liked teaching his boy about exercise. His own dad had been an amateur boxer, so Tommy had always known the value of sweat and pain. 'I'm actually going on a trip today for a few days. I need to get away and finish my book.'

'I know, Mom said. That's why Stuart's here, huh?'

Stuart was being quartered in one of several spare bedrooms in the house. Tommy wondered if the man even slept.

'Yeah, something like that.'

Chance stopped playing his game and looked up. 'Why do we need protection?'

'We're just being safe, Chance. That's all.'

'But why?'

'Because, believe it or not, your dad is pretty famous. And some-times famous people attract the attention of crazy people.' Tommy searched his son's eyes for fear and found only fascination. 'Stuart's job is to keep the crazy people away without interfering too much in our normal lives. But it's important you do what he says, OK? It's just for a few days.' *Hopefully.*

'Is he going to school with me?'

'No, Chance. I don't think so. But he might give you some pointers on how to be safe at school.'

'Is this like when you moved out a few years ago?'

Tommy tensed hearing the words.

'No,' he said. 'It's nothing at all like that, buddy. Just a quick business trip.'

Tommy braced himself for a deluge of more questions, but Chance merely absorbed this information and muttered, 'Cool.' Then he retreated back into his game.

Tommy envied him his ability to absorb and process information.

Downstairs, Tommy sought comfort in his espresso machine. He took his double shot and his iPhone over to the kitchen counter, checking his e-mail and voicemail. Nothing more from Elizabeth. She had receded back into the shadows as quickly as she had appeared, but that gave him no comfort. Her plan involved more than just scaring him, he was certain of that. He just didn't know what exactly she wanted.

But he *should* know what she wanted.

Tommy had been writing thrillers for years. Thrillers about women who killed. He had researched all types of dangerous and brutal women, enough so that he occasionally received calls from the FBI looking to pick his brain. Tommy was familiar with virtually every multiple murder involving a female perp over the last two hundred years.

Women killed for different reasons than men. This wasn't a universal truth, but it proved valid often enough for criminologists to be able to outline distinct differences in behavior. Male killers – especially serial killers – garnered far more media attention primarily because their crimes were often horrific in their violence. Jeffrey Dahmer was a prime example of this, among many others. Men killed for a variety of reasons, but the number one reason women killed was money. According to the Kelleher Typology, these women are called Black Widows.

Elizabeth hadn't killed Rade for money.

Nor was she a Revenge Killer, an Angel of Death, or even a Career Killer. From Tommy's few hours with Elizabeth and countless years thinking about her, he guessed she fell most closely into the classification of Sexual Predator, a defined type of female killer so rare that only one other person had even been classified as one in the US. Aileen Wuornos was convicted of killing seven men in Florida between 1989 and 1990, shooting them all after claiming the men had raped her.

Tommy thought back to that day. How Elizabeth climaxed after smashing the rock into Rade's skull. And what she had done with the other boys immediately afterwards. Yes, no doubt. Elizabeth was a Sexual Predator. He wouldn't be surprised to find out she had killed more than one person. In fact, he would be surprised if she hadn't. A Sexual Predator would never be sated with one kill. Tommy grabbed his laptop and opened the screen. The thought from earlier came back to him. The story needed truth. Real truth, and not just in the first chapter.

A feeling came over him that was both depressing and exciting. Depressing, because it involved throwing away a lot of hard work. Exciting, because it would be something he'd never done before.

He let the idea form just a little in his head and then he stopped it and tucked it away. It was the kind of idea not to be acted upon impulsively. It needed a little time to ferment. He would revisit it soon.

Perhaps, he thought, in Charleston.

TWELVE

Tommy felt the thickness of the South Carolina air as soon as he reached the jetway. It didn't feel like Octobers he was used to in Colorado. He fumbled for his phone and dialed Becky as he made his way toward the terminal.

'Hi, baby. Just landed.'

She sounded tired or disinterested. 'Good flight?'

'Pretty decent.'

'Great.'

'*Becky* . . .'

'Just be productive and then come home, OK? Maybe when you finish your book, you'll feel better about everything else.'

He didn't want to tell her that this book was far from being finished.

'I promise.'

'Good,' Becky said. 'Have you decided when yet or did you buy a one-way ticket?'

Ouch. Tommy shut his eyes and tried to keep his voice level.

'I booked it for Thursday,' he said. 'Hopefully I can come home earlier.'

Tommy walked into the terminal and saw it was largely empty, something he never expected inside an airport. He wondered why it felt so strange, and then he realized it wasn't the empty airport that gave him an unsettling feeling. It was the sense he was being watched.

'Try to come home earlier,' Becky said. 'I don't like the way you left. I don't like any of this. And having this goon here just creeps me out. I feel like a prisoner.'

Tommy looked around, searching for something that didn't seem right. 'I know. I know. Just . . . just trust me, OK?' *She's here*, he thought. She followed me to Charleston.

'The more you ask me to do that the less I want to.'

'Listen, I have to go. I'll call later to say good night to everyone, OK?'

'Fine.'

He pressed the phone hard against his ear. 'I love you.'

She was gone.

Tommy stood in the terminal, phone still pressed to his ear, and realized it wasn't really empty, not really. It just felt that way. The white noise of humanity he usually heard in an airport was replaced by a thick silence, which was all the more pronounced because of the fact that he did see people moving about, talking on the phones, greeting loved ones. But there was no life to any of it, and Tommy felt suspended, as if in a dream.

Tommy lowered his phone. He turned his head, to the left, and then to the right, and in a flash he saw the bounce of blond hair – attached to a tall woman – behind a row of books in the store near the rental car counter.

Tommy hesitated, then walked over to the bookstore. Upon entering, he found only two other people inside: the clerk, and an Asian woman browsing the magazines.

The clerk looked up, offered a smile and a faint hint of recognition, as if perhaps she had seen his image on many book jackets before.

Elizabeth was here. Maybe not in the airport, but she was here. In Charleston. He could feel it.

The thought didn't chill him. If anything, it was what he had expected. And if she was here, then it meant she wasn't in Denver, near his family. But there was something else.

It was *exciting*.

As much as he hated to admit it, and as much as he wished he could change the past, there was a kind of macabre thrill about Elizabeth being back in his life. For Tommy, it was almost like one of his characters had come to life.

He walked out of the store and dialed his agent.

'Dominic, listen, I need you to extend the deadline.'

'Very funny.'

'I'm serious. I want to go in a new direction.'

Silence. Then: 'Please tell me you're fucking with me.'

'Six months. I need six months.'

There was a moment of silence before the explosion.

'*Six months?*'

'I know. I know. But we have to. It'll be a better book.'

'Screw that.' Tommy could picture Dominic's puffy cheeks turning a darker shade of crimson. Whispers of sweat growing on his forehead. 'Tommy, you could end your book with a goddamn haiku for all they care. All the artwork is done – it's ready to roll. It's no longer about it being a good book. It's about it being a *timely* book.'

Tommy squeezed the phone.

'It's not about the ending,' Tommy said. 'The whole book is wrong. The characters . . . they turned out not to be who I thought they were.'

'Jesus, Tommy, how did three weeks become *six months*?'

'I'm Tommy Devereaux, goddamnit. And you know I never pull that card. OK, maybe every now and then I do, but I'm sure as hell justified in pulling it now. I write good books, sell millions of 'em, and never demand shit. I'm a publisher's dream. But not now. Now I'm going to be the pain-in-the-ass prima donna that *I've earned* the right to be. I need six months to finish this book. End of discussion, Dominic. Now go do your goddamn job.'

It was Tommy's turn to hang up. He felt guilty, but it had to be done. The book was wrong and making it right had suddenly become second in importance to keeping Elizabeth quiet. And the two things were intricately entwined. Tommy sensed that getting the book right might just be the thing to rid him of Elizabeth. It was a sense he hadn't quite figured out, but that was the beauty of such things: senses fed on instinct and feeling, needing no logic to let them grow.

Tommy went outside and found the taxi stand. One pulled up, and he half-expected Elizabeth to be driving, wearing a chauffeur's cap and blood-red lipstick. She wasn't. He gave the cabbie the address Mark had e-mailed earlier. The cabbie nodded without speaking and pulled into the traffic.

Tommy closed his eyes and thought about his book. He wondered what it would feel like to delete the existing draft of the book completely from his hard drive and his backup, erasing it forever. Would that free him, or would it make him feel like he wasted the last year-and-a-half of his professional life? He couldn't decide, so he let the rhythm of the cab's movements take over, and minutes later he felt himself drifting to sleep.

'—home?'

Tommy jolted, realizing the cab driver was talking to him. He straightened in his seat.

'What's that?'

'Nice address,' the cabbie repeated, his gaze ricocheting off the rear-view mirror, directly at Tommy. 'That your home?'

'Um, no. No. I'm just renting the place for a few days.'

'Pretty expensive, I'm guessing.'

It's free, actually. 'Yes. It is. Hope it's worth it.'

'Oh, it will be. You're right in the thick of it there. Been to Charleston before?'

Tommy looked out his window as they passed what was surely an ancient cemetery. Tombstones leaned in different directions, teeth loosened in a fight.

'No, I haven't.'

'Best city in the country, you ask me.'

Tommy felt the gentle rumble of the cab as it slowed from a smooth asphalt street to cobblestone. Out the window, dusk approached. A three-story Italianate house loomed above him, its intricate wrought iron fencing adorning the exterior balcony on the second level. Three dormers poked out from the third level, like eyes scanning the street below. It was a house suited for nighttime, gas lamps, and Victorian vampires.

'I don't doubt it,' he told the cabbie. Tommy suddenly wished he was here on vacation rather than to see Mark.

The taxi slowed a few houses past the vampire house to one different in appearance yet identical in spirit.

Three stories of white clapboard rose to the sky. Three windows per floor on the street side, with black shutters encasing each of them. Porches extended from the left side of the massive house on all three levels, the bottom porch fully enclosed. The house was almost perfectly square, and the symmetry of it was somehow beautiful and unnerving.

'Twenty-seven King Street,' the cabbie said. 'Knew it would be a nice place.'

Tommy looked up at his home for the next few days. 'It certainly is.'

'Didn't know it was a rental.'

Tommy opened the door and paid the driver. As the taxi rolled away, he climbed the four stone steps leading to the enclosed porch.

'Goddamn Tommy Devereaux,' a voice said. Mark Singletary was reclined in a wicker high-back chair, a hardback of one of Tommy's books in his hand.

Tommy opened the screen door and smiled. 'Goddamn Mark Singletary.'

Mark stood and Tommy walked up to him. If this was Jason – poor Jason, dead at the end of a rope – Tommy would have hugged his old friend, but there was something about Mark that didn't make such a gesture feel welcome. Tommy reached out his hand. Mark's grip was strong but not overbearing. The grip of a politician.

Mark smiled and Tommy took his old friend in, absorbing thirty years of changes in seconds. The man looked just like his web-page photo. He looked . . . practiced.

Thick, styled black hair had replaced dark unwashed hair. Shoulders and dimples had equally broadened, a testament to practiced exercise and smiling, no doubt. The man stood straighter, taller, and yet somehow more falsely than the old friend he knew. There was no substance to his bearing, and no bearing to his substance.

Though there were some similarities to his old self, the only constant from thirty years ago, from the boy Tommy once knew, were Mark Singletary's eyes. They were exactly the same as they had been back then. Small, discreet orbs, the color a bottomless brown, radiating an altogether different sense than the smile just below them. There was a malevolent intensity in those eyes, so well disguised you would have had to look at the mug shots of a thousand killers to recognize it.

Tommy recognized it.

Frustrated. The word from the day in the woods came back to him.

'You look great, Tommy,' Mark said. 'You were such a scrawny kid.'

'I spend a lot of time in the gym. Weights. Cardio. Some boxing.'

'Just like your old man. How is he?'

'Dead. Both my parents. Alzheimer's and cancer.'

'I'm sorry.' He said it with a trace of smile still remaining on his face.

'How are your parents, Mark?'

'They're still hanging on.' Mark slapped him on the shoulder. 'Come inside, I'll show you around.'

Tommy leaned down and picked up his bag, noticing the last sliver of the sun dip below the peak of the ancient house across the street.

He followed his old friend into the house.

Night was coming.

THIRTEEN

The house had a substantial library, rivaling even Tommy's. Tommy scanned the book titles and they seemed just random enough to have been put there by an interior designer. The two men sat in leather chairs, drinking Scotch as darkness crept behind the creamy sheer curtains.

'So what now?' Tommy asked.

'I don't know.'

A silence uncomfortable to Tommy and likely not so to Mark settled between them, and Tommy got the sense Mark wasn't quite ready to talk about the real reason Tommy flew halfway across the country.

Mark was already halfway through his first drink before Tommy had even touched his. 'I'm really proud of you, Tommy,' he continued. 'Of what you did with your life.' Mark said it as if Tommy had been on the verge of being a meth addict.

'Thanks.'

'The world needs storytellers. World's *second*-oldest profession.' He gave Tommy a wink.

'Looks like you've done a lot with yourself as well.'

'Oh, I have. I have. But this is just the beginning. State Senate is just a stepping stone.'

'To what?'

A shrug. Sip of the drink. 'Something bigger.' Mark looked around the room. 'I'll be honest, I was fortunate to marry into serious Southern money. This house is Mara's – that's my wife. Been in her family for over a century. Built sometime in the early eighteenth century. Rent it out from time to time, but use it mostly for friends and family coming into town.' He tilted his head back and he gazed at the punched-tin ceiling. 'Lots of ghosts here,' he mumbled. Then back to Tommy and back in focus. 'Point is, I married into money, and I know how to use that money. I financed my first campaign and won in a landslide. Re-election is looking certain. One more term here and then I'll do something on a national level.'

'Senate?'

'Wherever the people need me most,' he said. Tommy sensed the man actually believed what he was saying. 'Country is changing and we need to change it back.'

'We?'

Mark shook his head and smiled. 'I know, I know. Not a lot of your kind in our party.'

'My kind?'

'You know. Artsy-fartsy types.' Another wink, this one less playful somehow.

'You mean creative free-thinkers and successful business people?'

More insincere laughter. 'Same old Tommy. Scrappy to the end.'

What the hell did *that* mean?

Mark dipped the tip of his index finger into his Scotch and stirred it before sticking his finger in his mouth. 'Truth be told,' he said after a stretch of silence, 'Mara's family isn't as keen on financing my career as they once were.'

'That so?'

'Her mother thinks I've become . . . too *severe* in some of my views. What she calls severe I simply call God-fearing, and I won't change my views.' Mark sipped at his drink and kept his mouth on the glass for an extra moment, as if by not doing so he would reveal his fangs.

Tommy looked at the man who once was his friend. He wasn't sure what he was to him now, other than a direct connection to the worst day of his life. 'When did you get so religious, Mark?'

A heavy sigh. 'After.'

Tommy nodded, knowing what *after* referred to. It was the same in his own life. There was a *before*, an *after*, and a single, brilliant line of demarcation separating them. In Mark's *after*, the man found God and power. In Tommy's *after*, he wrote horror stories to keep the demons from burrowing too deeply.

It seemed Mark was ready to talk.

'Did you ever tell anyone?' Tommy asked.

'Of course not. Never.' Mark leaned in with a trace of panic on his face. 'You?'

'No,' Tommy said. *Except the whole world.* 'Except . . . except my new book talks about it. As fiction, of course.'

Mark nodded over to Tommy's book, which rested on an antique wood table between them. The brilliant red cover shone with the intensity of its title. *The Blood of the Willing.* That was Tommy's last book. The first chapter of his new book debuted at the end of the paperback version.

'Tommy, you didn't even change her name.'

'I thought she was gone forever. She was dead, for all I knew.'

'But she isn't. She isn't dead at all. And she can ruin everything. You should have known better.' Mark gulped down the last of his drink. 'How did you figure out Jason was dead?'

'My assistant did some research,' Tommy said.

'You're sure it's him?'

'Yes. I'm sure.'

Mark looked at his empty tumbler, as if it would suddenly reveal secrets to him. 'It seems strange. To have killed himself. I wonder . . .'

'Wonder what?'

Mark turned his head and looked out the window to the street. Tommy followed his gaze, seeing nothing of interest.

'Nothing,' Mark said, turning back to Tommy. 'Nothing.'

'Mark, what am I doing here?'

'You're here because you're scared,' Mark said. 'She told you to come here and you did. You're scared of the truth coming out, so you're doing what you're told.'

Tommy didn't like being told he was scared of anything, whether it was the truth or not. 'And you?' he asked. 'Are you scared, Mark?'

Mark looked at the floor. 'Like a little boy lost in the forest,' he said.

Tommy didn't believe Mark knew what that felt like at all.

'We all have things to lose, Tommy. We're just trying to hold on to them as long as we can. I'm not in a place where I can afford for any of this to come out.'

Tommy asked him the question he was used to only asking himself. 'Will you ever reach that place, Mark? Where you're ready to tell the world what happened, no matter the consequences?'

Mark walked around him and headed for the bottle of Scotch. 'I don't know, Tommy. I just don't know.'

'We were just kids, Mark. We didn't have a choice. He . . . the *Watcher* . . . would have killed us.' Tommy had told himself the same thing every day for the past thirty years. 'But we *could* have said something, Mark. Even a few years later. Given comfort to Rade's parents.'

Mark poured himself another drink, the Scotch splashing off the bottom of the crystal tumbler and sprinkling the silver serving tray. 'Tell me, Tommy. What do you lose if she reveals everything about that day?'

'I don't think anyone would believe her,' Tommy said.

'That's not what I asked. I asked what would you lose.'

'Hell, Mark. I can't even imagine.'

'Yes, you can. And you have. Say it out loud.'

Tommy felt a chill like a cold hand on his neck as he spoke. 'Assuming nothing could be definitely proven, I would lose a lot of respect from everyone I care about. I'd lose readership for sure. And if it could be proven . . . that I helped kill that boy . . .'

'You didn't kill him. *She* did the killing.'

'Doesn't matter,' Tommy said. 'It won't look like that. We all left our blood on the knife, remember? If they get a positive DNA match from the knife, then I could certainly go to prison.'

'Would your wife leave you?'

Tommy had wondered this as well. 'I'm not sure. I'd like to think she wouldn't, but I really don't know. We almost split up once before. And this . . . I mean. Shit, Mark. I just don't know.'

Mark leaned back against his chair and pointed at him. 'Exactly. You would lose everything. The moment you lose your family, you've lost everything. I feel the same way, Tommy. The same way. So the next question is, what would you do to prevent the truth from coming out?'

Tommy scrutinized the man in front of him, trying to find traces of the childhood friend he once knew.

'I'm not the only one at risk here.'

'You most certainly are not. I've got everything to lose as well. But there's a difference.'

'What's that?'

Mark took another sip. 'She's not interested in *me*.'

The cold hand now seemed to squeeze Tommy's whole body. 'What do you mean?'

'We spoke.' Mark's face betrayed the slightest of grins. 'Right here, actually. She sat where you're sitting right now.'

'*When?*'

'Couple of weeks ago. Before she contacted you. I didn't tell you that on the phone . . . I don't know why. Maybe afraid you wouldn't come out here, I suppose.'

'*What did she tell you, Mark?*'

Mark shrugged, as if sitting down for a drink with a killer was part of his everyday routine. 'She wants you to do something for her. I don't know the specifics, but her only interest in me is to help convince you to do what she says. The first step was getting you out here to Charleston. Mission accomplished.'

'So you're collaborating with her.'

'Not collaborating. *Obeying*. Just like you were when she told you to find me. I'm a proud man, Tommy, but I know when I'm backed in a corner. I don't have a choice. And neither do you.'

'Pride's a sin.'

'Everything's a sin, Tommy. That's why God invented forgiveness.'

'What else did she say?'

Mark looked at his watch and put his glass down. 'No time right now, Tommy. Sorry.'

'Jesus, Mark. What the hell's going on? Why can't you talk to me?'

'Gotta go – fundraiser. I'm coming up on an election. Time's a little tight to come by. I'll give you a call in the morning.'

Tommy stood, angered by the nonchalance of the politician. 'OK, so we'll discuss the possibility of us going to prison and/or being hunted by a killer at a more convenient time for you?'

Mark's expression hardened and his eyes narrowed. 'Tommy, I will tell you everything later. But I don't know much – just that she wants you to do something for her. I'm just asking that you listen to what she has to say. For both our sakes.'

'And why should I care about your sake?'

Mark walked up to him and placed both his hands on Tommy's shoulders. His glare softened into a practiced smile. Tommy smelled the Scotch on Mark's breath and it made him think of his father, who had consumed more Scotch than water in his lifetime.

'Because we used to be friends, and I would like to think we still are. Friends help each other out. If she had wanted something from me, I would have done it. For both of us.'

Tommy wondered how the man was able to keep his face so completely still. 'You really think God has forgiven you, Mark?'

Mark actually winced, as if the question caused him pain. It was then that Tommy saw his old friend was more than just scared about his past coming out. He was truly worried for his soul.

'I do, Tommy. I really do.'

'I think we're going to hell,' Tommy said.

Mark dropped his hands. 'Let me ask you something else, Tommy. That day. You didn't fuck her. Why?'

It was the last question Tommy expected, mostly because of how Mark asked it. Here was this man, this polished politician, who was so used to crafting language to appease the ears listening to him, and the word *fuck* just rolled off his tongue as if being muttered by the frustrated teenager from all those years ago. *Why didn't you fuck her, Tommy?*

'Because I knew if she controlled me then, she would control me forever.'

Mark's body stiffened. 'Is that what you think, Tommy? Do you think she controls me?' He wagged his finger. 'Let me tell you something. *Nobody* controls me. She just has better cards to play at the moment.'

'Seems to me she controls everything,' Tommy said. Then he took a chance, played a hunch. 'And I'm not so sure you mind that. Maybe there's something about her being back you like.'

Tommy couldn't be certain, but he thought that hit a nerve. Could Mark be happy about Elizabeth being back? Did he feel a nervous excitement about who she was and what she represented? After all, Tommy couldn't deny there was something deathly compelling about the woman, and he wondered if Mark felt it, too.

Mark didn't answer.

'Good night, Tommy,' he said,

Tommy watched as Mark waited on the sidewalk. Within seconds, a black Lincoln Town Car rolled up to the curb and Mark disappeared inside, whisked away to some other Important Thing To Do.

Tommy stood alone, inside the house of ghosts, wondering what the night would bring.

FOURTEEN

Tommy walked the cobblestone streets and alleys, feeling the weight of time surrounding him. Darkness blanketed Old Charleston. The late-summer evening was temperate, enough so that many of the restaurants lining the street still offered outdoor seating.

Though the messenger bag slung over his right shoulder was light, the straps seemed to cut into his skin, the weight of what was inside bending his thoughts toward it. Inside, on his Dell laptop, was his unfinished manuscript, the one that he ostensibly came here to complete. The one that brought Elizabeth back. The one that was completely wrong.

The same feeling he had at the airport returned to him, like a low-voltage current suddenly running through him. Tommy turned his head and scanned the faces closest to him, seeing no one who looked like Elizabeth. But it didn't matter. She was here, and she would find him. It was all part of her plan. Tommy's only advantage was he was no longer scared of her. She wanted something from him, which meant there would be a conversation before anything else could happen. Tommy wondered if that conversation was going to happen tonight. If it was, all he could do was wait and work on his manuscript until she slithered over to him.

Tommy strolled until he found a pub that suited his mood. He took a seat outside, one offering a view of an historic inn across the street that could have been featured in any movie about the Revolutionary War. After ordering a lager from the waitress, Tommy slid his laptop from his messenger bag and powered it up.

He scrolled through the book aimlessly, feeling the weight of all the work that went into it. In terms of fiction, he considered it his best work yet.

But it wasn't the story he was supposed to tell. As much as Tommy wanted to find the ending for his book, he knew he would never find the right one. He realized that as much as he wanted to unburden himself of the awful secret he had lived with for so long, it couldn't be done with half-truths and substantial chunks of pure fiction. It couldn't be done with *The Blood of the Young*.

He thought more about his idea, the one that depressed and excited him.

He flagged the waitress down.

'I need a shot of tequila. Do you have Don Julio Reposado?'

She smiled at him.

'I can check. You celebrating?'

Tommy thought about that. 'A bit of a celebration, and a bit of a funeral.'

She seemed to accept this as a common reply, and arrived a minute later.

'Congratulations and my condolences.' She set the glimmering ounce of liquid in front of him and left.

Tommy closed his eyes and brought the shot glass to his lips. He tilted the glass upwards and let the tequila slide down his throat, getting an oaky taste of both ice and fire.

He set down the empty glass and then did something he would never even have dreamed of doing. He closed the file on his computer and deleted it. Ninety thousand words, gone. Then he emptied his trash, assuring he couldn't get it back.

He attached to the pub's open Wi-Fi signal and logged on to his online backup system. He then deleted the manuscripts from all of his online backups.

The Blood of the Young was gone.

He did it all so fast he didn't second-guess his actions, which was the point. In just a few moments, over a year's worth of work vanished. All that remained were his memories of it, and, while that scared the shit out of him, it forced him to move on.

He was cleansed.

He would write something new. Something honest. And something far scarier than what he had just deleted.

How the hell am I going to tell Becky? Or Dominic?

Don't get distracted, Tommy. Feel the moment. Know the truth. *Write* the truth. And write it all, starting from the point she came back in your life.

Tommy opened up a blank manuscript template. Chapter one was easy. All he had to do was think back to the day she had come back into his life.

Tommy Devereaux stared out from the twenty-fourth floor of the downtown Hyatt, soaking in the expanse of the Rocky Mountains, laid out before him like a painting. The Peaks Lounge was one of his usual late-afternoon writing spots. The drinks and the Wi-Fi signal were both strong, and that's about all any writer needed. More than anything, though, the lounge always had a good buzz of energy, which he preferred around him when he was working. Ironically, a room full of people talking and laughing helped him to focus. And, when he needed the help, Tommy could look into the crowd and pluck out the perfect description for a character he was writing. Characters were everywhere; all you had to do was look.

And he wrote. Furiously. He wrote with a purpose he had never felt before, as if he was trying to get a confession out before his last breath left his body.

Hours passed. He looked down at an empty dinner plate and vaguely recalled a steak sitting on it at one point, but barely remembered eating. All he could hear was the staccato tapping of his fingertips against the plastic keys on his laptop keyboard. All he could see were words – new words – filling the screen, page after page. He would document everything that had happened since the moment Elizabeth came back. He would use real names, at least for now. And the words would express the fear and the anxiety he was feeling, because it was all real.

Best of all, he didn't have to think of an ending. The ending, however it turned out to be, would furnish itself.

'I'd love to see what you're writing.'

Tommy looked up.

Elizabeth sat down next to him.

FIFTEEN

A small breeze washed over Tommy, as if coming off Elizabeth's body. He looked down at the steak knife lying across his empty plate. He wasn't sure what he was planning to do with it, but he was glad it was there.

'Hello, Elizabeth.'

'Hi, you.'

Tommy felt a surge. A surge of what, he didn't know. Maybe it was the voltage of nearby evil, but he felt it pulse gently and steadily through him as Elizabeth sat, sliding her body against the back of the metal chair. She looked nothing like she did that day at the Hyatt, but Tommy still recognized her immediately. She looked, in fact, like the sixteen-year-old from 1981. Hair was still long and red, the same shade it had been that day in the woods. Her face was smooth and white, surprisingly wrinkle-free considering the time that had passed. Wide shoulders accentuated her perfect posture and her breasts, which were even more full and round than he had remembered.

Elizabeth had done a hell of a disguise job back in Denver. Truth was, she was gorgeous, and Tommy hated himself for thinking it.

The waitress came over before Tommy could say anything else.

'Are you dining tonight, ma'am?'

'No,' Elizabeth said. 'Just a glass of Merlot, please.'

'Certainly.' The waitress nodded and reached down to clear Tommy's plate. He removed the knife from the plate and placed it on the tablecloth.

'Will you be ordering more food, sir?'

'Not sure yet.'

She seemed ready for another question but must have decided against it. She walked away, leaving Elizabeth gazing at the knife on the table.

'You think you're going to need that?' she asked.

'I'd rather err on the side of caution.'

'If I wanted to kill you, Tommy, you'd be many years dead by now.'

He believed her. Tommy stared at her face, wanting so much to take a picture of her so he could compare it to the pictures of all the other killers he had researched over the years. Look for the shared traits. The common evil.

'Have you read any of them? My books?'

The waitress dropped off the glass of wine, her gaze staying on Tommy for a few extra seconds before heading back into the kitchen.

'She likes you,' Elizabeth said. 'I could see it in her face. She *wants* you, Tommy. How does that make you feel? A young little thing like that. Must make you feel powerful.'

'You didn't answer my question.'

'She kind of reminds me of your assistant. What's her name – Sofia? Gorgeous. She wants you, too, by the way.'

Tommy's stomach clenched. 'You don't know anything about her.'

'It's in her face when she talks about you. If I didn't think you were such a good little boy, Tommy, I'd assume you were fucking her.'

Tommy said nothing. He wondered if she knew the truth about him and Sofia.

Elizabeth sipped her wine. 'Yes, Tommy. To answer your earlier questions, I've read all your books. Of course I have.'

'So you're a fan,' he said, not sure what he meant by it.

'I've always been a fan, Tommy. Of you. Of Jason. Mark.'

'Meaning?'

'Meaning we share a bond few people will ever share. We killed together. Such things are not to be taken lightly.'

Tommy glanced around before leaning across the table.

'I didn't *kill* anyone. You know that.'

'You helped cover it up. Just as bad.'

'*Helped cover it up?*' His voice was a strained whisper. 'I didn't have a choice. Your . . . *Watcher* . . . had a shotgun trained on me. What was I supposed to do?'

'I don't know, Tommy.' Her face was glass. 'Be a man?'

'I was *fourteen*.'

'Man enough age for me,' she winked.

'Who was he? Who was your accomplice?'

'He was my first Watcher. The first of many.'

'And what's a Watcher?'

She winked at him. 'Stick around for a while and maybe you'll find out.' She took another sip, the red wine washing over her lips like blood. 'You know, Tommy, you were the only one who denied me that day. I thought at first maybe you were a faggot. But your eyes betrayed you. You *wanted* me. But you also wanted to hurt me.'

'Of course I did. You killed Rade.'

'He was my first, you know. You always remember your first.'

Tommy almost didn't want to ask. 'How . . . how many have there been?'

She gave a shrug and said in a faint sing-song voice, 'Thirty-eight.'

'I don't believe you.'

Tommy looked around at the other patrons on the restaurant patio, wondering if they saw a man talking to himself. Or, perhaps, this was all actually real.

Am I sitting across the table from a woman who has killed thirty-eight people?

Tommy accessed all the years of research in his mind. All the books, all the interviews, all the endless Internet articles about female serial killers. If she's telling the truth, he thought, she must be the third most prolific female serial killer in recorded world history.

She seemed to have read his mind. 'Another two and I'll tie for second. Belle Gunness was thought to have been responsible for forty deaths.' She gave a small laugh, as if they were sharing a recollection of a good time from the past. 'Of course, I'll never reach my namesake.'

'Elizabeth Báthory,' he said, snapping his attention back to her.

'Very good, Tommy. You know your killers well.'

'It's my job.'

Elizabeth Báthory was the greatest female serial killer of all time. Back in the sixteenth and seventeenth centuries, the Bloody Countess was said to have killed over six hundred young women, torturing them at length before finally draining their blood and bathing in it, hoping to prolong her life.

Tommy looked at Elizabeth's smooth, strong arms and thought she looked nothing like a woman in her mid-forties. Had she found her own secret to life through her bloodlust?

'Did you change your name to hers?' he asked.

'No, just fortunate coincidence,' she said.

'Is that what you're doing? Are you trying to be like her?'

'*Please.* Copycat killers are so vapid.'

Tommy ran his finger along the handle of the steak knife. 'I don't believe for a second you've killed thirty-eight people.'

'I don't need you to believe me, Tommy,' she said. 'But I think we both know I'm not lying. You, with all your wonderful research, should understand my behavior and what I'm capable of.'

'I don't know anything about you. And I don't want to. I just want to be left alone.'

A larger laugh. 'Oh, you know *that's* not going to happen.'

'And what's to keep me from turning you in?'

Elizabeth rolled her eyes. 'Gee, Tommy, I don't know.' She pushed her chair back from the table and scoured the streets with her eyes. 'There you go. A cop. Right there. Why don't you go up to him and tell him everything I just told you?'

Tommy turned and saw a patrol car. The cop driving it stopped at a red light and glanced over at Tommy, offering the slightest of nods.

Elizabeth grabbed Tommy's arm, making him jump. 'C'mon, Tommy, I'll even go with you! Just think, you'll be a hero!'

He pushed her arm away. 'Stop it,' he said.

Then Elizabeth changed. In an instant, Tommy saw the monster beneath the veneer. She stood and shouted as loud as she could. 'Don't you *dare* try to hit me!'

What the hell? Tommy thought.

Elizabeth's eyes nearly disappeared behind the slits of her eyelids as she screamed again. 'You won't! You won't treat me this way!'

Tommy looked around. Everyone was watching them.

Then he saw the cop pull up on to the sidewalk and get out of his car.

He hissed at her. 'What are you *doing*?'

He heard her wheeze in rasps of fury. Then another volley of rage: '*Goddamn you!*'

The cop came up to the table, his thumbs hooked into his utility belt. He looked Tommy's age but a hell of a lot bigger and blacker. He wore the calm look of someone who had kicked enough ass in his time to know not to panic.

'Evening,' he said, his deep voice laced with Southern charm. 'There a problem here?'

'No,' Tommy said.

''Scuse me, sir, but my question was directed at the lady.'

Elizabeth drained about half of the rage from her face. She turned to the cop. 'I'm just fucking tired of it all, you know?'

'Oh, yes, ma'am. I do indeed know. I know all about that. But that doesn't concern me. What *does* concern me is if you might be worried for your safety here.'

Tommy's mind reeled as he stared at the knife on the table. *Her* safety? She just confessed to having killed thirty-eight people, and the cop was wondering about *her* fucking safety?

'Sir, I didn't do anything,' he said as calmly as he could.

The cop turned to him and narrowed his eyes. 'Well, sir, that isn't exactly true. I did see you push her arm.'

'She grabbed me and I pushed her arm away,' Tommy said. 'That's all.'

Elizabeth leaned in at Tommy. 'You're a *fucking asshole*, you know that?'

The cop stood her straight. 'Let's just all calm down now. I need IDs from both of you.'

Ice water ran through Tommy. My ID? What the hell is happening here? And why aren't I just telling him everything?

You know why, the voice inside him said. *Because it's mutually assured destruction. Doesn't matter that you were only fourteen. Doesn't matter you weren't the one holding the rock. You've researched enough of the legal system and know enough about the reactionary public to know one thing is certain: talk now and it's over.*

'Please don't make me ask you again. IDs.'

Tommy pulled his wallet from his back pocket as he tried to avoid eye contact with the handful of other diners outside. Elizabeth quickly pulled hers from a small pocketbook and handed it to the cop.

The officer studied both of them, his gaze darting back and forth between them.

'Thomas Devereaux. Colorado.' He looked up at Tommy. 'Why does that name sound familiar?'

'I don't know,' he replied. Elizabeth remained silent, though a faint smile crossed her lips.

'I need to go run these back at the patrol car. Ma'am, would you care to come with me or do you feel safe staying here?'

'I'm fine, officer. I'll stay here.'

He gave her a small nod. 'You two stay right here and I'll be back. Do you understand?'

Tommy felt himself nodding vigorously. Elizabeth barely moved her head.

The moment the cop was out of earshot Tommy leaned across the table.

'What the hell are you *doing*?' he whispered.

Elizabeth leaned back in her chair and glanced up at the night sky.

'Research,' she said.

'What?'

'Research. Just like you do. I'm trying to get in the head of my main character.' She brought her gaze back to Tommy. 'How badly does Tommy Devereaux want his misdeeds to remain unknown? Enough to keep the police at bay, even when there's a vicious serial killer within arm's reach?'

Tommy didn't want to admit it, but it made sense. 'That's why you made me come here,' he said. 'To Charleston. Because you wanted to see if I would do it. You wanted to be able to direct me, predict my patterns.'

'And now I have my answer, which I already knew,' she said. 'Tommy Devereaux is quite eager to go back to his normal life and leave this messy business behind him. Tommy Devereaux just wants this woman Elizabeth simply to *go away*.'

Tommy looked down again at the knife on the table, thinking it was perhaps sloppy on the cop's part to leave a weapon on the table when he was questioning them about a potential assault charge.

'He knows people,' she said. 'The cop. He reads people for a living. That's what he *does*. He knows you're not a threat. Not to me. Not to him. Not to anyone.'

He searched her face. 'You don't think so?' he asked. 'You don't think I could hurt someone?'

'Oh, sure, if you had to. In defense. Anyone would. But to take an active stance to harm someone?' She folded her arms across her chest, appraising him. 'It's not as easy as it seems, you know. Hurting someone. *Killing* someone. It requires an inner strength that hardly anyone possesses.'

Tommy recoiled. 'What you call strength is actually called psychopathy.'

She winked. 'So quick to label.'

The cop walked back, and Tommy could see in his saunter that they would be fine.

'OK, folks,' he said, handing them back their licenses. 'Unless the lady wants to press charges—'

'Press *charges*?' Tommy said.

The cop scowled at him. 'Unless the lady wants to press charges, you two are free to go.' He turned to her. 'Ma'am?'

Elizabeth let the moment hang far too long for Tommy's comfort. 'No, officer, I'm fine.'

'How very noble of you,' Tommy mumbled, unable to contain himself.

'Just keep the arguments verbal,' the cop said to both of them. Then he turned to Tommy. 'Oh, and Mr Devereaux.'

'Yes?'

'Good luck with your next book.'

SIXTEEN

They walked side by side down the lighted cobblestone street, an arm's length distance between them. A long arm.

'So now the police know Tommy Devereaux is in Charleston and got into what appeared to be a lover's quarrel with someone who is certainly not his wife. Fucking fantastic.'

'And that's your biggest concern?' Elizabeth asked. 'Not that you're walking next to a serial killer?'

He looked over at her. 'First, I'm not convinced you're a serial killer at all. Second, like you said, if you wanted me dead it would have been done a long time ago.'

'You're the expert,' she said.

There were only a handful of people on the street. They passed the occasional bar, but those seemed mostly empty. It was growing late and Charleston was falling asleep.

'What do you want from me? From Mark?'

She pulled a long strand of red hair back behind her ear. 'Just walking with you is nice. For starters.' She folded her arms across her chest, and in doing so she pushed up her breasts just a bit.

Tommy's phone rang.

He pulled it from his pocket and looked at the screen. *Home.*

'Damnit,' he said. 'I completely forgot to call home tonight.'

'Understandable. Considering.'

He stared at the phone as if it were a lifeline. He knew answering it was a mistake, but he had to hear Becky's voice, even if it was only to tell her he would call her back.

'Hello?'

Becky's voice had no emotion to it. 'Your children are asleep, in case you're wondering.'

He didn't know what was worse: the longing he felt at the sound of her voice, or the chill from the tone of it.

'God, I know, Beck. I . . . I got so wrapped up here I completely lost track of time.'

Elizabeth leaned in and whispered close to his ear. 'Do you think she's fucking Stuart? I bet he has a *huge* cock.'

How the hell did she know he had hired private security for his family, let alone the man's name?

'Who was that?' Becky asked.

Tommy turned away from Elizabeth and snarled at her. 'I'm writing at an outdoor café. That was the waitress.'

'It's nearly midnight there.'

'I know. I told you, I lost track of time.'

'Fine. Try to call your kids in the morning. They would like to hear from you. Good night.'

'Becky, wait.'

Silence. Then: 'Yes?'

He pressed the phone hard to his ear. 'I miss you.'

More silence.

'And I love you,' he added.

'I love you too, Tommy. Now finish writing and get home. I'm tired of worrying and wondering about you.'

'What does that mean?'

Elizabeth reached out and brushed her fingers along Tommy's shoulder. He jerked away.

'I just don't like all this cloak and dagger stuff,' Becky said. 'And I don't like having Stuart here. The whole thing is just . . . just not like you.' She didn't add what Tommy knew was there on her lips: Becky wondered if this was all about something more familiar.

'I know. When I get home, we can let him go.'

'Just come home soon,' Becky said, then disconnected the call.

'Goddamnit,' Tommy muttered, sliding the phone into his pocket.

'She thinks you're having an affair,' Elizabeth said.

He turned to Elizabeth, feeling a rage well within him. 'No, *she doesn't*,' Tommy said. *Yes, she does*, he thought.

'That fear is there. In the dark side of her mind, where all the spiders nest.' Elizabeth reached over and tousled Tommy's hair, and he pulled back. 'You're everything to her, Tommy. Emotionally. Financially. If you went away, she'd be destroyed. So of course she can't help but think of that worst-case scenario from time to time. It's human nature.'

'Cheating on her isn't the worst-case scenario,' Tommy said. 'You're the worst-case scenario.'

She smiled. 'Quite true. And when you think about it, you are having an affair with me, aren't you? You came all the way out here to see me, and you'll do anything to keep me your little secret. It's an affair without the sex, which is a little boring I must admit.'

'Fuck you,' Tommy said.

'Such a charmer.'

Despite the slight chill in the air his face felt hot. 'And stay away from my family.'

'Your family doesn't interest me. Now, I must say I was a little tempted to kill Stuart, just to teach you a lesson about the futility of protection. You know, slice his throat and leave him for your kids to find.' She twirled a strand of her hair with her index finger. 'But he's just doing his job, and I do have *some* conscience. Plus it would have been a lot more planning that I really don't have the time or energy for, so Stuart gets to live. But you can get rid of him. Your family is safe. You have my word.'

'Which we all know is as good as gold, right? Is that your serial killer code?'

'It's no code at all. It's just logic. I know you would do anything to protect the people you love. You would sacrifice anything for them. You are more motivated if they are alive.'

He leaned toward her and lowered his voice. 'You're right,' he whispered. 'I would do anything for them. I swear to God I will kill you if you get anywhere near them.'

'You can swear all you want, Tommy. Swearing doesn't put a knife in someone's chest. Swearing is simply talk. Can you do more than talk when so much is at stake for you? Can you play dirty, Tommy? Can you *be like me*?'

He held his breath for a few seconds, thinking he could calm himself. 'What is it you want from me?'

Elizabeth ignored him and kept walking. Someone catcalled in the distance, and the sound stumbled along the ancient streets until it faded back into the night. She turned down a small, tight alley and he reluctantly followed her, walking away from the light of the larger street into the solitude of what felt like another time. He didn't feel danger, but he did feel an acute sense of awareness that heightened as the darkness consumed them bit by bit. Tommy forced himself to keep walking, though what he wanted more than anything was to run. Run away. Away from everything. He wanted to run back to the life he knew just a week ago, when the biggest problem he had was figuring out a way to finish his book.

Elizabeth started humming. Soft and quiet, a nighttime song for a baby. The peacefulness of it unnerved him. Tommy saw her only though his peripheral vision. She wasn't answering his question.

'You're a lunatic,' he said.

She shrugged. 'To*MAY*to. To*MAH*to.'

Suddenly he wished he'd kept the steak knife. 'Do you want me to scuttle the book? Is that what you're afraid of – that you'll get caught because of what I've written?'

She laughed, her tone soft and feminine. 'Yes and no.'

'Meaning?'

'Meaning I love that you're writing a book about me. But the book you've written is completely wrong.'

'How would you know?'

'Because I've read it.'

'*How?*'

She stopped and looked at him. 'You are incredibly naive, Tommy, you know that? When you write at the Denver Hyatt, you connect to their open Wi-Fi signal. You think it's that hard to hack into your computer and download all your files?'

'My God. You stole my book?'

'And *this* is what surprises you?'

'No. I suppose not.'

She turned and resumed walking, knowing he would follow. Her posture was perfect as she strolled.

'The problem, Tommy, is even though I find your book quite good, it's not right. It's not right at all.'

He kept a few paces behind her. 'I don't care what you think of it.'

'Oh, but you need to care. I want you to understand me the way I really am,' she said. 'You research, but you don't *understand*. I can't have you write me like that.'

He sighed. 'Then you'll be happy to know I deleted that book. Back at the restaurant.'

She pivoted around to face him, her eyes wide. 'Did you really now?'

Tommy felt a momentary wave of comfort. *Finally there's something she doesn't already know.*

He didn't tell her he wanted to re-write the book; he didn't like the fact that they both seemed to have the same idea about the finished product.

The sound of an empty glass bottle rolling on the ground emanated from fifty feet or so in the distance. Then Tommy heard mumbling, a man talking to himself. The sound of homelessness.

She moved her fingers lower and touched the buttons on his shirt. 'I want you to feel what I feel, so when you do write about this, you'll do it perfectly.'

He felt electricity go through him. 'Don't touch me,' he whispered.

She dropped her hand and took a few slow steps toward the mumbling man in the distance. 'You need to capture my essence perfectly. I want to be immortalized through your words but, as you said, as a fictional character. That, Tommy, is what I need you for.'

The simple questions always formulated first. 'Why?'

'Because I want to be famous.'

Tommy considered this. 'And if I . . . meet your expectations, then you'll leave me alone?'

'Forever and ever,' she said, moving her finger across her chest. 'Cross my heart and hope to die. And the beauty is, the faster you write and get it published, the faster I'll be out of your life. You get a little bit of control back.'

Tommy knew this was bullshit. The woman was a sociopath, and taking her at her word was the same as believing a crumb-laden five-year-old child who insisted someone else stole the piece of cake. But unless he wanted the truth to come out, all Tommy could do was follow her instructions until he came up with a better idea.

Tommy was waiting for the catch. 'And if you don't approve?'

'That's the tricky part, now, isn't it, Tommy?' She twirled on her toes aimlessly, left and then right, as if still dancing at the ball as the clock turned midnight. 'But I think you know the answer to that.'

Elizabeth walked deeper into the alley.

SEVENTEEN

'You'll tell the world what happened.'

She turned and beamed at him, a little girl staring into a pet-store window. 'In gory detail!'

'But then you'll sacrifice yourself in the process.'

She shrugged. '*Que sera sera*. I've had a good run. Don't get me wrong, I don't *want* to be caught, but it's a chance I'm willing to take. You know killers, Tommy. You know my actions since coming back into your life have been uncharacteristically brazen. That should tell you I'm willing to push the envelope a little here. I want to be immortalized by you, and this is my last shot.'

'What do you mean "last shot?"'

'It means now or never, baby. The timing is right. You do your job right, and we'll both be famous. But I'm a fierce critic. You need to capture my essence perfectly. I've read all your other books. Compelling, each one of them. But you don't understand the kind of mind it takes to do what I do. Not really. You need to understand me to write about me. You need to feel the lust. The desire. The raw energy that feeds me.'

'And you're concerned I won't be able to.'

'*Concerned . . .*' she mused. 'That's not quite the right word. I just need to make sure you learn how to play the game properly. Play it the way I do. Once you get that, you will see it all.'

The sound of mumbling increased. There was someone in the alley with them, and not too far away.

'So you want to teach me your game?'

She winked playfully as if responding to a flirt. 'Come here,' she said. 'I want to show you something.'

'What?'

'Just come here, you goose.'

Tommy walked toward her and the mumbling man. The alley stretched for another couple of hundred feet before feeding into a brighter street, the light from which backlit Elizabeth, rendering her into a simple silhouette of a woman. Nothing more. Not a killer. Not a monster. Just the curves and confidence of a forty-something woman with red hair that spilled down her back like water.

Elizabeth stopped walking and Tommy closed in, approaching her slowly from behind. When he was a few feet away he could see what – *who* – she was looking at.

'Homeless,' Elizabeth said. 'I passed through this alley earlier and he was there. Guess he hasn't moved.'

The faded light served only to highlight the filth of the man on the ground. He was sitting, his back propped against the brick building, his ancient army surplus jacket tattered and torn like a battle flag. Long milky whiskers hung from his face, and the dirt streaked on his cheeks and forehead accentuated his bright eyes, which were the only things lively about the man. Eyes that darted back and forth, looking at everything. Looking at nothing. Tommy guessed the man to be fifty, seventy, or somewhere in between.

An empty Seagram's bottle rocked back and forth like a baby's cradle between the man's feet.

'Spare change?' he grumbled, the words spoken with the automation of a Wal-Mart greeter.

'Yes,' Elizabeth said. 'Of course.' She opened her purse and took out her wallet.

Tommy didn't understand the sudden benevolence, or why she wanted him to see it. But seeing her wallet, something occurred to him.

'The ID you gave the cop,' he said. 'What name was on it?'

'Patricia Damotto.'

Tommy's jaw loosened. He hadn't heard the name Patricia Damotto in a long time. He had dated her for three of his four years in college and hadn't spoken to her since.

'Are you kidding me?'

'Yes, Tommy. Because I spent so much time researching everything about you so I could land a few good jokes here and there.'

'What . . .' The confusion began to overpower him. 'Why would you do that?'

'Because now there's possibly a police report indicating you were in Charleston with an old flame of yours. Having a bit of a lover's quarrel.'

'*But* . . . I haven't spoken to Trish in twenty years.'

The homeless man kept his gaze on Elizabeth's wallet.

'Your wife doesn't know that,' she said.

The urge to hurt her flooded over him. 'Why are you doing this? If this gets back to her she'll leave me. And I haven't done *anything*.'

'You should understand why I'm doing this, Tommy. It's not simply to fuck with you. It's to make you desperate. The more desperate you are, the more willing you will be to do what I want.'

She pulled a bill from her wallet and handed it to the man on the street.

'Here's a hundred dollars,' she said to him. 'It's probably pointless to say this, but please don't spend it on alcohol or drugs. You can still get your life back. I'm sure there's a shelter nearby. That can be your first step to a better life.' She leaned down toward him and reached out and stroked his long, gnarled hair. 'You can change yourself. *Anyone* can change.'

The man looked up at her but did not smile. He didn't seem to understand at all.

Elizabeth stood and turned to Tommy.

'It's all a game, Tommy. All of this. Can't you see that? Everything in life is a game. The goal is to see who can play it best.' She pointed at the homeless man. 'He's already lost the game. He's not having any fun at all.'

Tommy looked down at the homeless man, watching his head roll slowly from side to side.

'I've been having fun for quite some time now,' she continued, 'but you don't see that. You only see a chemically imbalanced sociopath. I need you to open your mind and play the game the way I do.'

Tommy couldn't reconcile the calmly spoken words with the madness that must be inside of her.

'Rade Baristow didn't have any fun,' he said. 'Rade Baristow died when he was only ten.'

She shrugged. 'We can't all be winners, Tommy, despite what society teaches. Some – most – will be losers. That's all just part of the game.'

'So this is fun to you? That's the whole point? Coming after me, and Mark, after all this time. That's just more fun for you?'

'No, Tommy. That's what you aren't seeing, and maybe you never will. I'm not here for me.' Elizabeth walked in a small arc and stood next to the homeless man, who was holding the hundred-dollar bill loose like a napkin. Tommy figured he'd be robbed, and maybe beaten, before he ever got a chance to spend it. 'I'm here for *you*,' she continued. 'I'm here to teach you how to play the game better.'

'And from that I'll understand you better.'

'*Exactly.*'

'And write about you the way you want to be written about. Have a bestseller about you. The world will know about you.'

'See? Doesn't that sound like fun?'

'So what about Mark?' Tommy asked. 'Why go to him as well?'

She looked down at the homeless man. 'We all have something to offer,' Elizabeth said. 'Mark has his uses. As did Jason.'

A chill swept under Tommy's skin, and it wasn't just the night.

'What happened to Jason?' he asked.

'That's a story for another day.'

In that moment Tommy realized she had killed Jason. But he wasn't ready to know about that. Now, he just needed to process what she was telling him.

'Hannibal Lecter,' Tommy said.

'What?'

'What if Hannibal Lecter wasn't just a character in a book? What if he were real, and Thomas Harris actually knew him? And everything he wrote actually happened? The world knows Hannibal Lecter, but no one thinks he's real. And somewhere, the real Hannibal Lecter is laughing, immortalized.'

Elizabeth smiled, and it was the first time the smile seemed genuine, the smile of a child running down a hill, the summer breeze licking her face.

'Now you're starting to understand,' she said.

Against all his better judgment, Tommy felt a little excited at the prospect of writing about the world's next Hannibal Lecter. He didn't trust Elizabeth, but if doing what she said helped his career and bought him some time to plan, he would do it.

'OK,' he said. 'Teach me the game.'

She laughed. 'Excellent, Tommy. *Excellent.*' Her bright teeth flashed in the dim alley light.

She stepped close, her breasts pushing up against him. Her nose was just inches from his, and though he told himself to pull away, he didn't. She didn't lean in closer, nor did she back away. She stood there, pressed up against him, gazing into his eyes, her arms at her side. He stared back at her, trying to understand her, trying to envision what things those blue eyes had seen since they first opened in the world. He tried to think of the horror, because it was the only thing he could do to distract himself from the fact that, indeed, she excited him. How easy it would be to reach up and hold her, pull her harder against him, kiss her.

He felt her fingertips run briefly against his thighs. For a moment he thought she was going for his zipper, but instead her hands reached into her purse. As Tommy glanced down she leaned in and put her mouth on his. His eyes closed, almost involuntarily. Almost. She didn't kiss him; she just rested her lips on his, breathing lightly inside of him. He accepted this for much longer than he should have. Maybe two seconds. He finally pulled his head back and opened his eyes. Then he took a step away from her.

Tommy looked at her right hand. She was holding a knife. He couldn't be certain, but it looked a lot like the steak knife from the restaurant.

Tommy's chest tightened.

There was a tissue around the blade. A tissue separating her fingers from the handle.

Panic seized him. *I am going to die*, he thought. *Right here.*

Elizabeth spun from Tommy and knelt on the ground in front of the homeless man. Then she swung her right arm in a beautiful, tight arc, displaying the control and purpose of a golf pro playing the Masters. A fraction of a moment later Tommy heard the sound of a steel blade sinking into a cantaloupe, a tight, wet popping sound. But it wasn't fruit the serrated blade had penetrated. It was the right side of the man's neck.

The man's expression barely changed.

She yanked the knife out and the teeth of the blade must have shredded his carotid artery, because blood launched from the side of his neck. Tommy jumped back, not knowing if it did any good.

The man slumped to the ground.

Elizabeth looked up at Tommy and grinned.

'Here's your first lesson.'

EIGHTEEN

In the seconds that followed, Tommy heard everything there was to hear in that alley. Elizabeth panting like a winded jackal after a short chase. Late-night and drunken voices in another world, shouting for attention, rewarded by peals of laughter. And thick liquid gathering in a pool. It seemed impossible that one could hear such a thing, but in those seconds Tommy heard it, that pool of blood, growing by the inch, forming a life of its own, being fed by the *thump thump thump* of a dying heartbeat, the percussion of the pulse slowly fading out like the last track on the second side of an album.

Elizabeth dropped the knife to the ground. The clanking of the blade against concrete rang in Tommy's ears like a single, dissonant church bell. Tommy watched as she squeezed her left breast and moaned, the killing clearly exciting her. Tommy's mind flashed back to the killing of Rade, where the boy's murder actually brought her to climax.

'That's number two for you,' she sighed. 'Thirty-nine for me.'

'What . . . *what did you do?*'

Elizabeth took her hand from her breast and radiated feigned surprise. 'Me? Well, Tommy, I didn't do anything. After all, those aren't *my* fingerprints on the knife.'

'You . . . I didn't . . .' Tommy felt the bile surging in the back of his throat.

Before he knew it, Elizabeth was digging back in her purse, this time unearthing a small cell phone. She punched three digits, the electronic tones of those numbers unmistakable in their unique tonal flatness.

Nine-one-one.

'There's a man bleeding to death,' she said calmly into the phone. The Midwest accent Tommy remembered her using back at the Hyatt had returned. 'He's located in an alley between Queen and Broad Street. Near the park.'

Tommy watched in disbelief as she calmly disconnected the call and held the phone up to him. 'Prepaid phone. God's gift to serial killers.'

'What are you doing?' he asked, really meaning *What do I do?*

'Teaching you the game,' she said. 'Hope you're a quick learner.' Elizabeth nodded up and down the alley. 'You have two choices: stay or run.' She pointed at the knife on the ground. 'If you take the knife with you, you risk getting caught with a murder weapon. If you leave it here, you risk your prints being on it. Now, your prints might not be on file anywhere, so you still might be fine. But who knows?'

Tommy felt his eyes water as the nausea welled within him. His body shook as if ravaged by fever.

'Don't puke,' she said. 'That's a lot of DNA to leave behind. Now, I was a bit vague in my location to the nine-one-one operator, so you should have at least three minutes. I'm leaving now, and will be in touch soon. Unless, of course, you're in prison, in which case I'll become a ghost to you again, probably forever.' She walked up to him and kissed him on the cheek. Tommy was too stunned to pull away.

'Ciao, baby,' she said.

Elizabeth plucked the hundred-dollar bill from the dead man's dirty fingers and walked down the alley, disappearing around the nearest corner.

He looked down at the body. The Seagram's bottle was motionless.

Laughter somewhere in the night. A group of women. Somewhere out there, someone was still having a good time. No sirens to be heard. Yet.

One minute, Tommy told himself. You can take *one minute* to make a decision, and then you have to choose.

Tommy closed his eyes, and the first thing he saw was his little girl. Evie was smiling at him. She asked him to watch her do a cartwheel. She barely made it though, her legs bent and flailing, but she landed on her feet, beaming with pride. *Want to see me do it again, Daddy?*

If he was blamed for this man's death, he would never see Evie do a cartwheel again. Right now, remaining free to see her do cartwheels suddenly became the most important thing in the world.

Tommy opened his eyes to the world around him. He reached down and snatched the knife, bending the blade back against the ground, folding it against the handle, making it smaller and easier to conceal.

Then, movement. Down the alley, maybe fifty feet away. He heard the sound of shoes against concrete and Tommy twisted his head. There. A man – it was a man, wasn't it? Running, not toward Tommy but away. The figure sped along the side of the alley, skimming the sides of the ancient buildings, avoiding the few shafts of light there were. Tommy could make out little except that the man was in a hurry and wanted to get the hell out of the alley. In fact, he couldn't even be sure it was a man, but the footfalls sounded heavy, hard soles slapping out a rhythm of panic.

Oh my God, Tommy thought. Someone else was here. Did they see what happened? If not, why were they running? If so, *how much did they see*?

Think, he told himself. Does this change your decision? I couldn't make out anything about that person, which means they probably couldn't see me, either. But what did they hear? Did Elizabeth say my name out loud?

His decision had already been made. He wasn't changing his mind now.

Tommy put the bent knife in his suit pocket and checked the bottom of his shoes, making sure he hadn't stepped in the blood. No footprints. Then he turned and walked back in the direction from which he'd come, his pace brisk but not hurried, his chest pounding, heading away from the sound of the siren, away from the sound of laughing women, away from the figure that disappeared deep in the night, and into the longest walk of his life.

NINETEEN

With each footstep Tommy felt the panic grow inside him. All he could think of was the cop who took his ID earlier. The darkness worked to Tommy's advantage, but in his mind it was daytime, the sun shining brightly down on the guilt and the panic that surely riddled Tommy's face.

But he ran into no one. Not a soul.

When he was one house away from Mark's, Tommy quickened his pace. He had to get inside, away from the light, away from any eyes peering at him through pulled-back curtains. Safe harbor. Tommy's fingers shook as he tried to put the key in the front door lock, and only on his third attempt was he finally able to unlock and open the door. He shut the door and leaned against it, halfway slumped to the floor.

The house held the dense silence of an empty stadium, the kind of silence that told him he was utterly alone in the world. Tommy suddenly needed light, and he raced around the house, stumbling down unfamiliar halls, flipping on switches.

The lights made it worse.

He went into the study, where he and Mark earlier that evening had shared cocktails, and poured himself three fingers of Scotch. He put his messenger bag on the hardwood floor and reached into his coat pocket, finding the knife. Tommy turned it over in his hands, examining it for the first time under the glare of the incandescent bulbs overhead. The blood left dull, faded streaks on his hand.

Tommy looked up from the blade and realized the curtains were still open, the windows black against the vast night. He dropped the knife on the floor and bounded to the windows, yanking the curtains closed.

For all that Tommy had researched murder and murderers in his life, he had no idea what to do. So he simply stood in the study, the weight of time settling upon him, staring at walls that threatened to swallow him.

Your phone, he thought. *Check your phone.*

He pulled his phone from his pocket. One missed call from home. He listened to the voicemail.

'Hi, daddy. I just wanted to tell you that I woke up because I had a bad dream, and mommy said I could call you. Well, I love you. Good night.'

Evie. Her voice was perfectly monotone and achingly beautiful on the message. He looked at the time stamp of the voicemail. Just about the same time the homeless man was bleeding out near Tommy's feet.

He couldn't call back. Even if she was still awake, he couldn't talk to her. Not now. He would lose his mind.

Tommy focused on his breathing, in and out. He closed his eyes and closed out everything that was around him. Tommy became an island, if only for a few seconds. In those seconds, a question came to him.

Why?

Why would Elizabeth put him in danger if she needed him so much? If she needed him to write a bestseller about her, he certainly wasn't going to do that from prison.

Maybe she was lying about needing him. Maybe, to her, this was all part of her fucked-up game, watching Tommy dance like the puppet she had turned him into. She was just enjoying the show.

Or . . .

Tommy's gaze swept vacantly over the rows of books in the study, seeing all of them. Seeing none of them.

Or maybe she hadn't called nine-one-one at all.

He considered both possibilities and determined that there wasn't any evidence to sway him in either direction. Even if she hadn't called the police there was still a very real and very dead man in that alley, and the knife used to kill him was on the floor near his feet.

Tommy looked at the knife. It seemed so harmless there, misshapen. As he gazed upon it, Tommy realized that sleep this night would be unlikely, if not impossible. He needed to get rid of the knife, but he didn't want to go back outside with it. Not at this hour. He was safe inside this house, and he was certain things would remain that way at least until daylight.

He went back to the window and pulled the curtain to the side, staring into the darkness at the rough direction from which he'd come. The alley was, what, maybe ten or twelve blocks away? Too far for him to see the pulsing strobes of emergency vehicle flashers, but the lack of sirens did bring him some comfort. He was certain he would hear those from this distance. So the body hadn't been discovered yet. Which meant Tommy was safe for now.

Except for the man in the alley. The runner.

Tommy couldn't dismiss the potential impact of that person in his near future, but neither could he do anything about it. That person either saw something or he didn't. He could either identify Tommy or he couldn't.

Faced with the idea of lying awake in bed all night, frantically thinking about the million different ways the next day's direction would take, Tommy decided to do something else. He would write. Write it all down, just like she said. For better or for worse, he had to press on. Right now. Tonight. He now understood what it felt like, to be fresh in the aftermath of a murder, and he knew this was the essence Elizabeth commanded him to capture. Capture the essence, write the book, be free.

Tommy grabbed the tumbler of Scotch and drank from it like a dying soldier sucking on a canteen. Then he sat down at the desk, positioned his hands over the keyboard, and let his fingers lead him where they wanted. Perhaps the words that formed on the screen would reveal the nature of Elizabeth's mind, arming Tommy with a knowledge he could use to drive her out of his life forever.

Or maybe the words would tell him something else entirely.

TWENTY

D usty sunlight penetrated the curtains of the old office, crawling along the hardwood floor and creeping up the side of the leather couch until finally, as the morning wore on, it found Tommy's face.

He stirred, letting out a small moan as he felt the massive knot that had formed in his neck during the night.

Tommy lifted his arm and looked at his watch. Just after ten. He hadn't gotten to sleep until sometime after four, collapsing on the couch in the office after being hunched over his laptop for three hours.

He wiped a thin film of drool from the side of his cheek and sat up. The laptop was at the desk where he had left it, the empty tumbler sitting next to it assuredly holding the residual smell of Scotch.

Tommy stood and walked over to the desk, barely able to keep his eyes open but wanting to see the results of his efforts. Scrolling the pages on the screen, Tommy was surprised by how much he had actually written. He couldn't resist stopping on one of the pages to read, and soon found himself absorbed by his own words.

This is goddamn good, he thought. *Why do I need horror in my life to write like this?*

Over four thousand words. Four thousand words in three hours. That was a record. One time, when writing the basement murder scene of *The Blood of the Young*, he knocked out nearly three thousand words sitting at the kitchen counter.

But this was something different. It was as if he had been possessed. Tommy thought back to mere hours ago, his fingers crawling over the keyboard in a controlled frenzy, his brain dumping on-screen everything that had happened, every mote of fear and angst, every wave of nausea, every hope and every crushing disappointment.

Every drop of blood.

The sudden memory of the homeless man's open neck seized Tommy and he fell back into the desk chair, squeezing his forehead with his hands. Then he peered through the slit of his fingers and saw the one thing that made the memory more horrific: the bloody knife. He'd left it out on the open desk. At the time, it seemed right.

The knife had been his muse for the night.

Now, in the harshness of daylight, Tommy had to face the black blood on the blade.

I have to get rid of it, he thought. *Now.*

His cell phone screamed, making Tommy jump. He reached over and looked at the screen.

Mark.

God, he thought. *What do I tell him?*

'Hello?' he answered.

'Tommy, it's Mark. How goes it? Sleep well?'

Tommy closed his eyes and grumbled into the phone. 'Like a peach.'

'You sound like shit. Tie one on last night?'

'Something like that.'

'Well, good for you, I suppose. Can you meet this morning?'

'Um . . . of course.'

'Great. My schedule's tight. I can be there in about an hour and can stay for thirty minutes. I might have some more time tomorrow . . .'

Tommy stared at the knife. 'Can you do something later today instead?'

'No can do. It's this morning or maybe tomorrow, but no guarantees on tomorrow.'

'Fine,' Tommy said. 'An hour.'

Mark hung up the phone without saying anything else.

OK, Tommy told himself. You have to get rid of that damn knife. You can do it now, or stash it somewhere temporarily and do it later, after Mark leaves.

Tommy looked at the sunlight coming through the drapes. He walked up to them and pulled the drapes to the side, looking at the bright, normal day outside. The day was just starting, and was certainly just another day to most people. But not to Tommy. No, this day—

There. Opposite side of the street, walking east. Two cops. Foot patrol.

Tommy pulled enough of the drape in front of the window so that just a sliver remained, enough for him to watch the movements of the two cops briefly. They didn't seem to be in a hurry, nor did they seem without purpose. They swept the street with their gazes, looking, assessing. They walked slowly but without stopping, and moments later they were gone from Tommy's view. He didn't want to pull the drapes back to keep watching them. Watching got people caught.

Tommy had no idea if foot patrols were common in Charleston, or if those two were out canvassing the crime scene periphery from last night, searching for clues. Information. *Suspicious activity.*

Now, Tommy told himself. Get rid of the knife now, before Mark comes over. And don't go out. Hide it close, but hide it well. Don't be sloppy. You're a smart guy. You research crime all the time. Don't be stupid with the murder weapon.

Tommy grabbed the bent knife and took it to the kitchen, spending several minutes scrubbing every millimeter of it with dish soap and scalding water, watching the blood turn from a dirt-brown to pink under the running water. He placed the cleansed blade in the sink and rinsed it one more time before using a paper towel to pick it up, while leaving the hot water running in the sink a while longer, making sure it washed away any residual traces of blood from the pipes.

Tommy turned the faucet off and looked at the knife in his hand, contemplating his next move in the silence of the kitchen.

Should I hide it in the house? Perhaps under a loose floorboard, or in the attic? It doesn't have any blood left on it, so if someone finds it they won't be able to prove anything, right? Maybe I should just throw it away. That's innocent enough. A bent knife is useless, so of course it should be thrown away. It's just garbage.

So many books about crime and criminals. So many scenes written about death and the evidence thereof. Tommy had spent so much time trying to keep his writing fresh and creative he had never really stopped to consider the *What would you do?* aspect of covering up the evidence of a murder. But in this moment, it was obvious. Adrenaline and fear consumed creativity. Panic swallowed up logic and decisiveness. In this moment, Tommy understood what Elizabeth wanted of him.

The image of broken earth suddenly flashed in his mind.

Bury it somewhere. Somewhere no one will find it. Bury it in the earth, where the soil will further destroy any evidence.

Backyard.

Tommy went to the back of the house and into the covered porch. The air still held some of the weight from the night, a hint of moisture. The backyard was small, almost non-existent, just a strip of manicured sod, peppered by fallen leaves from an ancient oak that separated Mark's house from the one just feet behind it. It wasn't ideal for hiding a murder weapon. It wasn't the woods.

Then he saw it. A small vegetable garden, measuring no more than four-by-six feet, at the far end of the backyard.

Tommy wrapped the knife in the paper towel and went outside, scanning the windows of the adjacent home for faces peering down, scrutinizing. No matter how well he hid the knife, it wouldn't do him any good if someone witnessed him burying something. The witness was the greatest enemy of all criminals. His need to bury evidence outweighed his fear of someone seeing him do it, and he briefly wondered if this kind of thinking was exactly how murderers were caught.

Still, he saw no one. He would have to move fast.

Tommy placed the wrapped knife under his shirt and made his way out into the backyard, keeping his head down. Once he reached the vegetable garden, he studied the soil, inspecting for recent disturbances. Nothing was growing and most of the plants had been culled, leaving nothing behind except for small metal markers – the shapes of insects – telling the world what had grown there that summer. *Squash. Strawberries. Tomatoes.*

The remnants of a withered tomato vine assured Tommy the garden wasn't tended every day, at least not at this time of year.

He knew he couldn't put the knife where seeds would be planted in the spring. Too easy for someone to find, even if he dug deeply.

In the corner of the bed sat an unpainted cement rabbit decoration, its eyes wide and blank, hunched in a frozen state of chewing, looking like something cast from a Pompeian mold.

Tommy lifted it and considered the dirt around it, concluding in an instant the rabbit hadn't been moved in a long time.

It would have to do.

But he didn't want to use his fingers.

He looked around, and a small shed stood like a sentry in the back corner of the yard. It was tiny, not much larger than an outhouse would have been at some point in time, and Tommy guessed there were gardening tools in there.

Unlocked. The door opened and Tommy immediately saw what he needed: a collection of trowels and hand rakes standing handles-up in a large bucket of sand. He grabbed a trowel and considered his good fortune. Well, that's a break in my favor, he thought. Maybe that's a good omen.

This, he soon realized, was exactly the kind of thought that got murderers caught.

Back to the rabbit statue. Tommy used the trowel to claw into the soft earth, making a small mound to the side with the excavated soil. He continued digging until the hole grew and he could feel the cold from the deeper soil breathing against his skin. Once he reached about a foot down he decided it was deep enough.

Tommy dropped the knife in the hole and quickly replaced the dirt, sprinkling on the last layer so the soil didn't appear recently disturbed. After putting the rabbit back in its place, he stood and surveyed his work.

Good.

He returned the trowel to the potting shed, sticking it deep into the sand. Back outside, he crossed the small yard and headed back to the kitchen. Something caught his eye. He shifted his gaze from his hands to the second-story window on the neighboring house. A slight movement. A flutter.

He couldn't be certain, but he thought a drape just pulled closed. Had someone been watching him? Did someone see him bury some object under the little bunny statue? Tommy's mind spun with the possibilities, creating a cause and effect scenario for each one in a matter of seconds.

If someone saw him, should he move the knife? Or would they watch him doing that as well, creating further suspicion?

The longer he stood outside the more exposed he felt, and Tommy realized he could very easily drive himself insane with second-guessing. He needed to trust his instinct, and his instinct told him all was fine and the knife was perfectly hidden where it was.

His instinct also told him to get the fuck inside the house.

TWENTY-ONE

Mark Singletary pressed his hand deeply into Tommy's grip. Tommy's flesh was still warm from a fast, hot shower, which, combined with a fresh set of clothes, made him feel more distanced from the last night's killing. Tommy looked over Mark's shoulder and saw the Escalade double-parked on the street, the driver looking down at a newspaper.

Mark stepped inside. 'Did you hear about the murder last night?' It was the first thing he said. Not *hi* or *good to see you*. 'My driver just told me on the way over. Some homeless guy, downtown.'

Tommy was able to retain eye contact, and in doing so he noticed that Mark's eyes actually seemed to brighten as he mentioned the killing. 'No, I didn't hear about that. Is that unusual?'

Mark picked a piece of lint off the lapel of his smoke-gray suit coat. 'Every city has crime,' Mark said. 'But when someone gets their throat slashed, it makes the news. You were downtown last night, weren't you? You see anything?'

'No. Nothing.' *Except for the cops patrolling the street this morning.*

'Where'd you go?'

Mark was probing, meaning he knew something. For all Tommy knew, Mark knew exactly what had transpired with Elizabeth during the evening.

'I forget the name of the place,' Tommy said.

'Hate to say it, but last night's murder is the kind of thing that only bolsters my campaign. My opponent is anti-death penalty. Probably the only opponent left in these parts.'

'Him and Jesus,' Tommy mumbled.

Mark shot him a look but said nothing further on the subject. Instead, he put an arm around Tommy and started walking him toward the kitchen, a gesture that felt insincere and borderline uncomfortable.

'And you, Mark? What did you do last night?'

Mark seemed surprised by the question, as if only he retained the right to interrogate.

'Campaign dinner. Fundraiser.'

'In Charleston?'

'Hilton Head. Why?'

Because there's something you're not telling me. 'Just curious.'

'You met with her last night. Didn't you, Tommy?'

Tommy folded his arms against his chest. 'I think you already know the answer to that.'

'I know far more questions than answers, Tommy.'

'I doubt that.'

Mark squinted at him, then took a step away and looked up at a painting on the wall above the living room fireplace. It was a portrait of an ugly man in a stiff gray uniform, his Ichabod Crane nose and weak chin somehow accentuated by the gleaming brass buttons on his jacket and impossibly long sword resting from his hip to the ground.

'That's Mara's great-great-grandfather,' Mark said. 'Isaiah Blackstone. Colonel in the Confederate army. Died in a tiny skirmish known as the Battle of Grimball's Landing in 1863.' Mark now had his full attention on the painting, and Tommy followed suit. He was trying to recall if he had ever seen a less impressive figure in an officer's Civil War uniform.

'How did he die?' Tommy asked.

'Crushed by a horse.'

'Who won the battle?'

'Inconclusive. In the end, the whole battle really amounted to nothing. Yet here he is, larger than life, always looking down at anyone who enters this room.'

'This bothers you?'

Mark shrugged. 'I wouldn't say it bothers me. I would say Mara's family places a little too much stock in false idols. If anything, for me it always underscores the idea that some men are destined in life to make a difference in this world, and some are destined to be crushed by a horse.' Now Mark turned and faced Tommy. 'Every time I see it I get inspired to do more with my life. Not to be a victim. Not to be known for the things I *didn't* do.'

'I'm sure he didn't intend to die that way,' Tommy said. 'I'm sure he would rather have been a hero.'

'Wanting and doing are different games,' Mark said.

Games. Just like Elizabeth had mentioned. *Everything's a game.*

'Is that what Elizabeth represents to you?' Tommy asked. 'Does she make you feel victimized?'

Mark ignored the question. 'Listen, Tommy. I'm going to be straight with you. I said I'd tell you what Elizabeth said when we sat down. Well, it wasn't much. She said she was going to bring you out here, and then she was going to meet you. What does she want from you?'

Tommy suspected Mark already knew the answer. 'She wants me to write about her in a way she approves of. And if I don't, she'll tell everything.'

Mark soaked in the information with a stony face, revealing nothing.

'Well, that doesn't sound so bad, does it?'

Tommy walked a few paces away from Mark and stared at the portrait of Isaiah Blackstone, who wore a sneer like a badge of honor. 'Sometimes I think it would just be easier to tell the police everything. I'm tired of letting her have all the control.'

He could hear Mark sucking his breath in. 'That's the worst possible thing you could do, Tommy. Please don't be stupid. We'd both be destroyed.'

Tommy turned. 'But we'd finally be free, Mark. Free of this nightmare. And isn't that what good Christians are supposed to do? Confess our sins?'

'I've confessed all my sins before Christ. I don't need to do it for the police.'

'And what about Rade's family? They just get to die never knowing what happened to their son?'

'It's not our fault, Tommy.'

Tommy walked back to Mark, noting the man's perfect posture and politician's half-smile.

'What else did she say to you, Mark? She just wanted you to bring me out here?'

Mark remained silent on the matter for a few seconds. Then: 'She wanted to make sure I understood my life would be over if you didn't do as she said.'

'Literally or figuratively?'

'I assume the latter.'

'So that's it, then? She wants to scare you to put pressure on me?'

'Yes, I assume that's right.'

'That doesn't make a lot of sense. What kind of pressure can you add that I don't already feel?'

Mark locked his gaze in. 'The pressure of friendship, Tommy. Knowing you would be hurting a friend as well as yourself if you didn't do what she said.'

'Is that what we are, Mark? Are we friends?'

'I think we are.'

Tommy studied him. It was time to jolt the man out of his pre-fabricated shell. 'Do you think about how she went down on you after the killing, Mark? Can you still feel her lips on your cock, even as Rade's blood spilled from his head?'

Mark's entire body tensed and his eyes squeezed shut. 'Shut up, Tommy.'

'Why did you do it? How did you let her do that?'

His eyes opened. 'Tommy, you have no idea what you're talking about. You denied her. I didn't. You can't possibly understand what that did to me.'

Tommy studied his old friend, reading his body language. The stiffness was so posed, so practiced, that it effectively concealed any true thought or feeling.

'What does she really want with you, Mark? Or, maybe the better question is, what do you really want with her?'

Mark pulled his hand back. 'Tommy, I want what you want. To move on with my life, and have her out of it.'

Tommy took a chance. 'I have to admit, Mark. As horrible as all this is, there's something a little . . . exciting about it. Don't you think?' Tommy walked away from Mark as he spoke, circling the room, not wanting his face to be read. 'Gets the heart pumping in a way I'm not used to. Here is this woman we only knew thirty years ago. A girl murderer. Now she's back, and we're left to try to understand her motives. We're left to wonder what other horrible things she's done in her life. And on top of it . . .' Tommy took a deep breath and forced the words out. 'She's pretty goddamn sexy. For a monster, that is.'

Tommy kept his back to Mark, but in the silence of the room he could hear Mark breathing. It was faster than before. Tommy turned and faced him. He saw true conflict in the man's face, and Tommy knew he had sparked something in him with his words.

'She still excites you, Mark. Doesn't she?'

Finally, Mark said, 'She represents an element of my life I'd rather bury.'

'You mean the past, Mark? You want to bury the past? Or does she represent a side of you that you don't want revealed?'

'Tommy, she needs to go away. For your sake. For mine.'

'What did she really say to you, Mark?'

'Tommy, I don't know what you're talking about. She wanted me to convince you to come out here. I did that. Now it seems the rest is up to you. Do what she says so we can all move on.'

'And you think she'll just disappear? Just like that? *Thank you very much, I'll never bother you again?*'

'She said she would.'

Tommy laughed, but it felt hollow. 'Mark, I think there's a possibility none of us will make it through this. Literally and figuratively. I don't know if her involvement with you is the same as mine, but don't underestimate her. I've spent my profession studying people like her.'

Mark's voice was a whisper. 'There is no one like her.'

Tommy stepped forward. 'Mark, don't get close to her. She'll destroy you.'

Mark held his gaze steady. 'She destroyed me a long time ago, Tommy.' He reached out and touched Tommy's arm, and the touch soon become a grab. It wasn't the grab of a threat, but the grab of a man seeking help. 'You have to do what she says, Tommy. For both of us. My faith is . . . tested . . . when she's around. I don't want to be like that. I can't be like that. *Please.*'

'What's happening, Mark? What did she do to you?'

For once the veneer faded and Tommy saw the face of his old friend. The face of frustration. 'I'm a weak man, Tommy. I always have been. I'm the man who will end up crushed by a horse. But not you. You have the chance to control the situation here. Just . . . just do what she says so she goes away. *Please.*'

Then Mark's face returned to its plastic self and he straightened his shoulders and smoothed his coat. 'I need to go, Tommy. And so do you. Set things right.'

'And when does it end, Mark?'

Mark studied his friend with detached curiosity. Tommy remembered a similar expression on Elizabeth's face.

'You could kill her.'

'Jesus, Mark.'

'It's not like you haven't thought it, Tommy.'

'Clearly *you* have. Why don't *you* kill her?'

'I'm too high profile. Way too risky.'

'And I'm not?'

Mark shook his head. 'Truthfully? I don't think either of us is capable.'

Tommy wanted to argue but couldn't. Mark put a hand on Tommy's shoulder, and Tommy was suddenly a little boy all over again, being lectured by his father.

'Then it ends when she says it ends,' Mark said.

Then Mark turned and walked away, out the front door and to the double-parked black Escalade, where its driver tore off down the street as if the State Senator from South Carolina had sustained a gunshot wound and needed immediate medical attention.

It would be the last time Tommy would ever see him.

TWENTY-TWO

T
ommy stared out the window from his first-class seat, through the scratches on the Plexiglas and out to the sky, its vastness consumed by layer on layer of blue, folding on to itself like the forged steel of a Samurai sword.

In moments of silence like these when the open sky was his only vista, Tommy's mind often pulled toward thoughts of guilt, like it did now. Guilt for Rade, whose cold, lonely bones remained a mystery to those who desperately wanted nothing more than to find them. Tommy might not have killed Rade, but he had killed the hope of anyone who wanted to know the truth. This guilt filled him when it could, spilling into the fissures in his soul, slowly eroding him as the years disappeared behind him.

And now there was another body, an anonymous man, homeless but human, who had bled out next to Tommy's feet. Once again, Tommy hadn't killed him, yet once again Tommy scrambled to hide the truth.

He squeezed his eyes shut and reminded himself once more why he allowed these secrets to remain buried. He saw the faces of Evie and Chance, and he tried to imagine what kind of emotion they would possibly feel knowing their daddy had done something very wrong. Wrong enough to be punished. Wrong enough to go to prison. The possibility of going to prison was more than a self-pitying fantasy. It was real.

After years of researching killers for his book, Tommy knew one thing for sure: the legal system was not to be fucked with. Sure, justice was often served. But Tommy also knew the system pulled innocent men and women deep into its vortex, sucking them down until they simply disappeared beneath all of its noise and weight.

If Tommy were arrested, his only chance would come from his money. He would have to hire the best lawyers in the country just to attempt to fight the charges of murder (*homeless man*) and accessory to murder (*Rade Baristow*). Somehow he'd have to convince a jury he buried a murder weapon solely out of fear and that he had nothing to do with killing the man in Charleston. He'd also have to convince them that, even though he was present at the killing of Rade Baristow, he'd no idea it was going to happen, and only agreed to help bury the body because he was threatened at gunpoint. He would have to plead for mercy. Mark, certainly, would face a similar fate, and the implication of an outspoken Republican politician in the sordid drama would assuredly be masturbation material for the watching eyes of every media outlet imaginable.

Tommy took a sip of the beer the flight attendant had just handed him. It was warm and bitter.

The trial would be a media sensation. The rich thriller writer caught up in a story so twisted he was actually making it the subject of one of his own books, certain to become a bestseller. *He was planning to get even wealthier on his own crimes*, the DA would shout at the jury. *Don't let him escape punishment because of his fame. Instead, send a statement to the world. No one is above justice.*

Best-case scenario was probably five years in minimum security, probation after a couple of years perhaps. And even in the best-case scenario, his children would forever know him as a killer, no matter how much he would try to convince them otherwise. Becky would divorce him. He would lose the only woman he ever loved and the children he loved more than all else. Not to mention his money would be gone, though at that point that hardly seemed to matter. She'd marry someone else – some nice fucking guy who everyone thought was just the kind of man she *truly* deserved – who would move into *his* house, and raise *his* kids.

Tommy Devereaux would become a shell of the man he was, and he couldn't let that happen. Despite all the mistakes he had made in his forty-four years, he was a *good* man, goddamnit, and he would not lose everything he stood for because a crazy woman wanted immortality through his words.

Which is why Tommy was not flying home. He was flying to Oregon. Back to his hometown. Back to the woods.

He was going to dig up that body. He was going to dig it up and bury it somewhere else, so at least she didn't have *that* evidence. It was the only thing he could do to assume some kind of control. Funny thing was, it didn't seem like a particularly crazy or horrific idea, though he knew the minute he was standing over the patch of dirt in the woods his whole body would be shaking.

Don't think about that now, he told himself. Just try to stay calm.

He felt his forehead beading with sweat and he wished he'd ordered something stronger.

Tommy glanced over at the woman sitting next to him. She was about his age, dressed in a business suit, working feverishly on her laptop. A PowerPoint presentation. Lots of bullet points and colors. For all Tommy knew, the woman was insane. Maybe she spent her day climbing the corporate ladder and her nights hacking off the limbs of kittens. Point is, you never knew who anyone really was. Everyone has secrets. Some are just a lot more interesting than others.

Just *focus*, he told himself. Don't try to figure out all the potentially awful outcomes of this next part of your life. Focus on what you can do in the immediate moment, and look out to the future only far enough to avoid the most calamitous of foreseeable events.

He glanced again at the screen of the woman's laptop as she was making some kind of fancy pie chart, which was both impressive-looking and achingly dull at the same time. Tommy's attention shifted to the title she had just typed.

Most Prolific Female Serial Killers

He read the words before they registered any meaning to him, and just as they did the woman deleted the title and re-typed:

Most Prolific E-mail Resellers

Tommy blinked. Had she really just written what he had thought he read?

He spoke without thinking.

'Did she send you?' he asked.

She stopped typing and looked over, a long strand of coffee-brown hair crossing her furrowed brow.

'Excuse me?'

He pointed at the screen. 'You just typed in something about female serial killers, knowing I would be watching. Then you changed it.'

She pushed herself noticeably away from him, exactly what anyone would do if they thought the person on the plane next to them was more than a little bit off. 'You're watching me as I work? What the hell is wrong with you?'

In that instant, from the look in the woman's eyes, Tommy knew he had miscalculated. This woman had nothing to do with Elizabeth,

and what Tommy thought he saw was nothing more than the conflu-
ence of stress and lack of sleep pushing his sanity to the brink. In
his research into insane people, he had often wondered what it felt
like to go crazy. Not *be* crazy, but the process of becoming so, when
there were still fleeting glints of light before fully entering the
dark tunnel. He wondered, in fact, if it felt a lot like what he was
experiencing now.

'I'm . . . God. I'm sorry. I don't know what's wrong with me.'

The consolation was too late. The woman pressed the flight
attendant call button on her armrest. Within seconds the first-class
attendant came over.

'This man is bothering me,' the woman said, 'and I don't feel
comfortable sitting here. You can re-seat either him or myself, but
one of us needs to move.'

'Look, I'm sorry. I thought you were someone else.'

The woman refused to look at him, keeping her attention on the
flight attendant.

'*Now*,' she commanded.

The attendant kept her lips pursed and her eyes just wide enough
to register alarm.

'Mr Devereaux, we have three C available. Maybe it would be
best if you moved over, just to . . . keep everyone happy.'

She used his name. If the woman picked up on who he was,
she'd be telling all her friends what a lunatic the famous author
was.

'Sure,' he said. 'That's fine.' He grabbed his laptop and messenger
bag and walked around his row mate. He considered apologizing
one last time as he passed by her, but decided against it.

Tommy settled into his new seat, not bothering to look at his
new neighbor for more than a second.

*Jesus, Tommy, get a hold of yourself. Going crazy isn't going to
help you, especially when you need to be more prepared than ever.*

He ran his fingers along the outline of the folded cash in his front
pants' pocket. There were so many things that could go wrong with
his plan it seemed almost pointless to be prepared at all, but he had
to do what he could. He had taken out enough money back in
Charleston to pay for a hotel room and the supplies he would need,
but his anonymity would only go so far. He had to fly under his
name, and he certainly needed to show ID to rent a car once he got

to Oregon. Any detective who wanted to trace Tommy's general route would easily discover he had gone back to Lind Falls, or at least the vicinity. But Tommy had at least to make sure no one could pinpoint his steps directly to the grave in the woods.

Moving the body was a desperate move. Only bones were likely left of Rade, and Tommy considered the fact that he wouldn't even remember exactly where these bones were buried. It was possible that Elizabeth herself had moved the remains years ago, just to be safe. But Tommy had to do something to be in control, because the only other thing he could do was what she *told* him to do, and Tommy doubted she would ever stop.

Elizabeth wanted to keep playing the game.

TWENTY-THREE

E lizabeth stands still, quiet. She is a perfect statue, her eyes unblinking. In fact, they aren't human eyes at all. They are the eyes of a doll, plastic brightness and hand-painted happiness. Lifeless.

She holds a serrated kitchen knife in her right hand. Shiny. New.

Tommy walks around her, inspecting her as if she were a car he just might want to buy. She does not move, though Tommy knows at any moment the knife could flash.

But it won't. Not yet.

There's a reason for what you're doing, he says. He lifts a strand of her hair and feels its natural smoothness, stroking it between his thumb and forefinger. Here, in this place, she is beautiful.

He looks around at the walls of the empty room. They are all the same, about fifteen feet wide and about infinity high. The floor seems only a surfaceless light that somehow the two of them are able to stand on, as if balanced on pure energy and nothing more.

There's a Van Halen song playing, but he doesn't remember the name. Something about shoes.

You think I don't understand, he says. And maybe I don't. But I know more than you think I do.

He notices something that was not there on first inspection. On her left rib cage, on the outside of her pristine white blazer, there is a bill feeder, the type you would see in the self check-out line at the grocery store.

Tommy reaches into his front pocket and finds a single dollar bill, folded once, crisp and sharp. He takes it out and unfolds it.

It's not that simple, he tells her. You're not doing this for money. If you were, you would have already told me.

He feeds the bill into her. It whizzes and whirrs, sucking the money in greedily.

She comes alive, but only her mouth moves.

Money isn't everything, she says, her voice as plastic as her eyes.

He looks down at the knife.

I've spent years researching the mind of the female killer, he tells her. She does not shift her lifeless gaze toward him.

What have you discovered? she asks.

I think something is wrong with you.

That's an understatement.

No, he says. Something wrong. Something different. You're being bold. You're coming out into the open, taking chances. You're taking greater risks to get your fill. In nature, only wounded animals do that.

What does that tell you? she asks.

He considers. It tells me time is important to you.

Before she answers, the homeless man appears, walking through the wall and into the middle of the room. He is partially flesh and mostly filth, yet Tommy smells nothing. The man drinks from a plain brown bottle, and when he is done a trail of viscous liquid snakes down his chin. He smiles.

Elizabeth bares her teeth, and with the speed of a car crash, the hand holding the knife lashes out. The man's throat rips open with video-game violence. Blood floats in the air for a few suspended seconds until showering on to the floor-light, covering it. The room now glows pink.

The man does not fall. In fact, he is no longer a man.

He is a boy.

He is Rade.

Rade is whole. He is perfect. He is as he should have been.

Why? Rade asks. Why did you do it?

I did nothing, Tommy says. She did it. She did it all. She killed you.

Rade does not listen.

You were my friend, he says. You said you would take me home.

It wasn't me.

You won't get away with it, don't you see? The boy's eyes are real, glistening with tears. You will have to pay, one way or another.

The boy disappears, sucked through the walls.

Elizabeth laughs, but she won't say why.

Tommy woke, a thin sheen of sweat on his forehead and the taste of stale tequila in his mouth. The stiletto shaft of a tiny feather poked though the thin, faded fabric of the cheap pillow, scratching his cheek.

He sat up in bed, trying to remember where he was. It took him nearly ten seconds, and then it all came back.

Oregon. I'm in Oregon.

Tommy turned his head and squinted at the outline of the forming day along the edges of the stiff, brown curtains of the motel. Dust motes danced lazily in thin beams of light.

He pushed the sheets off his body and wondered how long he would have to stay at the Fireside Motel. He had decided to stay a few towns away from Lind Falls and the Fireside Motel was the kind of place that wouldn't ask to see an ID. He had paid cash for two nights but hoped he would only need to stay one. Tommy opened the curtains and squinted at the parking lot. His rental was the only car in sight. The clouds seemed to have settled in for the day already, which was par for this time of year. The air would be heavy, but it wouldn't rain. He didn't even need to check the forecast. Tommy knew every type of Oregon sky there was. It wouldn't rain.

His phone rang. Becky.

'Hey, baby,' he said. He hadn't told her he was coming to Oregon; for all she knew he was in Charleston until Thursday, and here it was, only Monday, and his plans had completely changed. He couldn't tell her the truth. He didn't even want to imagine that conversation, so he chose to say nothing, which in and of itself was just another lie.

'Three more days?' she asked. No *hi* or *hello* or *go fuck yourself.*

'Yes, Becky. Three more days.' *Unless I get caught moving the remains of a body, in which case it might be a little longer.*

'Good. Do you want to talk to the kids?'

'Of course.'

Evie's voice bounced through the phone.

'Hi, Dada!'

And that was all it took. That little voice through the phone, and the world, which had somehow been held back by some massive dam, broke free and slammed into Tommy.

Tommy reeled and grabbed his chest, certain he was having a heart attack. He started wheezing and choking, trying to suck air in but failing miserably.

'Dada?'

Tommy disconnected the call, not wanting his daughter to hear anything. If he was dying, he'd be goddamned if his kid hearing it happen would be the last memory of him she ever had.

He collapsed to his knees and closed his eyes, trying to control his lungs.

Don't panic.

It was the number one rule in the world. The one thing he told his kids to remember no matter the situation. Don't panic.

It turned out to be a really hard thing to do. He couldn't breathe. He sucked in but could not exhale, but he kept trying, ensuring a faster death. His chest felt like it was collapsing on itself, a black hole. He closed his eyes and only saw the red of blood inside his eyelids.

Don't panic.

Slowly, he took himself away in his mind, far in another time, to a place with a towering tree surrounded by soft wild grass, a place he remembered at some age before he started remembering specific ages, where all he could remember was feeling, and the feeling at the tree was happiness and peace, the kind you could only know when you were too young even to know what that meant. Tommy, in that shitty motel room with the stiff sheets and the poky pillows and death shaking him like a rag doll, found that place now.

And then he started breathing again.

You're not dying, Tommy convinced himself. A panic attack.

That must be what it was. Just reality coming back to smack you upside the head a few times.

His wheezing slowed and he finally sucked in enough air to slow his pulse. He staggered to his feet and made it to the bathroom sink, where he vomited in three short, violent bursts. He hovered over the cracked plastic basin for a few moments before cleaning up, splashing water in the sink and on his face. When he was done, he looked up in the mirror, seeing a ghost of himself.

Tommy hadn't looked in a mirror in days, it seemed.

He didn't have to worry about someone recognizing him from the back of a dust jacket. His face was drained of any color it once had, and his eyes wore the bloodshot haze of an alcoholic on a binge. He had barely eaten or slept in days.

He stared at himself for a full five minutes, enough time, in his mind, to let his body absorb the blow of the attack. When he was done, he could feel something shift inside him. He felt looser, as if the panic attack released the pressure that had suddenly become too great to contain. Tommy felt weak, but he also felt better than he had in a week.

He called Evie back, apologizing for hanging up. He didn't tell her what had happened, but neither did he make up another lie. It was a small victory, but he fought to be honest where it didn't carry the risk of losing everything. Both kids told Tommy they missed him, and it had been a long time since he had been away from them long enough to hear that. It made him want to go home all the more, but he had a dirty job to do first.

His first stop was breakfast. He ached for a real meal, something that would give him the strength he knew he would need. Tommy slid inconspicuously into a back booth of a run-down diner and had the biggest omelet on the menu, chased with two cups of black coffee-water, sides of bacon and hash browns, and two glasses of orange juice.

Tommy took his time driving to Lind Falls, stopping at two different towns to buy supplies. In one hardware store he bought some work boots, heavy-duty gloves, and a duffel bag. In a different store he bought a shovel. Paid cash for everything.

In the mid-afternoon Tommy finally drove slowly into the place of his childhood. Lind Falls was a small town and Tommy's name was assuredly well-known there, but despite all the photos on the back of his book jackets, people rarely recognized authors, no matter how many books they had sold. Still, he didn't like the idea of doing what he had come to do during the daytime. Running into others was a possibility, and if someone recognized him Tommy's evidence trail would become more damaging.

But if there was one thing worse than digging up a body during the daytime, it was digging up a body at night. Tommy would take his chances.

He looked up at the sky. The clouds screamed rain, but Tommy knew better. Oregon clouds often lied. It wouldn't rain.

He drove to the woods.

TWENTY-FOUR

Tommy drove past his old house, which sat diminished by time and memory. The green and white clapboard was now painted beige and brown, making the house look like a big lump of 1950s ranch-house shit. The north side of the house had been popped out, adding more living area and encroaching on an already small backyard. The changes annoyed him, as if what was good enough for Tommy's family wasn't good enough for these people.

Three doors down was Rade Baristow's house. It hadn't changed at all, and Tommy wondered if that was done on purpose, just in case the missing little boy from decades ago stumbled back into town.

Tommy parked across the street, next to a park that was once a large field of dirt. He stared at the Baristow house from inside the car.

The disappearance of Rade Baristow had never been solved and, as clichéd as it was, his picture had indeed been placed on milk cartons back in 1981, at least locally. Most of Tommy's neighbors had been interviewed by the police to determine if someone had seen *something*. Tommy himself had been questioned, and it was, at the time, the second most nerve-wracking moment of his young life. He had barely felt his lips moving as he replied *No* to every question the officer asked. *Did you see him that day? Did you hear or see anything out of the ordinary? Any strangers hanging around the area?* The officer who had questioned him was Alan Stykes, at the time a newer member of the Lind Falls tiny police department. Tommy remembered the cold gaze of Officer Stykes in the brief moments Tommy had actually made eye contact with him. He had felt sure his guilt was wrapped around him like a book jacket, but he must have been convincing enough because he was never questioned a second time.

Mark and Jason were never questioned.

Nor was Elizabeth, but only because no one ever saw her again. She had been a ghost, whiffing away into a thin vapor trail that blew softly out of town. Tommy had asked a few questions about her, very delicately, here and there, but no one seemed to have heard of her. It seemed she had come to Lind Falls only to kill, and then, once satisfied, moved on. It had made no sense. Who were her parents? Or was she herself a teenager drifter, a character from an S.E. Hinton book?

Tommy had always assumed Rade's parents never really gave a shit about their boy. The assessment was based partly on the fact that Rade always seemed to be allowed to wander the neighborhood alone at any time of day, and partly on the fact that Tommy had been fourteen and wasn't really capable of understanding parental motives for anything. So what somehow came as the biggest surprise to him in the aftermath was the complete unwinding of Charles and Rita Baristow. Rita left within a year of Rade's disappearance, heading to California. Charles remained in the house but was constantly on the road for his job, selling insurance or some such commodity.

Rita killed herself in a Holiday Inn in Fresno six months later. Painkillers and vodka. Tommy remembered his parents discussing it at dinner. Tommy didn't eat much that night. Or most nights back then.

Tommy's gaze focused on the upstairs window, the one he remembered belonging to Rade's bedroom. Tommy wondered if Charles, the father, still lived there. Maybe Charles moved. If he did, who lived there now? Did they ever receive visits from the ghost of a boy buried less than a half-mile from here?

Tommy shook his head, as if flinging the thought from his head.

Focus.

You've got a job to do.

Tommy got out of the car and went to the trunk. He unzipped the duffel bag and put the shovel and gloves inside, then zipped it up and slung it over his shoulder. He then exchanged his leather loafers for the work boots before heading down the street.

He found the old path with ease, the one that led to the woods. From the start of the path, nothing had changed. The towering maples and oaks beckoned him. Even over the last thirty years, the economy of Lind Falls had never been good enough to encourage digging up the woods to add another subdivision, which was either a blessing or a curse.

The woods were exactly as they had always been.

The sky grew darker and the October breeze crept around Tommy's bare neck and snaked down the back of his shirt, chilling him. He had only the thinnest of jackets, not having been prepared for travelling from South Carolina to Oregon.

His steps were slow, not because he was unsure of his direction, but because he wanted to be aware of his surroundings. He wanted to see, to hear. If there was something to smell, he wanted to smell it. Tommy wanted to know what was out there with him.

Dry leaves crunched under his boots as he walked, and the noise seemed ungodly loud to him, making him feel exposed. He was carrying a shovel and gloves in a duffel bag, which, if questioned for any reason, he had no good answer for. But this was nothing compared to the thought of being caught digging up the body of a long-decomposed boy.

His plan was relatively simple, which always made for the best ones. Ideally, he would dig up Rade's body and rebury him somewhere else in the woods. Elizabeth would have no idea where the body was relocated, and thus she would have no real evidence with which to incriminate Tommy. The duffel bag was his backup plan. If he had to, he'd put the body in the bag and take it with him, disposing of it somewhere else. Tommy hoped to all hell it wouldn't come to that.

Can I really even do this?

His cell phone screamed.

'Fuck,' he muttered, cursing himself for the oversight of not turning it off. He yanked it from his jacket pocket and ignored the call, seeing Sofia's name on the screen briefly before Tommy sent her to voicemail. He turned the phone off.

A bird called in the distance. Three brief caws, then silence. Again, three brief caws, then silence.

A drop of rain hit Tommy on the nose and he looked up through the towering skeleton trees at the clouds.

'No,' he commanded them. 'I know you. You will not rain on me.'

No further drops came.

He was close now, and in his mind the trees were no longer bare but full and lush, reeking of soft earth and tender bark. The clouds were pulling apart, revealing blue skies above. The breeze no longer chilled him, but instead licked him with a hot tongue.

As Tommy finally reached the clearing, it was no longer a gray October day.

It was summer.

Summer 1981.

PART II

TWENTY-FIVE

Lind Falls, Oregon, 1981

'Holy shit,' Mark said. '*What did you do?*'

Elizabeth said nothing. Her eyes remained closed and her naked shoulders quivered, the faintest of smiles creeping over her face. She was still straddling Rade, who no longer moved, and whose blood had sprayed up on to his killer's naked chest, painting her skin with Pollock-like splatters.

Her breaths were heavy and slow.

A bird called high above, deep within the treetops. Three caws and then silence. Three caws and silence.

'Oh my God,' Jason said. 'Oh my God. Oh my God.'

Tommy's fourteen-year-old mind could not yet process what had just happened. He stood there, looking, absorbing all that was in front of him. Tommy looked at the death and the dirt. A movement to the right caught his eye, and he saw the squirrel coming back down the tree, inching toward them. Creeping closer, as if there had been nothing of interest until that young boy's head had split open, spilling out the possibility of food. In Tommy's mind he could hear the squirrel's tiny claws scuffle against the tree bark.

Elizabeth finally opened her eyes. They seemed brighter than what the filtered sunlight through the trees should have allowed.

'I just came so fucking hard,' she said. She reached up and gave her naked breasts a soft squeeze.

'You . . . is he dead?' Jason said. Tommy looked at him. Jason's bloodless face held eyes that did not blink.

She rose and stretched her arms high above her head, as if just waking from a long nap. Then she ran her hands longer over her naked waist, smearing Rade's blood across her skin until she was covered in broad strokes of pinkish hues rather than bright red splatters. She reached down and pressed her fingers against Rade's neck, to the place where life should be found.

'Yes,' she said.

The three boys looked at her, none of them speaking. There was so much to say. There was nothing to say.

Rade was on his back, the top of his skull crumpled like a Coke can, his dark hair matted and mushy with blood. Elizabeth had hit him a total of three times with the rock, but one time was probably all that was necessary. Rade's lifeless eyes stared up and back, as if still trying to see where the rock in her hands had been aimed. To Tommy, there was no question Rade was dead, but no one checked for sure. No one moved at all.

The bloody rock sat in the dirt, close to Rade's open fingers.

We have to do something, Tommy thought. That one sentence played over and over in his mind, yet he did not move. Whether it was fear or just the simple inability to process information, Tommy froze, and in his mind that made him a coward.

Mark will do something, Tommy thought. Mark is stronger than me. Mark will do *something*.

Tommy looked over at Mark, and as he did Jason and Elizabeth also looked at him. Mark's eyes narrowed as he kept his focus on the half-naked girl.

Elizabeth stood and began to move, confidently, a model on a catwalk, strutting over to Mark, her naked shoulders broad and straight, accentuating a narrow waist and the slight curve of her teenage hips.

She stood in front of Mark and placed a hand on his chest. Mark stared back at her, his gaze feral, but did not move. Elizabeth leaned in and whispered something to him. Still he did not move.

Do something, Tommy thought. His feet seemed cemented to the ground. *Do something, Mark. Smash her in the face or something.*

Then Elizabeth slowly went down to her knees, snaking down Mark's body like a raindrop on a window. Without any hesitation she opened the fly of Mark's jeans and pulled them down. Then she took him into her mouth, her head slowly working back and forth, her hand stroking his cock as her mouth consumed him.

Mark closed his eyes, almost wincing, as if trying to fight against the pleasure, but it was no use. Tommy could see he was already hard, and the hands he brought down, perhaps to push her away, were soon grabbing her red hair, pulling her face closer in to him. He shouted in fury as he came just seconds later, and she drank him in.

What is happening?

Elizabeth slowly wiped the corner of her mouth and she left Mark and turned her attention to Jason. Like Mark, he seemed powerless against her, and again she leaned in close and whispered something in his ear. This time she shed her remaining clothes and stood naked in front of him. She undressed Jason and led him by hand to the closest tree, where she turned and bent over, bracing herself against the trunk, offering herself to him.

Tommy saw the squirrel coming from the opposite direction, inching its way to Rade's open skull.

Jason thrust into her from behind while Mark and Tommy watched. In seconds it was over, and Jason withdrew and let himself fall into the dirt, naked and sobbing.

this isn't happening this isn't happening this isn't happening

Elizabeth let out a long, pleasured sigh and turned to Tommy.

Tommy watched as she now came to him, her feet crossing delicately one in front of the other as she walked, as if on a balance beam. Her long legs milky white and strong; her thin patch of pubic hair red like her hair.

Tommy felt certain he would vomit from revulsion at any moment, but he couldn't help feeling excited. He wanted to fuck her as much as he wanted to kill her, and the agony was knowing he would do neither.

She stood in front of him and placed a hand on his chest, brushing her fingertips from nipple to nipple. Then she leaned in close.

'We're family now,' she said, her breath hot and sensual. 'We have to make it official.'

Her hand lowered to his crotch.

Tommy felt his body light on fire and his breathing quickened. Her fingers deftly popped open the button on his jeans, and Tommy was certain he was going to let her do whatever she wanted.

But he couldn't. As much as he was no longer in control of what was happening in those woods on that summer day, he couldn't let this happen. He would not give in, because something told him if he did she would control him forever, and his soul would belong to her.

He pushed her.

'Get away from me.'

Her eyes flashed feral rage, but then almost immediately softened

into a hazy state of indifference. The crooked, playful smile crept
back.

'You some kind of faggot, Tommy?' she said. 'You like boys,
baby?'

Tommy pounced, throwing his body full force against hers,
knocking her into the dirt. His face pushed into her naked chest,
his chin pressing against one of her nipples. He could smell her
sweat and a lingering hint of perfume, both of which mixed with
droplets of Rade's blood that had sprayed her milky skin.

She tensed, her muscles taut and hard beneath her skin. But she
didn't fight back. In fact, she seemed to like it.

'That's right, baby. Take me rough. Any way you want it.' Her
breathing quickened. Tommy pushed off her. A small drop of blood
had smeared on the corner of her mouth, making her look like a
little girl who'd put on lipstick for the very first time. Whether it
was Rade's blood or her own Tommy didn't know.

Tommy staggered to his feet and leaned into her, screaming.
'What did you do?'

She said nothing. Then her gaze flicked to the left of Tommy,
and her eyes focused on something behind him. She looked at
Tommy again and smiled. The blood was still on her mouth.

Tommy turned.

Someone was coming toward them, from deep within the woods.
Not another teen. A man.

'I was wondering if you stayed for the whole thing,' Elizabeth
said.

The man's head was hidden beneath a black wool ski mask.
Tommy thought, in a detached, shock-setting-in kind of way, that
the mask must be insufferably hot. The man wore camouflage pants
and a tight black t-shirt, revealing some muscle, some fat, and deeply
hairy arms.

In those arms he held a shotgun, which was pointed directly at
Tommy.

Tommy looked first to Mark and then to Jason. Each boy stared
at the man with utter stillness. Jason's pants were still unzipped.

'He's not going to talk,' Elizabeth told the boys. 'He just wanted
to watch, and I wanted him to. I wanted all of you to.' She slowly
stood and brushed some dirt off her arm. 'It was fucking amazing.'

The man pointed the shotgun at the ground, gesturing. Tommy

looked down to what he was pointing at and saw Elizabeth's shirt. *Put your shirt on*, the shotgun said.

Elizabeth smiled, bent down, and put on her tank top, caressing her breasts one last time.

'Let me have your knife, baby.'

The man hesitated, then unsheathed a long blade from his belt. Tommy felt his stomach churn, hollowing itself, as if he could feel the tip of that blade piercing his white, hairless belly, the cool steel penetrating him millimeters at a time.

The man scuffled toward her, his black work boots crunching in the dirt. As he drew close, Tommy stepped back, but only a step. Two steps could've been a problem, he sensed. The man turned and Tommy saw soulful, brown eyes peering through the holes of the ski mask. There seemed no hate or danger in those eyes, and Tommy immediately determined himself a terrible judge of character.

The man handed Elizabeth the knife. As he did, they exchanged words, which floated over to Tommy's ears as unintelligible whispers. Elizabeth then reached up with her face and kissed the man's neck, and as she did Tommy saw the man's eyes close briefly. In pleasure? he wondered. Relief?

Then Elizabeth turned to the others and held the knife above her head.

'Like I said, we are *all* family now. And family helps each other out. I didn't expect to run into you boys here today, but I did, and that's that.' She nodded to the man. 'I'm happy I brought my friend here along to watch. Otherwise I don't think you would all do what now needs to be done. He can make sure you all do what I tell you to do.'

'You're fucking crazy,' Tommy said.

'Maybe,' she said. 'And maybe you're a faggot. All we can do is go off first impressions, right?'

'You wouldn't kill us all,' Tommy said.

'Is that a question or a statement?'

Tommy's chest felt like it was collapsing. He spun toward Mark, who always seemed to know what to do. 'Mark, *do something*!'

Mark said nothing.

Tommy ran over to him, ignoring the man with the gun. Mark stood there, a zombie at the moment of reanimation, blinking slowly, his shoulders hunched forward, staring at nothing.

Tommy grabbed him. 'Mark, c'mon man. We have to do something.' Tommy could hear his own high-pitched fourteen-year-old voice rasp and wheeze in short bursts of panic. He wanted to hug Mark as much as he wanted to pummel him. Anything. Anything to get some sense of normalcy back in his friend. But something about Mark had changed. Tommy could see that now clearly.

Tommy grabbed Mark's arm and pointed at the body. 'Look at that, Mark, man, that's *real.*' Tommy jabbed in the direction of the dead boy with his free hand. 'That's fucking real, Mark. I knew that kid. How are we just supposed to do what she wants us to do?'

The man spoke for the first and only time that day. 'I will kill all of you.' His voice had the light rasp of a pack-a-day smoker, and shook not once as he spoke. 'And then I'll go kill your parents. Brothers. Sisters. Pets. Everyone and everything. So you do as she says, and maybe I just won't. Maybe I will, maybe I won't.'

Tommy dropped his arm. After a moment, after another short burst of cawing from what was seemingly the only bird left in the woods, in between Tommy's heaving, plodding breaths, Mark finally moved. Just his hand. He moved it down to the crotch of his pants and slowly rubbed himself though his clothing. Back and forth. Back and forth. Four or five times. Then he looked up at Tommy, tears welling in his eyes.

'Jesus, Tommy,' he said. 'I'm still hard.'

'*What?*'

'I'm still hard.'

Tommy had no response for this, because how do you respond to a nightmare? That's what this all was after all, wasn't it? The day had started with such mundane clarity, a summer day full of empty minutes to fill, and yet had descended into shattered glass, impossible to see through even if the pieces could be put back together. Scrambled and jagged, just like a dream. Tommy could command sense into Mark no more easily than he could bring that dopey smile back on to Rade's face.

Mark stopped rubbing and started crying in earnest, as if the tears could douse his erection. 'We have to do what she wants.'

Tommy turned to Jason as movement caught his eye. The squirrel was now poking around Rade's head. Tommy picked up a rock and threw it at the squirrel, appalled at the thought of some creature crawling on the dead boy. His aim was perfect and disastrous, thudding into the dead boy's skull. The squirrel – its eyes tiny black marbles of curiosity and alarm – tore away up the nearest tree.

The man aimed the shotgun at Tommy. *Don't throw any more rocks.* Tommy turned to Jason, who had finally picked himself up. 'Jason?'

Jason would not look at him. 'Tommy, we screwed up, man. We screwed up.'

'*Jason . . .*'

Jason hissed at him as tears spilled from his eyes. 'I *fucked* her, Tommy. *I fucked her.* I didn't want to, but . . . I just couldn't help it.' Snot ran from his nose to his upper lip.

'Tommy, there's a shovel over by that stump,' Elizabeth said, letting Jason and Mark sob fitfully amongst themselves. 'Be a dear and go get it, will you?'

Tommy turned and saw the shovel, leaning against a rotted tree stump in the direction from which the man had come. He must have brought it with him.

'No,' said Tommy.

Elizabeth glided over to him. 'So defiant, aren't you, Tommy? Didn't think you had it in you, did you? You're probably proud of yourself. Your friends are over there, crying like little girls, but *you're* the strong one.' She took a step closer, and Tommy looked down at the knife in her hand. 'But I have a secret for you, Tommy. You're going to do everything I say, because you know you're alone.' Then she leaned in close and began to whisper. 'Your friend Jason is weak. He can't help it, because he's just a follower. Always will be. And Mark?' She rattled out a small laugh. 'He's actually excited by this. He doesn't want to be, but he is. Can't help it. Just how some people are. He's a sick fuck, and he's not going to help you at all. And *you*, Tommy . . .' She straightened and her voice was now louder. 'You're only as strong as your actions. And I'm guessing you're just a fourteen-year-old pussy.'

The blade flashed and Tommy barely had time to move before the tip swiped his forearm. Blood crested the small gash and spilled down his arm. Tommy let out a small rasp and tried to yank back his arm, but Elizabeth caught him by the wrist. She seized him with a strength that not only surprised him, but defied him. Elizabeth then pressed the flat of the blade against his blood.

'There,' she said, bringing the knife up and examining it in the filtered sunlight. 'Now go get the shovel.'

And so Tommy did. He went, the blood flowing slowly from the shallow wound, and every step felt heavier than the one before. As he reached the shovel he looked ahead, through the trees, knowing his neighborhood wasn't far. He could run. Wanted to run. How good was the man's aim? Would he really shoot? God, how Tommy wanted to leave. Run as fast as he could, anywhere away from *back there*. But he couldn't. He wanted to tell himself that he couldn't abandon his friends, but that wasn't exactly right, was it? He had to go back simply because he had to, and he hated himself for it.

He dropped the shovel at her feet and wiped his bloody arm against his pant leg.

'Now,' Elizabeth said. 'We need to dig several feet down, I would think.' She scanned the area, finally pointing to a dead elm tree in a small clearing about a hundred feet away. 'Over there.'

'I want to go home.' It was Jason, who was sobbing again.

'You will, sweetie,' she said. 'Soon, I promise.' She turned the knife over and over in her hand, examining it. 'We're all going to bleed a little on this knife today. Because we're a family. And that's what families do.'

Then she picked up the shovel and headed toward the clearing. The man grunted at the three of them, pointing the shotgun. Slowly, each of them began to move, following the girl. Tommy brought up the rear, and as they walked, the man poked the barrel of the gun between his shoulder blades, breathing heavily as he did.

Tommy glanced back once. The squirrel had returned. This time, Tommy did nothing about it.

TWENTY-SIX

Present day

Tommy looked down at his forearm and saw the faded white scar, the straight line left by Elizabeth's blade that had existed as a part of him for decades. It was buried deep enough in his arm hair that no one had ever asked about it, not even Becky. But he saw it every time he looked.

On he walked through the woods, and ten minutes later Tommy found the grave. He hadn't been sure he would be able to, as thirty years of memories had collected in his mind since he last stood here. Thirty years of thoughts, each new one eroding all earlier ones just a little bit at a time. But he remembered where it all happened. He remembered it perfectly.

Tommy stared at the clearing, the small path of scrub and dirt next to the dead elm tree. After all these years the dead tree still stood, crooked and defiant like an ancient tombstone.

The sky darkened as a bruise-colored cloud crept in front of the sun. A small gust of wind rustled the leaves on the floor of the woods.

Tommy looked around, expecting someone to come walking into the clearing at any moment and ask him what he was doing. The woods seemed silent and filled with noise all at once, and Tommy felt he could hear even the sound of a bird twitching its head. He would hear someone coming, he was certain, but it might be too late to do anything about it, especially once he started digging. He just had to hope for the best, which, as he had discovered in years of researching criminals, rarely worked out well.

Tommy's steps grew smaller as he passed the area where the actual murder had taken place. The pile of rocks, the one they sometimes used as a make-shift fireplace, was still there. To Tommy, this was unbelievable, as if no one else had bothered to come out this way since that summer day. He walked over and picked up one of the rocks, feeling its cold heft in his hand. It was about the size of the rock Elizabeth had used on Rade, maybe a little smaller. That rock, of course, was no longer in the pile. That rock was buried next to Rade, along with the hunting knife with all of their blood on it.

We'll cut ourselves, Elizabeth had said. *On the palm, just enough to bleed a little. And then we'll each put our blood on the knife, and that will make it official. Our secret forever. Our blood secret.*

Tommy hadn't needed to do it. She had already taken his blood, so he had stood and watched while Jason and Mark acquiesced at gunpoint. The Watcher hadn't participated in the ritual. He had simply watched.

Tommy remembered the moment of panic, way back in the early 1990s, when he heard about DNA testing being used to solve crimes. He had thought about all their blood on the knife, sitting next to the corpse of a child. But he had been too scared to do anything about it. What was he going to do – dig up the body? No, that would have been crazy. Twenty-something Tommy had been too scared to do anything, so he did nothing, just as he had always done.

But not anymore.

He walked around the old bike path and through knee-high wild grass to the gravesite. Flashes of that day stormed his mind. Their callused hands, unaccustomed to labor, blistering as they took turns with the shovel. It was *so much work* digging wide and deep enough to fit the small body. All the while the Watcher surveyed the scene, pointing his gun, resting his aim on each of them a few seconds at a time, back and forth, like an animatronic figure in an Old West theme-park attraction. Elizabeth had watched as she leaned against a tree, smiling and saying nothing. Then, with the hole finally big enough, they had to roll Rade into it, where he landed face-down with only the lightest of thuds. Kid probably hadn't weighed more than seventy pounds, after all. Then Elizabeth, Mark, and Jason added their blood to the knife and Elizabeth had thrown the knife down in the hole, where it landed sticking into the middle of Rade's back. It was at that point that Tommy had finally lost all bearing and fallen to his knees, a sweeping wave of nausea overcoming him until he puked in the dirt, retching as Elizabeth simply stared at the body with fascination.

Tommy remembered being thankful Rade hadn't been looking up at them when they again took turns with the shovel, this time spooning the cool earth on to the body, covering it a little at a time until the last thing visible was the handle of the kitchen knife. That, too, eventually disappeared under the dirt, until there was nothing left of Rade in those woods except his blood trail from the killing site to the burial site.

They had used dirt to cover that as well.

Tommy now entered the clearing as a small rumble of thunder rolled above. Almost immediately afterwards came the sound of rain falling on hundreds of leafless trees, a million matchsticks dropping from the sky. The clouds had lied to Tommy.

'Hell,' he muttered, dropping his supplies to the ground and keeping only the shovel in his hand. He had thought digging up a body would be the worst part of all of this. He hadn't thought about digging up a body in the rain.

Holding the shovel with both hands, he scanned the small clearing where he would have to dig. Leaves covered the dirt beneath, and near the middle of the clearing they had gathered into an unnatural-looking pile, as if someone had built a small monument from them. Tommy stared at it, a sense of dread spreading over him, and fought to understand what could have caused the mound of leaves to form in that exact manner.

It was at that moment Tommy realized he wasn't the first one to have been here.

TWENTY-SEVEN

He stared at the pile of leaves as the rain came down harder. The trees would shelter Tommy for only so long. Soon he and all the earth around him would be soaked.

Yet he did not approach the . . . thing. It was no bigger than a football, but something was there. *Under there.* Under the leaves. Yes, it was a *thing*, of that he was certain.

A lightning bolt cracked nearby, close enough to make Tommy jump. Pellets of rain made their way through the bare trees and began assaulting Tommy and everything around him. Within seconds, the top layer of leaves covering the small mound on the ground began to peel away.

The thing underneath was white.

Tommy bent over, wanting to look but not yet ready to touch.

Another leaf fell off.

Tommy saw ears. The white thing had ears.

Rabbit ears?

Tommy reached out and scraped off the remaining leaves, their once-dry skin now wet and slimy. He recognized the object immediately.

It was an unpainted cement rabbit, its eyes wide and blank, hunched in a frozen state of chewing. And it wasn't just any common garden ornament. This one had meaning.

It was the exact one Tommy had buried the knife under in the back garden of Mark Singletary's home in Charleston. The knife Elizabeth had used to slice open the homeless man's throat.

Tommy snapped his head to the side, staring deeper into the woods. She was here. Watching him. Must be hiding behind a tree. Laughing. But he saw no one.

Then he looked back down. The rabbit was no longer a rabbit. The rabbit was nothing but a large white rock.

He reached out and touched the rock, seeing if it was real. He felt the cool surface of the stone, the uneven bumps. It looked nothing like a rabbit at all, just as the PowerPoint presentation had suddenly morphed on the airplane.

Tommy had done his share of drugs in his life, but never anything that made him hallucinate. Now he was hallucinating, and it was so disconcerting that he had to sit down on the cold floor of the woods just to ground himself.

The rain didn't give a shit if he was sitting or standing. It still came down on him.

'Fuck,' he muttered. He rubbed his eyes, as if that would cure insanity. 'Fuck.'

Someone had been here at some point, Tommy thought, but Elizabeth wasn't here now. She was a monster, but she wasn't supernatural. If she moved the body, she did so at some earlier time. The rock was just a signal for me, he thought. But she's not hiding behind a goddamn tree, or going to rise out of the ground.

She's just a person, he told himself. An evil, fucked-up person. But just a person.

Tommy kept his eyes closed for another few moments and felt the drops roll down his face. He focused clearly on the sensation, letting it be the only thing he felt on his entire body. Water tickling his cheek, falling from his jaw. It cleared his mind, if only a little, and when he reopened his eyes he felt refocused.

Tommy wiped the rain from his eyes and willed himself to ignore the deep chill that was starting to course through his body. He was ill equipped for this weather, but it was too late to turn back. He was going to do what he came here to do.

Tommy picked up the stone and threw it as far as he could deeper into the woods. He kicked away the remaining pile of leaves from the mound and grabbed his shovel.

Another lightning bolt flashed just as his shovel pierced the mud for the first time. It was like shoveling sand. With each clump of wet earth he heaved to the side, more water filled the growing hole in the ground, until he was eventually scooping a thick, slushy mixture. It felt fruitless – it would take him forever to reach Rade, if Rade was still down there.

He kept digging, sweating through the chill of the rain, and his shoulders began to burn every time he flung a scoop of mud behind him.

Faster. Deeper.

He grunted as he picked up speed. His clothes were now soaked, and from the knees down his jeans were caked in wet earth. He struggled to keep his footing, and slowly his feet disappeared deeper into the rain-soaked earth. Yet he continued on, harder, faster. Deeper into the pit. The grave. The floating tomb of a little boy. Tommy drove into the ground with all his might, not even caring that his repeated spearing with the shovel could bisect the remains at any moment.

Sweat now mixed with rain and fell into his eyes, stinging them. His back screamed in protest, yet still he drove on. He could barely see into the hole, but the faster he went the more progress he could actually see. He was clearing out more water than was going in, and if he could maintain this pace he might actually see what, if anything, was down there.

Go, Tommy. Keep going. You came all the way out here, so you *have* to see what's down there. You can't give up now, because giving up was what got you here in the first place. You gave up thirty years ago when you were too afraid to tell anyone what had happened. Too scared the Watcher would come back. Too worried no one would believe your story, that they would think instead the three of you boys had done the deed. Elizabeth had disappeared, after all, so wasn't it reasonable to assume no one would believe you?

No, Tommy told himself.

You and Mark and Jason could have told the police. Told your parents. Told *anyone*. You could have led them back to the woods. To the body. And what then?

Tommy shouted at the collapsing ground as he kept digging, working with the frantic energy of a man scooping water out of his sinking lifeboat.

'I don't know!'

Of course you do, Tommy. Of course you know. If you had said something back then, then Rade could have been her first and only victim. She could have been locked away. No one else would have died. You would have been a hero, but instead you said nothing. You did exactly as she told you.

'Fuck you,' Tommy grunted. 'Fuck you.'

Yes, Tommy. You thought you were brave for not letting her *fuck you*, didn't you? Yeah, you sure stood up to her. You thought that was being brave enough, but it wasn't. Not by a long shot, Tommy. Not by a country mile. You just fed her will, and look where it's led you. You're losing your mind, Tommy, don't you know that? Look at you. You haven't slept a full night in days. You're barely eating. Writing like a maniac, pushing your brain into some realm it's not used to. *Hallucinating*. And now. Covered in mud, digging for something you know is no longer there. You *do* know that, right? You do know she's already moved the body, right? Why else would she put that rock there? She wants you to know she was here. She wants you to see that, no matter what you do, she's *smarter* than you. You have to be different this time, Tommy. You have to think like *her*. It's the only way, Tommy. The only way you can win.

The pain overwhelmed him and Tommy let the shovel fall to the ground, then he raised his face to the blackened sky and wanted to scream, scream to release it all. But he couldn't. He didn't want to risk the noise, and the incompleteness of the act made him feel plastic. So he just stared at the sky and hoped for a lightning bolt. The rain went on, but Tommy could no longer.

He looked down at the hole in the ground, which was quickly being overtaken by water now that his digging had stopped.

There was something there. Something floating to the surface.

Tommy bent down and stared at it.

What was that?

It dipped below the surface. Tommy wanted to reach in, but he recoiled at the idea of what he might grab if he stuck his hand into the brackish water.

Or what might grab him.

Then it popped up again. This time it pointed at him.

Tommy was staring at a small hand.

TWENTY-EIGHT

T ommy wiped the raindrops from his face, which were immediately replaced with new ones. The floor of the woods
seemed to darken by the minute, but nothing was blacker
than the water-filled grave at his feet. Which made the sight of the
little white hand so goddamn unnerving.

He bent forward and stared at the tips of the fingers, three of which
poked just above the surface of the water, floating like a fishing
bobber. The fingertips were an unnatural white, and no longer seemed
to have any nails on them. If they were thinner, Tommy would have
guessed them mere bones, but they were thicker and had more shape
than that. He knew that a body could last for years in the ground
before decaying to bone, but thirty years? No way. Not in these woods.

Something wasn't right.

Tommy took a deep breath and plunged the shovel one more
time into the hole, driving it as deep as he could, well beneath
where the little arm floated near the surface. This time, as he heaved
up, he brought with the mud and the muck something else.

It was the rest of the body the arm was attached to. But it was
not Rade's body. In fact, it really wasn't a body at all.

It was a doll. A Pinocchio doll. A large one, nearly two feet long,
and dressed in his telltale red and yellow costume, with a mud-
stained yellow peaked cap adorning his head. Half of the yellow
hat seemed to be missing, but Tommy then noticed it wasn't just
the hat. The top of Pinocchio's head was caved in, as if it had been
smashed with a rock.

Tommy looked down at the wooden doll as it dangled over the
side of the shovel's blade. Its limbs had many joints, its legs and
arms articulated like those of a skeleton. Pinocchio stared up at the
trees, his little black eyes dead to the world, his stained wooden
face repelling every raindrop landing on it.

Then Tommy noticed the nose. This Pinocchio doll did not have the
standard-size nose, the one Pinocchio earned whenever he was
truthful. This doll had the other nose. The long, pointed one, the

one that told the world he was a liar. This nose, streaked with blackness, pointed directly at Tommy.

Of course, he thought. It wasn't enough to move the body, she had to replace it with something else. Something that sent a message to me. She's telling me *I'm* Pinocchio, and I'm the one lying to the world.

Tommy lowered the doll to the ground, not letting it fall but instead gently letting it slide off the shovel blade and on to the mud, face up. She has the *real* body, he thought.

Tommy then crouched over the hole and reached into the dark water with both hands, feeling. He moved slowly, not wanting to stab himself if the knife was still there, but he knew it wouldn't be. Tommy felt nothing but the cold of the water and the slime of the wet earth. He pulled his hands back, knowing the doll was the only thing left in the decades-old grave. She has the evidence of the crime, he thought, including the knife with all our blood on it.

A voice boomed from behind him. A man's voice.

'What are you doing?'

Tommy spun around and saw the police officer approaching through the sheets of rain.

Tommy dropped the shovel to the ground.

TWENTY-NINE

The cop seemed to float toward him, boots absorbed by the water and the muck, his black utility slicker puffing out from him, rendering him almost formless. But there was no question the man was a cop. The hat he wore outright declared it.

'I asked what you're doing.'

Tommy was grateful not to be holding human remains at the moment.

'Research,' he said.

The cop finally drew close. He was a hulking, overweight man who at one time had probably been an impressive figure. Tommy guessed him to be in his mid-sixties.

'Research? What the hell kind of research?'

Tommy drew up straight. *Don't act guilty.*

'I'm sorry, officer, am I doing anything wrong?'

The cop squinted and his eyes seemed to disappear into the fleshy mass that was his face.

'Well, *sir*, I figure I'll tell you if you're doing anything wrong after you tell me what exactly it is you're doing.' He nodded at Tommy's shovel. 'Strikes me as odd to be out here in the middle of a rainstorm, digging in the woods.' His gaze went to the doll on the ground. 'Is that Pinocchio?'

'It is.'

The cop kept looking at him, waiting for an explanation.

'I'm a writer,' Tommy said. 'I'm doing some research for my next book, which entails . . . digging.'

'That so?'

'Yes, sir.'

'You writing a book about mud and holes and Pinocchio dolls? Sounds like a real page turner.'

The rain had eased from a downpour to a cold annoyance.

'Look, officer, I'm sorry if I'm not supposed to be digging on public land. I just figured that—'

'I need to see your ID.'

It was the second time in a week a cop had asked for his ID.

Tommy fished out the wallet from his back pocket and handed him his license. The cop studied it as raindrops spilled down its laminated surface.

'No shit? Tommy Devereaux?'

'Yes, sir.' Fuck. It was exactly what Tommy wanted to avoid, having his steps retraced, especially first-hand by the police. He was naive to think this plan would ever even work.

The cop handed him back his license. 'You're a bit of a celebrity around here. I remember you when you were a kid. Alan Stykes?'

The name flashed in Tommy's mind, followed by an image. The image of a younger and stronger face, peering at him.

Seen anyone strange around here lately?

Alan Stykes was the cop who had questioned Tommy the day after Rade's disappearance. Tommy had stared at his shoes and covered the fresh wound in his forearm with his hand as Officer Stykes asked him the last time he had seen Rade.

Tommy stuck out his hand as his stomach muscles tightened into a knot. 'Sure, I remember you.'

Stykes took the hand. His grip was firm despite the rain.

'I talked to you about the Baristow boy. Back in eighty-one. Remember that?'

Tommy felt his eyes being drawn toward the ground but he forced himself to make eye contact as he sucked in a deep breath. 'Sure I do.' He paused. 'Ever solve that?'

'No, sir. That and a few others over the years.'

'Others?'

'Three more. Then the disappearances stopped. All of 'em kids. Never found a one of them.'

The rain slashed at Tommy. Three kids? he thought. How had he never heard about this? Tommy had researched the killing of Rade as best he could in the months and years that followed, but it remained an unsolved disappearance and that garnered little attention from the media. Once Tommy realized nothing new would be written about the Baristow disappearance, he had simply stopped researching it. Three other kids had disappeared in Lind Falls? Hadn't Elizabeth left town?

'So you've come back, have you?'

Tommy nodded. 'For a couple of days.'

'You here alone?'

Tommy wanted to lie, but saw no point to it.

'I am.'

'Well, Tommy, big shot writer or not, gotta say you look pretty damn stupid out here covered in mud and holding a doll. What say you go get cleaned up now?'

Tommy nodded. He would have agreed to anything as long as he could just leave those woods without handcuffs on him.

'Then you're coming over to my house for dinner tonight,' Stykes said.

The words stopped Tommy. 'Oh, well, Alan . . . I really need to work on my—'

'I insist. Otherwise I'm writing you up for vandalism.'

'Seriously?'

Stykes burst out laughing, which soon turned into the hacking cough of a smoker who had finally reached the point of no return. 'Hell, son, I got you good. But you *are* coming over for dinner. You're a goddamn celebrity.'

Tommy acquiesced, mostly because he couldn't think of any easy way out of it. Besides, he wasn't caught with a body, so he figured one lousy dinner wasn't too steep a price to pay for fate cutting him a break.

'C'mon back to the squad car and I'll give you my address.'

Tommy grabbed the shovel and the doll and put them in the duffel bag. Then he trudged behind Stykes, who seemed not only comfortable, but even happy to be sloughing through the mud.

As they eventually emerged from the woods and back into the comfort of suburbia, a thought occurred to Tommy.

'How did you even know I was out there?'

Stykes grumbled a deep chuckle, as if the answer was self-evident.

'Well, that's just the thing, Tommy. There isn't anything in Lind Falls I *don't* know about.'

THIRTY

Night came early to Lind Falls, swept in on the back of thunderheads, which hovered and menaced like massive alien ships. Tommy's exhaustion was nearly complete and probably needed only a drink or two to land the final punch.

He pulled up to Stykes's house just after seven, a half-hour later than he was expected. Fresh clothes had replaced the mud-caked ones from earlier, and a long hot shower had restored Tommy to something resembling his normal self. He had called home, feeling anxious and guilty about talking to his family while pretending to be in South Carolina. Again, he debated telling Becky everything, wondering how bad things would have to get before he finally admitted he could no longer do this without help; but he had to push through the guilt. This would end, he kept telling himself. He could deal with this. He would shelter his children from a darkness they didn't deserve to know about, and he would make things right with Becky. Things would be normal again. Just a little longer.

Tommy nestled his rental car against the curb in front of Stykes's house, which was only four blocks away from where Tommy himself had lived. Tommy knew this block well; he had passed by it on a daily basis walking to school.

A dying bulb spat bursts of light on to Stykes's porch, from which old paint peeled skyward. The lawn, brown for the dormant season, looked as if someone once tried to care for it but then found something better to do. Like most houses in this section of Lind Falls, Stykes's was small and simple. It was likely built in the 1950s, when the lumber industry first began attracting people to the area. In the ensuing decades, the owners of these houses either renovated and upgraded their simple homes or just seemed to let them run their course. Stykes's situation was the latter.

Alan Stykes opened the door before Tommy could ring the bell, impressive considering both his hands were full. In his left hand was a Budweiser. In his right hand was a dog collar, which was attached to a snarling Rottweiler.

'Saw your headlights,' Stykes said, pushing open the screen door with his elbow. 'If you'da rung the bell she'd have gone crazy, and we don't need all that barking.'

The dog had not yet barked, but dogs like that didn't need to. The Rottweiler looked at Tommy as if he could be some kind of fun toy to play with before snapping his neck.

'That's a hell of a dog,' Tommy said. He held a bottle of red wine in his right hand, which he now thought of more as a potential weapon to use.

'Aw, she's all right. Name's Panzer. She just needs to sniff ya a bit before you come in.'

Tommy walked up the porch and hesitantly reached his hand out, wondering why people so implicitly trusted crazy dog owners when they said their dogs were harmless. For all Tommy knew, this would be the last time he saw the fingers on his left hand. And he *needed* those fingers to type, goddammit.

Panzer sniffed and pushed against his hand, transferring a dollop of viscous drool in the process. But she didn't remove his fingers, and Tommy even thought he saw a change in her expression, one that said Tommy wasn't a threat. Like a nightclub bouncer, Panzer backed up a bit and let him in.

'Welcome,' Stykes said.

Tommy stepped into the house and immediately knew he didn't want to be there. He didn't want to have dinner with some old cop from the town, talking about some endless bullshit for God knew how long. Tommy's life was too complicated for such things at the moment. The question was how to extract himself as early as possible without upsetting the man.

'You live here alone, Alan?'

'Yup. Carol died coming on twenty years now. Cancer. Which is why I invited you over. Don't get much chance to cook for anyone these days.' He glanced toward the kitchen and then back to Tommy. 'Real special to have a guest.'

Tommy looked around and wondered if Carol would've allowed for a messy house when a dinner guest was coming over. He also wondered if Carol let Alan smoke in the house, for surely he did now, as stale cigarette smoke hung in the air, attaching itself to any other scent and beating it into submission. 'Well, I thank you again for inviting me, Alan. Just have to warn you, Alan, I'm not feeling one hundred percent.' Tommy patted his belly. 'Not sure what it is.'

Stykes beamed, as if Potential Vomiting and Diarrhea was a comedy duo. 'Well, now, suppose that's what you get for traipsing around in the mud and rain. Maybe picked up a bug.'

'Maybe. Just hope I can stay for dinner.'

'Oh, you *have* to stay for dinner, friend. I cooked up a stew that'll set you right.'

Tommy forced a smile. 'Sounds great.' Stew sounded awful.

'And I want to be able to say I cooked dinner for a famous author, so I gotta admit there's a bit of a selfish side about me wanting you over here tonight.'

Tommy walked further into the house and stuck his hands into his pockets, as if by doing so he wasn't fully committing himself to actually being here. The hardwood floor creaked as he walked and there were several deep grooves next to the door, evidence of Panzer's enthusiasm to rip apart someone ringing the doorbell. Or attempts to escape.

'Come in, come in,' Stykes said. 'Can I get you a beer?'

'Sure, Alan. Beer sounds great.' Tommy set the bottle of wine he brought on a small table holding unopened mail and a pack of cigarettes.

Stykes disappeared into the kitchen and Tommy looked around the room, noting the complete lack of anything on the walls. No art, no photos, nothing. In fact, the only photos he saw anywhere were contained in a metal collage frame that was sitting on top of a weathered and ring-stained end table next to the couch. Tommy leaned over and looked at the frame, counting five photos within it.

Stuffed animals.

They were old Polaroids – the shape and white border of the prints unmistakable. Each photo showed a collection of stuffed animals, all arranged neatly and facing the camera, as if waiting for something exciting to happen. A chill ran through Tommy, the kind of chill a clown gives when he smiles just a little too much.

Why the hell would this man have photos of old stuffed animals on display?

Tommy straightened just as Stykes returned with two Buds, handing one to Tommy. Tommy sized up the man in front of him, turning him immediately into a character in one of his books. Alan Stykes was the man who never had too many dreams, and when he made it into the police academy at a young age he pretty much realized it was the best he was ever going to do, so he clung to the job like a piece of driftwood in the middle of the open sea. Married young, was a decent husband to a plain-looking woman, grieved hard and long at her death, and made his way about life doing the same thing he'd done for decades: making sure the good folks of Lind Falls slept well at night, all the while committing a slow suicide through nicotine and solitude.

The beer had already been opened and Tommy took a sip. Warm. Tommy spied an ancient-looking golf club in the corner of the room.

'You a golfer, Alan?'

'Nope.' Stykes smiled, as if it was a joke.

Tommy wanted to ask why he had a golf club if he didn't golf, but instinct told him to let it go.

'So you've been a cop all this time?'

'Deputy sheriff, actually. Going on thirty-five years now.'

'I'm sure Lind Falls appreciates your commitment.'

'Oh, I believe so, Tommy. I believe so.' Stykes walked into a small living room and let his weight collapse into a faded brown recliner with duct tape along the sides. Panzer followed suit, resting at her owner's feet. Tommy moved a newspaper – dated three weeks earlier – off a loveseat and sat across from his host.

'But you're the big celebrity around here, Tommy. I always hear your name. You've done good for yourself.' Stykes raised his beer and tipped his head.

'Thanks, Alan. I'd appreciate you keeping my visit to Lind Falls on the down-low, though.' *Jesus*, Tommy thought. *Did you just say down-low? You've never said that in your life.* 'Kind of helps the creative process to keep my research quiet.'

'Well, don't you worry about me. I'm a private man myself and I haven't even mentioned you to anyone.' His face then settled into the placid stillness of a mountain lake and he seemed to look distantly through Tommy. 'No one knows you're here tonight, Tommy. No one.'

Tommy paused. That was an odd thing to say. 'Thanks, Alan.'

Stykes leaned forward and cracked a smile. 'Now tell me, Tommy. What were you really doing out there today? Because I'll tell you what, I've seen a lot of weird shit in this town and that's right up there with the weirdest. I mean, what was that business with the doll? That is, if you don't mind me askin'.'

Tommy studied Stykes's face and remembered it from all those years ago, asking simple questions that felt loaded with the weight of a mountain. *Investigating questions.*

'It's kind of a . . . treasure hunt,' Tommy said.

'Treasure hunt?'

'Has to do with my next book.'

'*The Blood of the Young*,' Stykes said. 'I read the first chapter.'

'I'm flattered.'

'That killing. Of that little boy. You set that in Oregon.'

'I did. Right here, in fact.'

'Now why would you do that?'

Tommy felt his breathing quicken.

'I grew up here. I know those woods. Makes it easier to write about.'

Stykes absorbed this and leaned back in his chair. 'Yeah, I suppose it would at that.' He studied the label of his beer as if it was different than the thousands of identical ones he'd likely seen in his lifetime. 'I thought maybe your book had to do with Rade Baristow. Or the three other kids.'

Tommy froze and dropped his gaze to the floor, just as he had done thirty years earlier with this man. Did Stykes know something?

Was this whole dinner a fucking setup to get him to confess to the murder?

Tommy hated that Stykes could probably spot a liar. 'What makes you say that, Alan?'

'Well, we had four missin' kids in this tiny town, and you wrote about a boy the same age as Rade Baristow gettin' cheesecaked with a rock. You set the book at that same time as when he disappeared. The connection just kinda came to me after that.'

Tommy nodded and tried his best to mix honesty and bullshit in a combination that would pass a taste test. 'I won't lie that Rade came to mind a bit. Guess I was always disturbed by his disappearance.'

'Not solving those cases will forever make me feel like I've failed in my job as an officer of the peace.'

Tommy nodded. 'I never even heard about the other three. How is that possible?'

'Well, because you got the fuck outta Dodge and never looked back.' Stykes barely raised his beer in a half-hearted salute. 'Good for you, is what I say. 'Sides, those other three . . . well, the kids were a bit older, and most folks thought they were all runaways. Delinquents for the most part. Got a lot of press locally but not so much outside, I expect.'

'Boys or girls?'

'All boys. Disappeared in ninety, ninety-two, and ninety-seven. None after that.'

Pretty big spread in time, Tommy thought. If Elizabeth had killed them all, that was a slow pace given how many she currently claims to have murdered. Or maybe she would just come back to Lind Falls from time to time to get one in? None of it seemed to follow a pattern, but Tommy had so little information finding a pattern would be nearly impossible.

'Well, I hope they were all runaways and not . . . something else.'

'Amen, Tommy. But hope is for country singers and religious folk, Tommy. And I ain't either.'

Tommy wanted the questions to stop, but he figured Stykes might keep drilling at him until Tommy sprung some kind of leak. There was no way he could stay for dinner. It would be hell, if not worse. He needed to tell Stykes he was sick, but he had to go use the bathroom first at least, so his excuse for departure seemed plausible.

'Can you tell me where your bathroom is, Alan?'

'Sure thing, buddy.' He pointed to the solitary corridor the house seemed to contain. 'Just down the hall to the right.'

Tommy rubbed his stomach as he stood, as if signaling to Stykes that all was not right *down there*.

He turned into the corridor, leaving Stykes's gaze. He already felt better just not being in the line of sight of the cop. Stykes *was* a fucking cop after all, and Tommy felt the guilt draped over him, visible for all to see. He felt like he had walked into some kind of sting operation, and by the time stew was served, Tommy would be confessing.

Why did I even come here? What was I thinking?

The voice of reason, a small little fellow with decreasing job responsibilities, answered in a weak voice.

Because if you had turned down the nice man's offer of dinner, he might have told the whole town what you were doing. You're just saving your ass, Tommy, so just play it cool and everything will go fine. You'll see.

Tommy wasn't so sure. He wanted to leave, and leave *now*. But he also suspected Stykes wasn't buying the whole upset stomach routine.

He found the bathroom, which was just before the end of the hallway, where a door stood half-open, revealing a room with an unmade bed and a small pile of clothes on the floor. Master bedroom, Tommy thought, thinking the term more grandiose than the room warranted. The lights were on.

The art on the wall above the bed caught Tommy's eye, not because it was particularly stunning or absorbing, but rather because it was the only thing on any wall Tommy had noticed since he'd first walked in.

He stopped in front of the bathroom and stared at the wall in Stykes's bedroom. There were four small framed prints there, each stuck in a simple black frame, the kind you'd buy at Target for twelve bucks. Together, the prints formed a loose square on the wall.

They were photos. Landscapes, Tommy thought. Trees. Lots of trees.

He began to step into the bathroom but something nagged at him, telling him to take a closer look at what was hanging on Stykes's bedroom wall. There was something familiar about those photos, wasn't there? Familiar, but in an unsettling way, like suddenly remembering a piece of a recurring childhood nightmare.

Tommy looked back down the hall. He could hear Stykes humming in the other room, a low, nostalgic hum of some tune that sounded vaguely like a military march.

Tommy pushed the door open fully and stepped into the bedroom. It only took one more step toward the wall for him to realize what one of the pictures was. The photo on the upper left. The first photo.

It was a picture of the woods he'd been in just earlier that day. And it wasn't just the same woods. The photo showed the exact spot where Tommy had been digging. Elizabeth's voice whispered in his mind.

Rade Baristow is buried four feet beneath the dead elm tree, thirty paces west of the clearing in the woods behind the Jackson Creek subdivision in Lind Falls, Oregon.

Tommy tried to process what he was looking at.

A photo of Rade Baristow's grave is hanging on the wall of Alan Stykes's bedroom, he told himself. At least his grave before the body was moved.

Tommy took another step closer, so now he was just a few feet away from the wall. The photo was behind dusty glass, but it looked old. It wasn't some shiny, glossy art print, this was an old 35 mm photo that had been enlarged. Was it thirty years old?

Tommy's stomach twisted.

Get the hell out of there.

But he couldn't. He couldn't move at all. All Tommy could do was stare at the photo and try his best to think of any reason that Alan Stykes wasn't the Watcher from the day Rade died.

See anyone strange around here lately?

Tommy forced his gaze to the other three photos. They were also landscape shots of woods. Tommy didn't recognize any of the exact locations, but they were similar enough to the first photo that he was fairly certain they were all taken in Lind Falls.

Three other boys had gone missing.

Three more photos.

Elizabeth and Stykes killed them all. And these photos were Stykes's trophies. He slept beneath their graves every night.

Fresh cigarette smoke wafted past his nose.

'You like them?'

Tommy jumped. Stykes was standing just a few feet behind him in the doorway to the bedroom. He held a lit cigarette between the fingers of his meaty right hand, its long ash threatening to plummet to the floor.

'Jesus, Alan, you startled me.'

'Didn't mean to.'

No, not at all, Tommy thought.

Stykes's hulking frame completely blocked Tommy's exit from the room.

'Took those myself,' he said. 'Right around here.'

Tommy tried to calm himself, but knew his face must be giving his real emotion away. 'That so?'

'Yup. That one there is where you were today, matter of fact.'

Tommy refused to turn and look at the photo. He didn't want his back to this man. 'Thought it looked familiar,' he said.

'Kind of a weird coincidence, don't ya think?' Stykes took a drag on his cigarette and the ash finally fell, scattering about the floor. He exhaled his smoke directly at Tommy.

'It certainly is.' I'm going to die here, Tommy thought. In this bedroom. And no one knows where the hell I am.

And then Tommy thought of something that hadn't yet occurred to him. *I can take this guy*, he thought. I might be smaller, but I'm younger and stronger. I know how to fight. I'm in good shape. He's just an old cop who probably hasn't had a real physical challenge in decades. This guy might be a killer, but I'll bet he's not expecting me to put up a real defense.

Tommy subtly shifted his right foot back and assumed a defensive posture. And then he decided to ask a question.

'These photos have some kind of meaning for you, Alan?'

Tommy saw in Alan Stykes's face a man calculating, best as someone like Alan Stykes could calculate. Weighing what to do. If Stykes *was* the Watcher (and how could he not be?), he must have been wondering why Tommy came back to exhume the body. And was he even surprised to see there was only a doll in the ground? No. Of course not. Elizabeth must still be in contact with him. She must have told Stykes what she thought Tommy was coming back to Lind Falls to do. It was probably Stykes who had moved Rade's remains.

And if he was truly still working with Elizabeth, he would have to know that she didn't want Tommy harmed. Yet.

The calculation became simple at that point, Tommy figured. If he was right, there wasn't anything Stykes could do, and there wasn't anything Tommy could do. Stalemate.

'Nope,' Stykes said. 'Nothing special. Just kinda liked the look of those places.'

Stykes remained in the doorway.

'Why did you invite me over here tonight, Alan?'

Stykes's face softened, just enough to make him look suddenly very tired. 'I wanted to see what you turned into,' he said. 'To see if . . . well, ya know.'

'To see if what?'

Stykes's large eyes widened, growing sad. 'To see if you became like me.'

Tommy said nothing in response, as if even denying he was at all like Stykes would still be some kind of admission of guilt.

'I'm going to go now, Alan. OK?'

Stykes nodded. After a few seconds, he stepped back from the doorway. Tommy braced himself as he slid past the man in the hallway, but Stykes did not pounce. He didn't even move. He just stood there, a sad old man who had killed three children, and Tommy had to figure out what to do about that.

Stykes called out as Tommy reached the front door.

'Careful not to let the dog out. She wouldn't survive one damn night out there on her own.'

THIRTY-ONE

The smell woke him up.

Tommy stirred. The faint headache that had clung to his brain like a barnacle all night had slipped away. He smelled flowers. Faint. He almost wondered if he imagined it, and then he opened his eyes.

A light was on in the motel room. At the table, near the door.

Elizabeth was sitting in the chair at the table, looking at Tommy's laptop.

Tommy froze, but it was too late. She knew he was awake.

'Her face was smooth and white,' she read from the screen, 'surprisingly wrinkle-free. Her shoulders were wide, accentuating her perfect posture and her breasts, even more full and round than he had remembered.'

She looked over to Tommy. 'Somebody thinks I'm hot,' she said in a sing-song voice.

Tommy sat up in bed, suddenly aware of his naked upper torso. 'How'd you get in here?'

She looked at the cheap motel door, which didn't even have a deadbolt. 'Please,' she said. 'If you were staying in a Westin, I'd be hanging out in the lobby. But a piece-of-shit place like this? No easier lock in the world to pick.' She ran her gaze over his body. 'You're in pretty good condition yourself, Tommy. Yummy.'

'What the hell do you want?'

'You spend a lot of time asking that.'

'I think I'm entitled.' Tommy glanced at the clock. Just after four in the morning. After coming back from Stykes's house, he'd spent some time researching the other child disappearances in Lind Falls before succumbing to a fractured sleep.

Elizabeth stood, her long hair spilling over the crisp folds of a black leather trench coat. She was well dressed as always, Tommy thought. Just like SS officers always were.

'You're the expert. What do you think I want?'

'I think you want to fuck with me.'

She smiled. 'Drop the "with".'

Elizabeth unbuckled the belt of her trench coat and left the coat to open by itself. It didn't reveal much, but enough to see she was naked underneath.

He wasn't tempted by Elizabeth, but that didn't mean he wasn't excited. And he didn't want to feel excitement now, but how do you control that? He couldn't deny that she was, in truth, beautiful. Sexy. The visual definition of woman. But she was a killer, and not an interesting, fictionalized assassin for hire, like a character Angelina Jolie would play in a movie. She was a sick fuck who had actually killed innocent children with her own hands and watched their stunned faces as their life seeped out of them.

Tommy felt a rush to his loins and hated himself for it.

'No,' he said.

'You sure?' She cocked her head. 'It would help you understand my character.'

'You disgust me.'

'Not according to what I just read.'

'Close your coat.'

She smiled and did just that. 'Maybe later,' she said.

'Is that how you do it?' he asked.

'Do what, Tommy?'

'Your men. Your *Watchers*. You use sex to lure them in?'

'Sex is used for everything, Tommy. It's the currency of the universe.'

'You didn't answer my question.'

She took a step toward him, the spikes of her stiletto boots plunging into the decades-old motel carpet.

'So now you want to ask me questions? After all this effort spent running from me, are you finally ready to ask me questions, Tommy?'

'I'm not running from you,' he said. 'I'm just trying to live my life and you keep showing up.'

'Well, we both know that's not true. You're desperately trying to cover up your past, and you're just digging your grave deeper.' She pulled a strand of hair back behind her ear. 'You think you don't need me, Tommy. You think you don't want me. But the truth is I'm your muse and you know it. I inspire you.'

'You revolt me.'

'Those aren't mutually exclusive sensations, Tommy. Everything you have you owe to me. And we're more alike than you want to admit. The homeless guy in Charleston? A lot of people would have stayed. Waited for the police. Told them the truth.'

'That wasn't an option,' Tommy said. 'You know that.'

'Of course it was an option. It was another calculated risk, just like the rest of what you're faced with.'

'If you need me, why would you have called nine-one-one and risked me getting picked up by the police?'

'Oh, sweetie. You're adorable. You think I actually called nine-one-one? Truth is, Tommy, I think you enjoy all this. I think you *want* me in your life. Pretty good team we would make, don't you think? I get to do what I do and you get to write about it.'

'You're delusional,' he said.

But isn't your new draft the best thing you've ever written? Haven't you written more words in the shortest amount of time since she's been back in your life? Can you really say she's not your muse?

He pushed the thoughts away as he pulled the covers off him and stood. He turned and walked to where he'd left his t-shirt and jeans on the floor, feeling her gaze on him.

'Damn, Tommy,' she said. 'I could eat you alive.'

Tommy put on his clothes and ran his fingers through his hair, smoothing it out. This was done from habit, he told himself. He didn't want to think he was actually concerned about how he looked in front of her.

He turned to her. 'Yes, I do have questions. And I think that's why you keep following me. You want me to understand you, as much as I can. Right?'

'That's right, Tommy.'

'So let's do it. Right now.' He pointed at the small wooden table where she had just been sitting. 'Right here. Then maybe you can leave me alone for a while so I can write this fucking book.'

She paused, then walked to the table and sat down. Her jacket pushed open just enough for him to see the soft curve along the top of her right nipple.

'OK, Tommy. Whatever you want. Ask and it shall be answered, and then I'll leave you alone. Until . . .' Her voice trailed off, inviting him in, which he accepted.

'Until what?'

'Until you need to write the ending.'

THIRTY-TWO

Tommy reached into his messenger bag and pulled out a small digital recorder.

'No,' she said. 'No recording. No pictures. No video. Just notes.'

He placed the recorder back in the bag, sat opposite her, then opened up a blank document on his laptop. His fingers poised over the keyboard.

'Tell me again how many,' he said. 'How many murders.'

'You mean you can't remember?'

'Just tell me again.'

She sighed. 'Our friend in Charleston. He was number thirty-nine.'

Tommy began typing. 'The beginning. Start from the beginning.'

'Well, you know my first.'

'Before that,' he said. 'Your parents.'

'What about them?'

'Are they alive?'

'They were at one point. Then, not so much.'

'Did you—'

'Of course not. Though sometimes I wished it.' Tommy saw her drop her gaze to the table. 'They died in a car crash when I was nineteen. On vacation in Puerto Rico. My father had rented a car. No one really knows what happened, but they went off the road and into a ditch. Car caught fire.'

'Where were you at the time?'

'College.'

'What college?'

'Well, Tommy, I can't tell you *that*. I'm supposed to be a fictional character, remember? Just like I won't give you the names of my victims.'

'Well, I know Rade's name.'

'Which will be changed before you send this to your editor. In your teaser, you used the name Brian. That works.'

'So. College. East Coast?'

'Yes, East Coast*ish*. Two years. I dropped out after my parents died.'

'What was your major?'

Elizabeth considered before answering.

'Psychology.'

Figures. 'And then what?'

'Then I used the life insurance money from my parents to find a nice little place to live and act out my fantasies.'

'We'll get to that in a minute. Siblings?'

'What do you think?'

Tommy knew. 'None.'

'Bingo.'

'So you never had to work?'

'I've never needed a job, if that's what you mean. I'm able to live off what my parents had and . . . the means of others.'

'Others? You mean your victims?'

'No.'

'The Watchers?'

'Yes.'

'I want to know about them,' Tommy said, not looking up from the glow of the screen.

'I'll bet you do.' Elizabeth stretched one hand along the table and slowly rapped her blood-red fingernails against the wood.

'The murders,' Tommy said. 'They fulfill you sexually, don't they?' He was surprised at his ability to ask the question so dispassionately. But he had interviewed killers before Elizabeth, so a part of this felt like basic research. He just needed to keep thinking of it that way. *She's just another murderer.*

'The answer to your question is yes,' she said. 'But I don't think you and I define "sexual" the same way.'

'Define it for me.'

She took what would be her longest pause of the whole interview. Finally, she said, 'I can have sex without killing. And I can kill without sex. But neither of those things, in absence of the other, feeds me. Only when they are combined can I continue to thrive.'

Tommy considered this. 'So sexual homicide isn't pleasure for you. It's food.'

Elizabeth nodded. 'That's a way of putting it.'

'So you feel no guilt in killing, just like I feel no guilt over eating a hamburger.'

'Not exactly. I do feel guilt, though it doesn't manifest itself in a way where you would perceive it as such. Still, I've had periods where I stop myself, because I know what I'm doing is wrong. But when I stop, I grow weak. My body breaks down.'

'But it's not food. If you stop eating, you die. The same thing doesn't happen if you go without sex. Sex isn't essential to live. To create life, yes. But not to survive on your own.'

'I don't ask that you believe me, Tommy. I'm simply saying that's how my body works. I know this for a fact. I need . . . to do what I do, just as I need to eat. To drink.'

'What's the longest you've gone without killing?'

'Three years and thirteen days.'

'When did that end?'

'In Charleston.'

Tommy stopped typing. 'That was your first killing in over three years?'

'Yes.'

'Why did you start again?'

'He wasn't for me. He was for you.'

'To frame me?'

'That's how you chose to see it. And maybe there's an element to that. But you needed to see blood. Real, flowing blood. You needed to see his face as he died. It had been too long for you, and you needed to be reminded.'

This was the moment Tommy remembered he was sitting across from a killer, one who might still be planning to slice his throat open as well. He sat back in his chair.

'Why did I need to be reminded?' he asked.

'Because you need to write it. Describe it. Know the sensation. The horror. The . . . the energy of it. You can't get that from an interview.'

'So you think I know you enough now? After seeing what you did.'

She slowly shook her head. 'No, I don't. Not quite yet.'

The way she said it was unsettling, like a doctor telling you the test results *weren't quite what he'd hoped for*.

'Alan Stykes. He was the man in the woods that day, wasn't he?'

'Bravo, Tommy. I understand you went over to his house for dinner.'

'I didn't stay very long.'

'He wouldn't have killed you, you know.'

'Because you're still working with him?'

'No, because you're not his type.'

Tommy paused. 'You killed four kids with him.'

'Incorrect,' she said. 'Just one. The other three were all his.'

'So—'

'So the deputy sheriff of Lind Falls has a thing for little boys. The other three boys were just the ones I know of. For all I know there are countless others.' Her gaze wandered. 'Little bitty graves, here and there, where no one can find them. Lonely-sounding, isn't it?'

Tommy stared at his fingers but did not type. He just sat there and tried to steady his mind. Alan Stykes is also a serial killer, he thought. And he just drives around Lind Falls all day, trolling, and everyone knows him and trusts him.

He took a deep breath and continued. 'Were you abused? As a child?'

'Here we go. Let's make sure we put the serial killer in the correct little box. Abused as a child, enjoyed torturing animals.'

'Were you abused?'

She flashed her eyes at him. 'It doesn't count as abuse if you like it,' she said.

Tommy recoiled at the casualness of the statement. 'Your father?' he asked.

'Mostly.'

'How old?'

'Until I went to college. I really missed him when he died. I didn't really give a shit about my mom.'

Tommy had never heard a victim of childhood sexual abuse say they enjoyed it. And many of the killers and rapists he'd interviewed over the years for his research were horribly abused. Most fantasized about killing their abusers. Some of them had.

'How . . . how did you first equate sex and killing? Did you learn that from your father?'

She released a soft laugh that sounded more at place at a cocktail party. 'You can't learn something like that, Tommy. *You just know.*'

'Did you know that day with Rade? Were you planning to kill him?'

She considered this. 'I knew that was what I wanted. I just wasn't sure I could actually go through with it.'

'How did Alan Stykes get involved?'

'I was fucking him, too. Met Alan when he busted me for smoking weed near the trailhead by the creek.'

Tommy knew the exact location she was referring to.

'I blew him and he let me go. We hooked up all summer long after that. Classic love story.'

'And he knew what you wanted to do.'

'I told him I fantasized about sex and death. I remember saying it very coyly, like I was just saying something to shock him. I wasn't sure how he would react, but I had a sense about Alan. I knew there was darkness underneath that uniform, just as I knew it existed in myself. I just had no idea how deep that darkness went.'

'Was . . . was killing Rade his idea?'

'No, but watching was. He suggested a young boy – someone I could overpower. But I think he just had his own fantasies he wanted fulfilled.'

Tommy tried to separate the memories of that day from his questions, but the blood and the leaves and the dirt and the skin all flashed at him as he kept typing. He felt his stomach jump at him, either wanting food or wanting to empty itself through his mouth.

'Did you know we were there that day?'

'No clue. Alan suggested Rade because he was always playing alone away from his home. Easy target. I found Rade and convinced him to come with me, but I really didn't have that much of a plan.'

'I find that hard to believe.'

'It's true. I didn't have a weapon, because that would have made it too certain. Too real, perhaps. I told Alan I'd figure something out, but I think the reality was that Alan would have come along and choked the kid out himself if I hadn't finished him.'

'So I led him into the woods,' she continued. 'And then I found you, Mark, and Jason. I almost just ran away, but then I convinced myself I could do this. I could control you. And then suddenly I realized it was supposed to be that way. I was supposed to find you there. You were going to watch it all.' She grew more animated as she spoke, her gaze toward the ceiling, her hands moving back and forth. 'And the idea of all of you watching me excited me more than I thought would be possible. You would be *right there*. Seeing everything. Smelling everything.' She touched her neck, wiping away invisible sweat.

'And then . . .'

'And then I was on top of him. So young. So perfectly young.'

Tommy felt the nausea well within him.

'I saw the rock,' she continued. 'It was right there, as if placed there just for me. The moment was just . . . right. It was what I was *supposed* to do.' She looked at Tommy. 'This, I know, you will never truly understand, because you and I are fundamentally different. I can only try to describe it to you.' She sucked in a deep breath and exhaled it gently over toward him. 'I came harder in that moment than I ever have before or since. I've been chasing that feeling for thirty years, and I've never matched it. I hear the first one is always the best.'

Tommy slammed his hand against the table and then pushed himself away from it. 'Goddamnit, *he was just a kid*! He didn't do anything to deserve what happened to him.'

Elizabeth shrugged. 'Does a lion hesitate before killing a young antelope?'

'A lion has to eat,' Tommy said, trying to steady his breathing.

She smiled. 'So do I, Tommy.'

Tommy closed his eyes and tried to remind himself why he was doing this. What his objective was. *You have to understand her to write about her, and when you do, you'll be closer to getting her out of your life.*

She remained quiet, as if listening to the argument Tommy was having with himself. After a minute, Tommy let out a long, slow exhale, opened his eyes, and pulled himself back to the table and to his laptop.

'Tell me,' he said. 'Tell me about your victims.'

'I can't be specific,' she said.

'Do what you can.'

She closed her eyes and remained quiet for nearly a minute.

'All male,' she said at last. 'Rade was the youngest. After that, they were between, oh, say twenty and fifty years old.

'Afterwards,' he said. 'After . . . Rade. You tried to seduce all of us.'

'I wanted to make you the same as me. I wanted you to feel what I felt. But I knew I couldn't. You were all different. You weren't like me. Except . . .'

'Except?'

'Mark. Except Mark. Mark is more like me than he is like you. I just knew.'

What the hell?

'Are you saying Mark . . . has . . .'

She cut him off. 'Mark has dark, violent thoughts that he hides under a thick blanket of Jesus and America.'

'You think this or know this?'

'With me, there's no difference. That's the beauty of megalomania.'

Tommy wanted to add this accusation to the list of things that made her crazy, but something about it seemed . . . correct. Mark was definitely not the man he portrayed to the public – even Tommy could see that. But violent?

She interrupted his typing.

'Jason was a Watcher, you know.'

'Jason?'

'He was my fifth Watcher.'

'What the hell are you talking about?'

'Oh, he didn't want to do it. Trust me. He was a lot of work, that one.'

Tommy leaned slightly over the table. 'You're talking about Jason Covington.'

'That's the one. The one who fucked me and cried.'

'He moved to Texas.'

'I know. I tracked him down. I forced him to come to New York.'

'I don't understand.'

She rolled her eyes, as if the logic of her thought process should flow as easily through those who didn't enjoy combining sex and murder.

'Finding a Watcher is a tedious, long process, with great risk associated with it. You have to identify the right person, which is only an extremely small percent of the population, mind you. Then you have to develop a relationship with them and slowly introduce the idea, which they almost always reject outright. It takes great skill and a lot of patience. Years, sometimes. And sometimes even then it doesn't work, and then you have to start all over again. Trust me, I wish my . . . desires . . . weren't so attached to the concept of having another person watching me. But that was all cemented on that day thirty years ago, and thus has it been ever since. The process owns me. I don't own the process.'

'But Jason wasn't the type,' Tommy said.

'No, but he was vulnerable. He could be blackmailed, after all. He didn't want to relive that day any more than you do now, and he was willing to do anything to make me go away. Don't you see? I didn't have to go through all the work of the recruitment process. I could just go straight to him.' She lost herself in thought. And Tommy wondered what it must feel like to think the way she did. 'It was a mistake,' she said.

'Jason?'

'Yes. It didn't give me the satisfaction I needed. He hated every minute of it, so my pleasure was minimized.'

'What did you do?'

She grinned at him. 'You mean *who* did I do?'

'I suppose.'

'It was 1991. New York City. I set myself up as an independent escort. Back then there were no websites. No Craigslist. I placed ads in the *Village Voice* and priced myself to attract the Wall Street type. Worked like a charm.'

Tommy forced himself to keep typing. 'What happened?'

'I got a banker to come to my apartment, where Jason hid in the bedroom closet. He watched through the wooden slats of the closet door as I fucked the banker. I remember it so vividly. The smell of him. Cheap cologne on a guy who was probably a millionaire. Cheap cologne and sweat. Whiskey breath. He fucked me from behind and pulled my hair, saying things like, "Yeah, you like that, don't you, you dirty fucking whore?" I mean you could just tell he had done this a thousand times before, and it had always gone his way. Just as he planned. Fucked the whore and then tossed some crumpled hundred-dollar bills at her as he zipped up and left.' Her eyes grew wide with the innocence of a five-year-old finding money from the Tooth Fairy for the first time. 'But not *this* time. I almost came just with the excitement of what was about to happen, but I held back. Not yet, I told myself. Wait for *the moment*. It's so much more powerful to come when I'm actually feasting, you know?'

You know? Tommy thought. How the hell would I know about any of this?

'So I told him I wanted to be on top,' she continued. 'And when we switched positions I pulled the knife out from under the mattress and hid it just under the sheet. I rode him and told him to close his eyes. I felt myself close to climax, so I reached back and grabbed the knife. Kitchen knife. A Henckels. They're the best, by the way. And as I pulled it out from under the sheet, I heard Jason gasp in the closet. Loudly. Like a *huhhhhh* sound. Then the john opens his eyes and says, "What the hell was that?" Only he doesn't get quite that far because he sees the knife in my hand, and gets maybe only half the sentence out. Good thing he had a couple of drinks in him and I have quick reaction time. Before he could do anything I stabbed down at him. I only had one real shot at that point and made it happen. Right into the chest. His eyes screamed but only air came out of him, through both his mouth and the hole I had just made in him.'

'Fuck,' Tommy muttered.

'And then I heard Jason crying in the closet. Crying. I need my Watchers to be excited by the feast. Not crying. My orgasm immediately ended the moment I heard his sobs.'

Poor Jason, Tommy thought. Poor, poor Jason.

She flicked her hand as if dismissing an indolent servant. 'He hanged himself three days later. Saved me the trouble.'

'Trouble of what?'

'Killing him myself, of course.'

'That was your plan?'

'It usually is. I can't have Watchers just walking around willy nilly. Despite their own complicity.'

Tommy considered this. 'Except, of course, for three of us.'

'That's right. Alan Stykes, Mark, and you. You are my three little loose ends.'

Three little loose ends, Tommy thought. It's all about that, isn't it? She's covering her tracks, after all these years. She wants me to write her story, and then what? And what about Alan and Mark – are they on her endangered species list? And why now? What's so special about this point in time?

These were thoughts he had had before. In his dream of her, Tommy saw her as desperate. Taking chances she normally wouldn't be taking. Signaling that, after thirty years, time was suddenly of the essence. That was just a dream, but he found himself wondering again, *why now?*

He stopped typing and looked up at her. In doing so, he realized that in their brief time together he had never *really* looked at her. He had looked at what the image of her was in his mind, but for the most part he'd avoided looking directly at her, as if she would somehow steal his soul if he did. But now he looked, and what he saw was a beautiful woman . . . almost. There was something behind that beauty, some trace of frailty that was not just age. There was fatigue in her eyes that she tried to cover up by blinking a few too many times, and there was a lack of color in her face that she tried to cover with a little too much makeup.

And then Tommy knew.

THIRTY-THREE

'You're sick,' he said. 'Aren't you?'

She said nothing for a few moments, assessing Tommy's face, searching his eyes.

'Very good, Thomas.'

'What is it?'

'Ovarian cancer. That somehow feels ironic, but I'm not sure how.'

'What stage?'

'Three.'

'That's early enough.' Tommy blurted the words out automatically, as if he was encouraging her to get treatment and get well. Her dying could actually be the best news he could have received.

'I'm not treating it.'

'No?'

'No.'

'So why go to the doctor at all?'

'I didn't know what was wrong with me. It's a sensation I'm not used to.'

'So . . .'

'So this is how I will die. After all I've done, it'll be something as dull as cancer that kills me.'

'That's what you meant when you said you get weak. You hadn't killed in over three years. You stopped because you knew it was wrong. And you think that abstinence gave you cancer? Because your body feasts on the sexual high you get when you kill?'

'Yes,' she said.

'But the body doesn't work like that. It's basic biology.'

She shrugged. 'It's what I believe. And it's too late to do anything about it.'

'Why did you stop?'

'I was tired of being controlled by my needs.'

'So that's why you're here. Now. Because you're running out of time.'

'I was always planning on writing my memoirs, and now I'm afraid there's not enough time. And you are the perfect person to memorialize me, all through fiction. It needs to be a bestseller, Tommy.'

'But you'll be dead.'

'I'm hoping they have libraries in hell.'

'I could just wait for you to die,' he said.

'No, you can't.' She sat up and gave a small cat stretch. 'Your book needs to be on the shelves within the next calendar year, and it needs to reach at least number ten on the *New York Times* list. I will need a draft in six months that I approve, and the final version cannot deviate substantially from the approved draft. I will need to be represented as a fictional character, and all references to any real crime will have to be changed enough to be untraceable. And, most importantly, you need to capture my essence, and only I will be the true judge of that.'

She's really thought this out, Tommy thought. 'Or what?'

'Or else my written history of that day in the woods and the location of little Rade – and all the wonderful evidence with him – will be released to the media and the police. I have a very good and expensive attorney who does what I ask and asks very few questions in return. He will continue to work on my behalf after my death.'

'But then you won't get what you want. You'll be known as the killer you really are, not some romanticized fictional antagonist.'

She nodded. 'I'm betting your willingness to withhold the truth is greater than mine.'

Tommy soaked in the information. None of it really surprised him. It all made sense, in a cosmically fucked-up way.

'So you don't want me dead?' he asked. 'Even after I write the book, there won't be some hired associate of yours waiting to carry out your last will and testament?'

'Tommy, no matter what happens, I'm not going to hurt you. You might go to prison if you don't fulfill my wishes, but I'm not going to hurt you.'

He wanted to believe her but he knew better. Elizabeth was a manipulator, and doing what she wanted would only fuel her desire to demand more. But if she was truly sick, Tommy could do what she wanted and her death would finally end their relationship.

So that was it. This was the end. It might take a few months, but Tommy knew he could do what she wanted. He knew his book would break in the top ten – it would be a first if it didn't. And he knew the manuscript was truly one of a kind – the best he had ever written. His book would come out, Elizabeth would be dead, and Tommy would go back to his life. He would be free. Free to be the husband he needed to be to Becky, one who held no secrets. Free to be a father without the looming threat of being taken away from his kids.

But what about Alan Stykes? Tommy couldn't possibly go back to his normal life knowing a child murderer was watching over the town of Lind Falls. But he could do something about that. An anonymous tip to the FBI, perhaps. He could call one of his friends who—

'There's one more thing,' she said, pulling Tommy from his thoughts. 'One last thing I need you to do.'

'Which is?'

'You need to understand me fully.'

'You've already said that.'

'But I need you to know what it feels like. There is someone I need . . . to go away.'

Tommy knew immediately.

'Alan Stykes.'

'Correct.'

It instantly unfolded before Tommy. She was going to ask him to be a Watcher while she killed Stykes. The homeless man in Charleston wasn't enough – it was too spontaneous. She doubted Tommy's abilities to understand her process, her *system*, in that one, random killing. She needed him to be there, in anticipation, while she feasted. He would be Jason in the closet. An unwilling accomplice. He would watch as she executed Stykes, and then at last she would believe in his ability to capture her essence in his words. Bestselling words.

He felt revulsion at the thought. He still carried the sound of the tearing flesh of the homeless man to bed with him every night, and the vacant, dead eyes of Rade Baristow greeted him each morning. But Stykes? Stykes was a certified, genuine, made in the US-fucking-A child killer. Could he not take some comfort in that? For the sake of all that he had to lose, could he do this one, last horrific thing?

He didn't know the answer.

And then Elizabeth spoke and rendered worthless his brief dilemma.

'Alan Stykes,' she said. 'I want you to kill him.'

THIRTY-FOUR

Tommy stared out the dirty car window, watching the leaves on the trees around him plunge to their deaths. Technically, they were already dead, but suicidal thoughts seemed to fit his mood.

He was parked outside his old house, on the opposite side of the street, the part nestled against open space. In the two days since he'd gone into the woods with a shovel, the owners of his old place had put up some cheap Halloween decorations. Grocery-store variety.

Wind swirled and growled outside the car. Dead leaves danced.

Tommy had no idea why he was here. He needed to go home, back to Colorado, but somehow it was important to come back to the neighborhood, even if it was just to look at what had changed. Maybe looking at his old house was supposed to show him how all things change, and despite that (or because of it), life goes on. But instead it was just fucking depressing. His dad would never have put up cheap, grocery-store Halloween decorations.

Tommy had a decision to make. He came here for an answer, and instead he found emptiness.

Elizabeth hadn't said much more. She didn't need to. She wanted Tommy doing the killing, for only then could he have the best chance of understanding her. When he had countered that the two of them were chemically different, and what motivated her did not motivate him, she accepted his argument as essentially true and told him it didn't matter.

She wanted what she wanted, and that was all that mattered. She thought the killing would make Tommy a better writer. Tommy disagreed. She didn't give a shit.

So he had a decision to make. And he had three days to give her his answer.

He put the car in drive and slowly pulled away from the curb, taking one last look at the house and still feeling nothing close to any kind of inspiration. He wasn't sure he was supposed to feel inspiration, but he damn well needed to feel something.

Three houses down he drove by Rade's old house. No Halloween decorations.

Then he saw someone. On the porch. An old man.

Tommy stopped the car, wondering if it could be who he thought it might be.

He pulled once again to the curb and made eye contact with the man sitting in a cheap metal chair on the front porch. The air was frosty but the man didn't seem to notice the cold. He looked to be on the ugly side of seventy and carried a stare that said *don't bother me*. But the age was about right, and Tommy decided to take a chance.

He got out of the car and crossed the street. The old man's eyes seemed buried by wrinkles around them, so Tommy couldn't tell if he was staring at Tommy or beyond him. When Tommy reached the sidewalk in front of his house, he got his answer.

'I don't entertain solicitors. That's how I've always been. Nothing against you. Just the way it is.'

Tommy stopped walking.

'Mr . . . Mr Baristow?'

The man shifted in his chair.

'Who's asking?'

'It's . . . I'm Tommy Devereaux. I . . . I used to live here a long time ago.'

Tommy thought he could see the trace of movement on the man's mouth, but couldn't be sure.

The wind kicked up again and raked frosty fingers though Tommy's hair.

'Tommy Devereaux. Now there's a name I hear every so often around here.'

'Can I come up?'

'Suppose it's in your mind to anyway.'

Tommy took that as a yes and walked up the path to the house. Three concrete steps led to a wooden porch that begged for repair and staining. Charles Baristow watched him every inch. An empty chair sat next to Charles, but Tommy remained standing.

'You're some kind of writer now I hear,' Charles said.

'Some kind, yes.' Tommy had a sudden moment of horror thinking that Charles had read the teaser of *The Blood of the Young* and realized the story of the killing was about his own boy.

'I never read any of it. Just how I am. Never been much of a reader.'

'Quite all right, Mr Baristow.' He expected to be told to call him Charles, but the invitation didn't come. 'I . . . I was just in the old neighborhood. Just waxing nostalgic, I guess.'

The man's eyes flashed with emotion for the first time. 'Nothin' here but nightmares, Tommy Devereaux. I suppose you know that. If not, it don't matter, because I certainly do.'

Tommy lowered his gaze. 'Yes, I suppose I do know that. I haven't been here in ages.'

'Left to go to college. Never came back?'

'No, I never came back.'

'Best decision of your life.'

Tommy shrugged.

'How are your parents?' Charles asked.

'Dead,' Tommy said. 'Within the last five years for both of them.'

Charles nodded as if that was just about the right answer. 'Never knew them all that well. Moved away not long after you left for college.'

'My dad got a job in California.'

Another nod. 'Your mom. She made me some dinners after . . . after Rita moved out. Damn nice of her.'

'I remember that.'

Charles looked across the street, the hazy sunlight warming over his milky cataracts.

'Why did you come back, Tommy Devereaux?' He didn't ask it as a question so much as some kind of accusation.

Tommy once again fought to keep his focus on the man's face and once again lost.

'I'm doing some research,' he said, hoping it didn't sound as lame as it felt.

'That so?'

A quiet settled upon them, but not a comfortable one. Tommy wanted to ask what he wanted to ask, but felt hesitant. Charles Baristow seemed to slip in and out of this world.

Finally, Tommy said, 'I want to ask you about Rade if I can,' he said. 'You can tell me to go away and I would understand.'

Charles seemed not to hear him, his gaze still across the street, lost in the depth of the trees in the woods. Then, like a hawk spying movement from above, his gaze shot to Tommy.

'This part of your research?'

Yes, Tommy thought.

'No.'

'Well, I suppose you can ask. Then I'll decide if I'm of the mind to answer or not.'

Tommy took a deep breath. 'Did . . . did you ever find out what happened?'

Tommy saw the man's jaw tense and then release.

'No.'

'The police. They . . . they dropped the case?'

The response was grumbled in old-man drawl. 'Well, the police will tell you one thing and then another, but they'll never tell you they dropped the case. They just move on to other things, which I suppose is what they ought to do. But nothin' ever came of my boy. One day he was here. One day not. So it goes.'

So it goes. Tommy recognized the line from *Slaughterhouse-Five*, but didn't know if Charles was quoting it or just making an observation about the ebb and flow of life. It was a book about death, and

Charles wasn't much of a reader. Tommy felt the queasiness rise in him, but he couldn't stop himself. 'Do you keep looking?'

'No place left to look. A person can grow crazy turning over stones, once you turn over enough of 'em.' Charles looked down and cleared his throat of a day's worth of build-up. 'Course, a person can grow crazy lots of different ways. Happened to Rita. She stopped looking and still went crazy. Killed herself. Don't know if you knew that.'

'I remember hearing that. I can't imagine what you went through.'

'No, Tommy Devereaux. No you certainly cannot. And I hope you never will.'

'Any . . . any theories about what happened to him?'

'I don't have much use for theories. All theories do is let you imagine a million different horrible things and never let you know which one is the truth. Just another thing to drive you crazy.'

For a second Charles's face broke its stoic mold, and in that instant Tommy saw the pain. The pain of a man who had lost so much he had nothing left to lose.

Tommy felt the weight of it all on him again, just like in the days immediately after it had all happened. The guilt and the shame. The incredible, dense pressure of a knowledge he couldn't – *wouldn't* – share. Tommy didn't have a theory about what happened to Rade. Tommy *knew* what happened. And he could tell Charles the truth. Right here. Right on the old man's front porch. Charles probably wouldn't believe a word of it, but that was just another excuse to Tommy. Tommy had lots of excuses, some of them downright logical. He didn't want his family destroyed. He didn't want his children hurt. He didn't want to go to prison. These were all real and valid excuses for the kind of man Tommy had become, but they all fell under the one large umbrella of *the real reason*. The real reason Tommy wouldn't say one word about the truth to Charles Baristow was because Tommy was a coward, and he hated himself for it.

Charles's rigid expression returned, but Tommy would never forget the sense of loss he saw in that one instant on the man's face.

'Tell you what,' Charles continued, trying to force his words back into an emotionless tone. 'Alan's the only one who seems to give a rat's ass anymore, and he's not even a detective. State police don't even return my calls anymore, but Alan still searches for leads here and there.'

'Alan Stykes?'

'That's right. Solid man.' Charles nodded in conviction. 'A *good* man. And it's not just Rade. There were some other kids missin' from this area. You hear about them?'

Tommy felt his stomach muscles clench. 'Yes, I did.'

'None of them was ever found either. But that Alan Stykes, he keeps looking. Solid man, like I said.'

Alan Stykes was tormenting Charles Baristow. Probably did the exact same thing with the parents of the other kids he had killed. Probably gave him some immense sense of power. This wasn't an uncommon characteristic among serial killers, Tommy knew, but he'd never felt the all-encompassing sickness of it until now.

'Does he . . .' Tommy felt himself struggling to get the words out. 'Does he have any theories?'

'Like I said, I don't listen to theories much. But once in a while – on his own free time, mind you – Alan will take a shovel, go out in them woods, and just start digging in a spot that doesn't look right to him. I've seen him doing it with my own eyes. Never amounts to nothing, but he's a damn fine man for trying.'

Jesus Christ, Tommy thought. *I can't hear any more of this.*

'I don't know what to say, Mr Baristow.' Tommy reached out his right hand and felt the sweat on it. Charles took it and gave him a single, limp pump. 'I didn't mean to bother you today. Don't . . . don't give up hope that the truth will come out.'

Charles's gaze returned to the woods, and now Tommy understood why he fixated on them. That was where Alan Stykes searched for his little boy.

'I just want my little boy to come home. That's why I never moved away from here, much as I wanted to. This is the only house he knows.'

Tommy didn't know why he said it, but he did. 'I guess he wouldn't be so little now, though. Right? He'd be just a bit younger than I am.'

Charles Baristow looked at Tommy as if he'd just declared himself the King of Prussia.

'I'm just waiting for my little boy.'

THIRTY-FIVE

Tommy pulled away from the curb and watched Charles Baristow shimmer into a fading ghost in the rear-view mirror. The trees in the woods to his right slowly paraded by, their branches stripped bare by the October winds. Tommy stared straight out the dusty windshield and tried to think about anything other than the conversation he just had. He tried not to focus on the lifetime of pain he had helped cause that man, or the fact that, in a few simple sentences, he could make it all go away.

It was time for Tommy to go home.

He approached the lone stop sign in the old neighborhood and rolled through it, just as he had always done. As he did, he spied the police cruiser parked on the adjacent street. Waiting.

Tommy turned his head and saw Alan Stykes staring directly at him. As Tommy passed by, he saw the cruiser's overhead lights spring to life, exploding like fireworks against the pale, gray Oregon sky.

'Damnit,' Tommy muttered. He pulled over to the curb, wondering. Was Stykes just there fishing, or had he been trailing him?

He watched in the mirror as Stykes heaved himself out of the cruiser and made his way up to Tommy's car. Stykes was in no rush, his steps small, as if wanting Tommy to spend a little extra time wondering what was going to happen next.

Tommy rolled down his window.

'Hello, Tommy.'

'Hello, Alan.'

Stykes leaned down and Tommy saw himself reflected in his mirrored aviator sunglasses. He barely recognized himself.

'That stop sign back there? I call it my cash cow,' Stykes said. 'I sit there every so often and, by God, someone always just rolls through it. Guess that person is you today.'

'Guess so.'

Then Tommy knew. He knew Alan Stykes had been trailing him. He could feel it in the man's words. The tightness of his voice. Alan

Stykes didn't want things happening in his town without him knowing about it.

'Shame you couldn't stay for dinner last night,' Stykes said. 'Gets kinda old eating alone. How about tonight?'

Tommy slowly shook his head, wondering how long they were just going to keep pretending. 'I'm headed home today,' he said.

'Well, OK then. Rain check?'

'Rain check.'

Stykes turned his head back down from where Tommy had come. 'Saw you talking to Charles Baristow back there.'

'Did you.'

'Yup. That I did. Mind me asking what you were discussing?'

Tommy tensed. 'I don't see how that's your business.'

Stykes grinned, revealing ashen teeth. 'No, I don't suppose it is exactly, but then again I don't think we're bound to strict social protocols, you and me. I think we have a bond that lets us ignore such things from time to time.'

Tommy lowered his gaze for an instant and considered the gun holstered on Stykes's hip. He heard Elizabeth in his mind, assuring Tommy that Stykes wouldn't kill him. *You're not his type*, she had said. But they were beyond pleasure killing now, weren't they? Wouldn't Stykes kill just to keep from getting caught?

'I just wanted to say hi,' Tommy said. 'I saw him on the porch and I wanted to say hi.'

Stykes nodded. 'You ask him about his boy?'

'I did.' Tommy paused and took in some of the outside air. 'Said you still help him out from time to time. Looking.'

Another nod. 'That I do. That I do.'

'Very noble of you.'

Stykes removed his glasses and searched Tommy's face. Tommy forced himself to return the gaze.

'Well, now, not sure how noble it is. Just doing my job is all. Not a lot of mysteries around here 'cept those four missing kids, so when things are a bit slow, which is just about always, I need to keep looking for them. Like I said, it's my job.'

Tommy felt his fear becoming injected with anger. Anger at this man who had killed four little boys and continued to live his fantasies out around their disappearances.

'Will there ever be a time you give up, Alan?'

Stykes blinked. 'Give up? You mean give up looking?'

Tommy felt himself nod but didn't answer, because he didn't mean that at all.

'No,' Stykes said. 'It wouldn't be fair for me to give up looking now, would it? Too many families still live here with a lot of pain, and if I can help in any way, then I need to. Even if that means pointless looking.' He turned his head and looked back at the stop sign Tommy had rolled through. 'Well, now I guess I'm not gonna write you up, Tommy. Like to think I don't show favoritism and all, but you are a celebrity around here. Hell, everywhere, I suppose. So I'm going to let you off with a warning.'

Tommy stared into the eyes of a murderer. 'That's very kind of you,' he said.

'Just mind yourself a little better next time,' Stykes said. 'Mind yourself, and then we won't need to have these little talks anymore.'

'Understood, Alan.'

Stykes stood, and the holstered gun was right next to Tommy's face. Tommy pictured himself locked alone inside a small concrete prison cell, waiting for Stykes to come in and dispatch his own version of Lind Falls justice. Tommy pictured his own grave, larger and deeper but otherwise identical to four others in the woods. Tommy wondered how long it would take before someone found his bones. Probably a long time, he concluded. Maybe even thirty years.

Alan Stykes turned around and walked back to his cruiser. Tommy didn't want to leave first, so he sat there in his rental car waiting for Stykes to pull around him. As he drove by, Stykes turned toward Tommy and flicked him a little salute, a casual *take 'er easy*.

Tommy exhaled, closed his eyes for a few seconds, and then pulled his cell phone from his pocket.

He dialed Becky and she answered on the third ring.

He knew immediately from the tone of her *hello* something wasn't right.

'I'm coming home,' Tommy said.

There was a long silence. Then she said one thing before hanging up.

'Don't expect us to be here when you arrive.'

THIRTY-SIX

Home.

Tommy did a quick visual scan of the house as he pulled up the driveway. Becky's car wasn't in sight, but she usually parked in the garage anyway. He glanced up at the windows. No lights. No movement. Again, not unusual.

What *was* unusual was Becky hadn't answered any of the dozens of calls he'd made since leaving Oregon. Not one. Not a solitary text. Not even the courtesy of a *fuck you*. He'd called the security company he'd hired, hoping for some more information, but all he was told was that Mrs Devereaux had suddenly terminated the contract and had sent Stuart home. Then he'd called Sofia, but all she was able to tell him was that Becky wasn't returning her calls either. He'd even called Becky's best friend in Denver. Nothing.

Tommy pulled into the garage and the smallest flame of hope he still possessed was snuffed. Her car wasn't there. He walked from the garage into a dark kitchen. The granite countertop was empty. No note.

'Becky?' he shouted.

Silence.

'Evie? Chance?'

He waited for the sound of running feet. Nothing.

The knot in Tommy's stomach tightened, and the worry that had been consuming him began morphing into anger. *How dare you take my kids*, he thought. *Think what you want about me, but don't just take my kids. You're just going to decide that they can't be around me? No way.*

His breathing quickened as he ran upstairs and searched room by room. Clothing and toys were strewn throughout the kids' rooms. It didn't necessarily mean anything, but it sure as hell looked like someone had gone through and packed their stuff in a hurry. Next he went to the master bedroom, where he finally had his answer. They kept their suitcases in the master closet, a cavernous space

mostly containing Becky's clothes. Three suitcases were gone. *Three.*
That was enough to hold at least two weeks' worth of things for
Becky and the kids.

Tommy slammed his fist against the hollow closet door. 'Goddamnit!'

It was all unraveling. For thirty years, Tommy had worked to
protect his greatest secret and heal his soul. And now, in less than
a week, everything was being destroyed.

'No, no, no,' he muttered. He dialed Becky's number again and
waited, squeezing his eyes shut as he hoped for her live voice and
not a recording. He was disappointed again.

'Becky, I'm home. *I'm home*, OK? I'm here *right now*, and it's
obvious you've left. Trust me, OK? I know that's asking a lot
considering what I've done in the past, but I am not having an affair.
And even if you don't believe me, you can't just take the kids.
That's not the best thing for them. Even if . . .' *Even if what, Tommy?*
He squeezed the phone until his fingers hurt. 'I would never do that
to you, no matter what I think you did. I would never just snatch
the kids and take them from you.'

He disconnected the call and sat on the bed, squeezing his hair
with his fingers.

The phone rang five minutes later. Tommy stared at the screen,
hoping against hope.

It was her.

'Becky,' he said.

'You're right,' she said. Her voice was hollow. 'I can't just keep
the kids from you. I'm sorry.'

Tommy let himself breathe.

'But we'll have to figure something out, because I don't want to
see you.'

'Becky, what's going on? Just tell me.'

'You tell *me*, Tommy. You tell me why you said you were in
Charleston but were really staying at some motel in Oregon.
You tell me why I call you and I hear a woman laughing in the
background. All the suspicious phone calls? The death threats?
You're full of shit, Tommy. But I have to hand it to you, I'm
impressed at your creativity and the effort you've put into
hiding your affair. Must be nice being a writer, huh? All those
great ideas running through your head all day? Must be goddamn
nice.'

How the hell had she known about Oregon?

The answer leaped at him. He had to use the credit card for the rental car. Becky never looked at their charges online, though he had shown her several times how to. But she had gotten suspicious and decided to check for the first time when he was away.

He couldn't let her continue to think what she was already thinking. He had thought he'd let her believe anything but the actual truth, but now, facing the actual moment, he couldn't.

'Becky, whether you choose to believe this or not, I am swearing to you, right now, that I'm not having an affair.'

She was silent for a moment.

'You're lying about something, Tommy. What am I supposed to think it is?'

His mind raced back to when this all began. God, had it actually only been five days ago? And it all began with a lie. The note Elizabeth had left for him in the bar at the Hyatt. He had lied about who had called him on the phone. He had lied ever since Elizabeth had come back into his life.

He knew if he lied any more, it was over. She never would believe him again. She would be gone.

'Yes,' he said. 'Yes, I have lied.'

'About what?'

'Becky . . .'

'Was it the note? Did you lie about the note?'

He sighed. 'Yes.'

'I *knew* it. So, the note I read. About threatening us . . . our *kids*. You made that up?'

'Yes.'

'Oh, you asshole. You fucking asshole. And Stuart, hiring that wanna-be Secret Service prick, that was all for nothing? That was just some kind of added layer to your bullshit? All the fear that you put us through. For nothing?'

'No,' he said. 'He was hired for a real reason. I was worried about the safety of the family.'

'Why, Tommy? What the hell is really going on?'

'Becky, everything I've done . . . I've done for us. All of us. I've done it to preserve all we have.'

'Tommy, just tell me. Right now. This is your chance. You have me on the phone. If you ever want me to come home, this is the moment.

This is the one, single chance you have not to throw everything all away. Right now.'

Tommy took himself away, in his mind, to his childhood place of safety and comfort, the place he escaped to after his panic attack in the Oregon motel room. To the soft sloping hill with a towering tree surrounded by long, wild grass, a place he remembered at some age before he started remembering specific ages, where all he could remember was feeling, and the feeling at the tree was happiness and peace, the kind you could only know when you were too young even to understand what that meant.

It was time.

Tommy took a deep breath and then he began to speak. From the beginning. From the day Rade bled out in the woods until when Tommy left Oregon for home. Every detail. Elizabeth's ID, on which she used the same name of Tommy's old girlfriend. The murder of the homeless man in Charleston. Elizabeth's truths. The killer cop in Lind Falls, who buried little boys like garbage. He went through every lie he'd told, and every desperate thing he'd done, just to keep from being caught. Finally, he told her what Elizabeth had asked him to do. He told her the only way out of everything was to kill a man.

He didn't even pause, because if he did he knew he would be tempted to create some kind of story to excuse his behavior. Maybe come up with a small lie here and there to soften things. But he didn't stop. He just spoke as the words formed in his head, and what came out of his mouth was as honest and raw as the revised manuscript he'd been writing. And as he spoke, the world slowly lifted off him, a millimeter at a time, and he found himself breathing again. The relief of pressure was so great it made him nearly euphoric. And then he knew he should have been honest with her all along, because she was his partner and she deserved to know. Most of all, he was madly in love with her and telling her was the right thing to do. She was a forgiving person, and he knew she loved him. She would help him. Instead of running from her, he should have been asking her to stand with him. She was the reason for it all, and he was wrong not to have believed that from the beginning.

The more he spoke, the happier he became, despite the horrific things he was saying. Finally he had someone to help him. To confide in. To tell him he wasn't a horrible person. Becky would tell him the right thing to do. She would be strong. She would save them.

And then he finished. When he did, he paused a few seconds, waiting for her to speak. But all he heard was his own breathing, still quickened from his excitement.

Then, without a word, Becky hung up the phone.

THIRTY-SEVEN

Tommy woke to the sound of his phone. Bright sunlight streamed through the linen drapes of the master bedroom. The other half of the bed was still made, underscoring Becky's absence. Tommy pawed out from the sheets for the phone. *Please*, he thought. Please let it be Becky.

He saw Sofia's photo on the screen.

'Hey,' he muttered.

'Tommy, I just heard the news.'

'What news?' he asked.

'About your friend. Mark.'

'Mark? Singletary?'

'Yeah, the one you had me research.'

Tommy froze, imagining a number of things that Mark could have done or said. The worst possibility was he spoke publicly about Rade Baristow. But Tommy couldn't imagine that. Mark would never do it.

'What did he do?'

A pause. 'So you haven't heard?'

'No, damnit. Just tell me what he did.'

'He . . . he's dead, Tommy.'

'What?' Tommy swung his legs out of bed and pressed the phone hard into his ear.

'Friday night.'

'What happened?'

'Car accident.'

Tommy stumbled toward his laptop that he'd left in a bedside chair and flipped it open. He Googled *Mark Singletary*.

'Hang on,' he told Sofia. 'I'm looking it up.' He clicked on the first story that appeared.

NC State Senator Killed in Car Accident

(Reuters) South Carolina State Senator Mark Singletary was killed late Friday night in a car accident in his home city of Lantham. Singletary was driving alone after a fundraising event in advance of next month's election when his car swerved off State Road 35 and into an embankment. A witness driving behind Singletary's car described no unusual or erratic driving prior to the accident, and road conditions were dry. Investigators on scene said the Senator was not wearing a seat belt and was ejected from his car, and he was believed to have died instantly.

Singletary's death comes at a particularly inopportune time for the Republican Party, who were counting on—

'Oh my God,' he said.

'I'm sorry. I figured you knew.'

Tommy stared at the floor. 'I had no idea.'

'Well, at least you weren't too close to him, right?'

'Sofia, I had drinks with him last week.'

'You did?'

Tommy closed his eyes and turned his face toward the sun. 'That's where I went last Saturday. To meet Mark. There were some things we had to discuss.'

'Tommy, what the hell is going on? You left for a week and no one really knew what you were up to. Then Becky takes off with the kids. And now your friend from thirty years ago, who you suddenly wanted me to research, dies right after you see him?'

'Sofia—'

'Tommy, we're friends. Maybe I can help you. Just tell me what's going on.'

'You're right,' Tommy replied, squeezing his temple. Just a day ago, he was willing to do anything to make sure the story about Rade never got out. Now his desperation was so intense he was on the verge of telling everything to a second person. 'Can you come over?'

'On my way.'

Sofia disconnected the line as Tommy re-read the top part of the story. And again. Making sure the name was spelled the same way. Making sure it was really Mark they were talking about. Mark Singletary. Holy shit, Tommy thought. I stayed in his house less than a week ago. I sat in his office and had whiskey with him.

Tommy finished reading the article, which offered no more information on the actual cause of the accident, then re-read the first paragraph yet again.

Why would the car suddenly swerve? A million reasons, Tommy thought. The most likely one was that Mark fell asleep at the wheel. It must have been late at night. Maybe a little too much to drink? But the witness said he hadn't been swerving prior to the accident. Suicide was also possible. Maybe Mark was convinced the story about Rade was coming out. Maybe Mark had other hidden gems that were about to be discovered. Who the hell knew?

Tommy Googled the story to find any other information on what happened. Google smugly told him it had found over four hundred articles on the subject. Tommy read the first five displayed and found many variations of the same information. None of them said – or even hypothesized – why Mark's car flew into an embankment.

Or why he was driving alone.

That thought grabbed Tommy by the shoulders and shook him. Why didn't he have a driver? Where was the guy who had been waiting for him outside the Charleston house last week? Did State Senators often drive themselves around, especially late at night after a fundraiser?

Tommy walked downstairs, the slapping of his bare feet loud in the empty house. The lights downstairs were still on, just as he'd left them the night before. An empty house was bad enough. An empty dark house was unbearable.

Like a rat trained to retrieve a food pellet, Tommy went through the motions of firing up his espresso machine: turning it on, checking the water levels, and making sure there were enough beans in the silo. He looked down at the phone again and checked for any relevant mail, meaning any kind of message from Becky. Something.

Nothing. Just a collection of e-mails from his editor wondering where the hell he was and if work was progressing on the latest draft, considering it was all due when they were several months younger.

Tommy put his phone on the counter and waited for Sofia. He felt himself grow old as he stood there, doing nothing but trying to avoid his own thoughts.

Ten minutes later Sofia arrived.

He opened the door and took in the sight of her. She looked how she did when she was most likely to make him catch his breath: kinked hair back in a ponytail, no makeup, perfect smooth cheeks leading to wide green eyes. She walked into the foyer and took a sip from the cardboard Starbucks cup she was holding.

He fought back tears as he walked up and hugged her.

'Yeah, good to see you too, Tommy. Want to tell me what the hell is going on?'

'I do,' Tommy said. 'But I've only told one other person, and that was Becky. She hung up on me and I haven't heard from her since.'

'That's why she took the kids and went away?'

'No, she thought I was having an affair. Which I'm not.'

The word 'affair' hung in the silence, and in that brief moment the weight of their own relationship pressed down on him. He'd had an affair with Sofia, yet they still worked together. He'd also spent his whole writing career under the influence of another woman, a woman who'd been in the shadows but had just stepped out of them. He so easily welcomed women into his life, but had difficulty letting them leave.

She raised her eyebrows at him. 'So what you told her was worse?'

Tommy shut his eyes and nodded. 'Just . . . just stay and listen to me, OK? And try not to storm out of the house when I'm done talking.'

'No offense, Tommy, but I'm not your wife, so I have a much higher tolerance of bad behavior from you than Becky has. I mean, I have my limits, but they're pretty high.' She gave him a smirk. 'As long as you haven't fucked any kids, I think we'll be OK.'

Tommy immediately started laughing which, in the span of seconds, turned to tears. Hot, scalding tears that tore at his eyes. He didn't understand why he was crying, but it felt so goddamn good. Such a release. And so much more meaningful to have it in front of someone who cared about him.

Sofia took a step back. 'Jesus, Tommy, I was joking. Tell me you didn't.'

He shook his head. 'No,' he said through his hands. 'God, no, of course not. I . . . I don't know why I'm . . . I don't know what else to do.'

Sofia turned and went to the liquor cabinet. She pulled out a bottle of expensive tequila; she had given it to him when he signed the contract for *The Blood of the Young*. It was still unopened, but she quickly changed that. She pulled out two shot glasses and set them on the counter, then poured out two perfect shots, each the color of a honey sunrise.

'It's nine in the morning, Sofia.'

'I know it is. But I think this will help. And I think I'm going to need one as well.'

'Yes, you are.'

They each reached for their shot and held it delicately before them. Under his breath, Tommy counted to three, and on three they let the tequila burn down their throats. It wasn't Tommy's accustomed practice to do shots, and certainly not in the morning, but he had to admit it was a damn fine tequila.

Two empty glasses slapped the counter. Tommy wiped his mouth. Sofia didn't.

'From the beginning,' she said. 'Tell me from the beginning, and don't stop talking until you're done.'

And then, for the second time in less than a day, Tommy told his story.

THIRTY-EIGHT

T hirty minutes later, Tommy stopped talking. He looked at Sofia, who said nothing. Telling her had been a relief, but now that he had finished his story he questioned if he should have done it at all. He was sure she would remain quiet, but why had he needed so desperately to tell her? Was it because he craved some kind of sympathy? Becky had hung up on him. Did he need Sofia to tell him he wasn't a horrible person? Or was it because Sofia was different? An ex-lover, but a current confidante. Sofia knew him intimately enough to understand him, but was still removed just enough not to judge him for the myriad faults he had.

She stared at the empty shot glasses on the table, their insides streaked with tequila wisps.

'Please say something,' Tommy said.

It took her another minute before she spoke.

'You told all of this to Becky?'

'I did.'

'What did she do?'

'She hung up on me. I haven't spoken to her since.'

Sofia stood from her chair in the kitchen and walked away from him, pushing her fingers up through her thick hair.

'Don't walk away,' Tommy said.

'I'm not walking away. I just need to move. I . . . goddamnit, Tommy. This is all really true?'

'All of it.'

She turned to him. 'And you've never once thought about contacting the police?'

'I think about it every day,' he replied. 'I obsess over it.'

'Yet you don't ever call.'

Tommy looked at the floor. 'No, I don't.'

'Tommy, if this is true, there're two killers out there walking around. Freely.'

'I know.'

'And you don't call the police? Why?'

'You know why,' he said.

'I want to hear you say it.'

Tommy took a long breath and let it drain from his lungs. 'Because I don't want to lose everything. My family. My career. Because I'm scared.'

Tommy lifted his gaze and saw her looking at him. No, she wasn't looking at him, she was *judging* him. She was trying to reconcile the man she knew with the man she just met.

'Bullshit,' she said.

'Bullshit?'

'Yeah, Tommy. Bullshit. You're not scared of losing everything.'

Confusion washed over him. 'What are you talking about?'

Her tone stiffened. 'I mean, sure, OK, you're scared. I get that. You've built up this amazing career and you have this wonderful family, and this would expose a dark part of your past.'

'Sofia, what I did back then was a crime, and everything I've done since then, especially in the last week, has just made things worse. I'm . . . I'm in it too deep now.' Like a desperate gambler going deeper into debt hoping for the big payoff, he thought. Yet that never seemed to work.

'It's not too late, Tommy. Go to the police now, before it gets worse.'

'How could it possibly get worse?'

'Tommy, you have to. I'm sure you'll be fine, as long as you don't wait any longer.'

'Really? How do you define "fine"? Prison? Divorce?'

'But you told Becky everything, so by your own logic, you've already potentially lost your family. It wouldn't even have mattered if she heard the name of your old girlfriend associated with your trip to Charleston. The reality is much worse. The reality is what will make you lose your family.'

The words punched Tommy in the gut. 'I didn't lose them. Damn it, Sofia, I didn't lose them.'

'When we slept together, it was a mistake. I'm not going to say I regret it, because I don't. But it was a mistake, and you nearly got divorced over it. So you know what it feels like to nearly lose everything you love. Why would you do it all over again?'

'This isn't just about divorce. This is about my kids growing up hearing their father is a criminal. It doesn't matter whether or not I had anything to do with it. People will call me a murderer, and my kids will hear it.'

She didn't seem to hear him. 'Yet everything you've done since the moment you let her back in your life has only dug the hole deeper and deeper for you.'

Now Tommy stood. '*Let* her back in my life? I didn't *let* her come back. She just came back.'

'I don't think so.'

Tommy paused. 'What the hell are you talking about?'

Sofia took a step toward him, and to Tommy that one step seemed somehow aggressive. Defiant.

'You need her,' Sofia said. 'You want her in your life, because she's always been there.'

'Sofia, what the h—'

'Your whole career is because of her. It makes perfect sense. Every book you've ever written has been about her. Every villain

that has paid for everything in your life is her. She is your success.'
Another step closer. 'Your face lit up when you talked about her,
Tommy. You looked excited. Energized.' Closer. 'She's your muse,
Tommy. She's your *fucking* muse.'

'That's not true,' he whispered. The words sounded flat, hollow.
He repeated them, but they felt just as impotent.

'Tommy, step back and look at things. That's why Becky hung up
on you. Not because of what happened when you were a kid. Not even
because of all the lies in the last week. She hung up on you because
your whole life has been dedicated to another woman. Don't you see
that? Do you know how much strength it took her to trust you again
after . . . after us? And now she finds out there's yet another woman.
You might not be fucking her, Tommy, but she's still your mistress.'

'Stop it, Sofia.'

She raised her voice. 'It's *true*, Tommy. You know it's true. You
haven't gone to the police because you don't want this to end, do
you? You're not scared of losing everything, Tommy. You're scared
of losing *her.*'

'*Stop it.*'

But she didn't stop. Sofia was now thinking out loud, and every
word she said was a link in the chain that Tommy always knew
existed but never wanted to acknowledge.

'You practically said it yourself, Tommy. The new manuscript
you're writing now, the story of her coming back into your life. *You*
said it was writing itself. *You* said it was the best thing you've ever
written. Isn't that what you just told me?'

Tommy started to walk away, but she followed.

'Tommy, you have to end this. She's going to . . . do something
to you.'

'No, she's not,' he muttered.

'Can't you see it? If everything she told you is real, do you really
think your friend Mark died in a car accident? She's getting rid of
witnesses. And now you've told Becky? And me? Aren't you putting
us all at risk?'

I'm not going to hurt you, Tommy.

That thought chilled him. In Tommy's sudden haste to unburden
himself of his secret, he hadn't considered the liability that came
with his knowledge. But then Mark died, and Tommy was no longer
convinced Elizabeth wasn't trying to cover her tracks.

'We're not in danger,' he said, trying to convince himself as much as Sofia. 'She needs me.'

'But not for much longer. Once that manuscript is turned in to the editor, you're open game.' The faster she spoke the more the pitch of her voice increased. 'Think about it. If she actually . . . if you die, then that will make your book even more anticipated. *Tommy Devereaux's final book, the most haunting one ever.* Can't you see it? Her character will be exactly what she wants it to be: emblazoned into literary culture forever. It's the perfect plan.'

'I don't want to talk about this anymore.'

She reached out and pulled his shoulder until he turned and faced her.

'You can't just ignore me, Tommy. You can't ignore the simple truth: this is not going to end well if you let her stay in control. *You* need to end this, Tommy. *You* need to go to the police.'

'They won't believe me!' he shouted. 'Don't you understand that? There are too many things I've lied about. Covered up.'

She pointed a finger at his chest. 'This is bigger than you, Tommy. This is about a father still hoping for his son to come home. This is about a monster who has killed thirty-nine – God, I can't believe I'm even saying this – *thirty-nine* people. And it's about another monster who kills little boys. You can end all that, Tommy. You *have* to end it.'

'That's what I'm planning to do.'

'What, by doing what she says?' Her eyes flashed. 'By actually killing that sheriff in Oregon? Can you really do that, Tommy? And what then? Hope she doesn't kill you? Hope you don't get caught for killing a police officer? *Are you insane?*'

'*I'll take care of it.*'

'And what about the bodies, Tommy? What about all the families wondering what happened to their loved ones? Are they just left to wonder for the rest of their lives?' She covered her face with her hands. 'I can't believe this is all really true.'

Tommy turned and walked toward the front door. He opened it, and fresh morning air washed over him, somehow making him even more angry. The air felt so damn normal. Everyday air, the kind he used to breathe when he'd leave the house for a run, or head to his favorite coffee shop for a morning latte. He just wanted things to be back to the way they were.

He stood back and held the door open. 'I think you should leave now,' he said.

She finally seemed to have nothing to say. She stared at him with anger in her face, which eventually gave way to a look of searing disappointment. Tommy could bear it no more, and he looked at the ground as he repeated his request.

Sofia passed through the doorway and was a few steps on to the gravel pathway when she turned around.

'This is bigger than you, Tommy.'

Tommy said nothing as he shut the door in her face.

THIRTY-NINE

He woke, feeling the coolness of the leather couch under his face. He didn't remember going to sleep, and he had no idea how long he'd been out. The position of the shadows along the living room floor suggested it was late afternoon. Of what day he wasn't certain.

He knew he hadn't slept during the night. Tommy had written, and he'd written everything. The laptop hummed next to him, and Tommy reached out from the leather couch and swiped his finger along the touchpad. The screen came to life and Tommy saw the last words he'd written.

Tommy said nothing as he shut the door in her face.

He thought of the look in her eyes as he dismissed her. Sofia was just trying to help. Trying to be a friend, convince him of the right thing to do, and he had shut her out, just after he had been the one to let her in. Not even let her in. Beg her to come in.

Tommy squeezed his eyes shut, as if he could hide within himself. He had become very good at disappointing the women in his life.

His cell phone was on the side table. Tommy realized he could reach it without actually having to sit up, so he did. It was cool to the touch. He had turned it off the moment Sofia left, and now he was ready to connect back to the world. After the phone booted up, Tommy checked the time and did the math.

Thirty hours.

Thirty hours had passed since Sofia had told him that he needed Elizabeth in his life.

Thirty hours of no communication with anyone. No contact. No calls. No leaving the house, and barely even leaving the living room. Thirty hours of nearly non-stop writing, and his fingers, now rested, felt brittle as lifeless twigs.

He checked the phone history. Fifteen missed calls, none from Becky or Sofia. One number was unlisted. None of the four voicemails was urgent.

One text message.

Steps of Red Rocks. 5 p.m. E.

Once more, Elizabeth commanded him. She wanted to meet him inside Red Rocks Amphitheatre, just west of the city. Tommy knew it well and had memories of watching some of his favorite bands performing there over the years.

This time there would be no band, and it would be he who was expected to perform. But Tommy was starting to feel a shift in his attitude. Maybe it was because he had finally told Becky everything, and it exploded in his face. Maybe it was because all that he hoped to protect was so close to being permanently gone he stopped worrying about consequences. Maybe he was just finally getting really fucking pissed off.

Whatever it was, the change of attitude felt good. Tommy just wondered if he was going to do anything with it.

FORTY

The sun disappeared behind the mountains around six in early October, and it was well on its way as Tommy pulled into the parking lot of Red Rocks Amphitheatre. The venue was carved into the red sandstone that gave it its name, and being to the west and at a higher elevation than Denver, it offered amazing views of the city.

Tommy got out of his car and scanned the blood-red sky. It was warm for the time of year, but the temperatures would plunge quickly after dark.

No other cars were in the lot.

He wondered if he was here before Elizabeth and, if not, where her car was. It was odd to think of her driving. Tommy just thought she could magically appear any place she wanted to be, without having to use any mode of transport.

He made his way alone inside the gates and walked along the dirt path down toward the venue. As Tommy walked in along the lowest part of the amphitheatre he looked up at the long, curved rows of seating that climbed up toward dramatic rock outcroppings. The sun, large and wax-like, hung low in the western sky above them.

Tommy scanned the entire arena and saw one person standing alone in the center of the uppermost row. A woman. Elizabeth.

She stood there and looked at him but did not move. He was too far away to make out her face, but he knew those cold, blue-jean eyes were trained directly on him.

She didn't move, and neither did he.

After a minute, her message was clear.

You come to me. I don't come to you.

So Tommy did. He climbed the steps, keeping his pace steady, feeling the growing burn in his thighs.

He reached her row and walked slowly toward her, letting his heartbeat slow. Elizabeth turned toward him, her impossibly tight jeans drawing a curved line down her legs and into the four-inch heels of black leather boots. Her long hair was unrestrained; the early-evening breeze pushed and lifted the outermost hairs around her face. The remaining sunlight glinted off her oversized sunglasses, and as Tommy got closer he saw himself in those lenses, the curve of the glass making him appear larger than he felt.

'Hiya, sexy,' she said.

'You killed Mark,' Tommy replied.

'Well, that's not the greeting I was hoping for.'

'You killed Mark. Why the hell did you do that?'

A hand went to her hip. 'And now why do you think I killed Mark?'

'Because he knew the truth.'

'The truth? OK, Mulder. What truth are we talking about here?'

'You know what truth. About Rade.'

'Shit, Tommy, he knew the truth for thirty years. Don't you think if I was worried he was going to say anything I would have been a little more proactive?'

'You're cleaning up everything. Before you die.'

She laughed. 'You're paranoid.' Elizabeth pulled the hair away from her face. 'Next thing you'll be telling me is Mark was in the alley the night we killed the homeless man. That he was a Watcher.'

She winked at him and the temperature of the air dropped ten degrees.

Images of Charleston flashed through Tommy's mind. Standing there, alone in the alley, the blood of the homeless man pooling near his feet, deciding whether to stay or run. And then the movement, the sound, and then the sight of someone else there that night. Someone else running away, down the alley, fading in and out of the shadows before disappearing into the night.

Mark.

It was Mark. He *was* a Watcher. The killing, which seemed almost random, was planned well before that night. That murder wasn't for Tommy. It was for Mark.

'My God,' he said. 'He was there. He saw the whole thing.'

'You see, just like I said. *Paranoia.*'

Tommy stared out over the city to the east, as if he could see all the way back to that night. 'That was why you wanted me to go see him. So he could be a Watcher. You two planned it all along. He was . . . he was like you.'

Mark's dark side extended well beyond what Tommy assumed, and now he was dead because of it. Watchers always died.

'No one is quite like me, Tommy. Besides, you're the one coming up with this story, not me.'

'You haven't denied it.'

She removed her glasses. Her eyes nearly disappeared in the light. Tommy hated thinking she was beautiful.

'And if I denied it, would you believe me?'

'No.'

'So let's not waste our time here.'

'Are you planning to kill me, too?'

Her tone was that of a scolding mother. 'Now, Tommy . . .'

'I asked you a question.'

'Again, would you believe me if I said no?'

'No.'

'Then we're just going in circles here.'

'So why am I here?'

'I need an answer,' she said.

Tommy turned his head, more than anything because he didn't want to look her in the eye. His gaze swept over all of Denver, which glowed against the eastern plains.

'This is crazy,' he said.

'Life is crazy. Get over it.'

'You don't need me to do this. I can write the book without . . . without going through with it.'

'It doesn't matter how you feel about it. There are two choices, and two choices only. Kill Stykes in the manner and time period that I demand, or don't kill him and deal with the consequences of that decision.'

'I already told my wife, you know. And my assistant. I told them everything.' Tommy hoped to shock her, but he knew immediately from her expression he hadn't.

'There's a difference between the people who love you knowing your dirty secrets and the whole world knowing. You know that, Tommy. And I think you'll still do everything I want you to in order to keep your secret quiet.' She reached up and touched his shoulder. 'Tommy, Alan Stykes deserves to die. The man is a child killer.'

Now he looked at her. 'So are you.'

'Just that one time. But Stykes makes me look like a saint. What he did to those other little boys is . . . even beyond me.'

'You know, I only have your word that he's responsible for those other missing kids. You might be making all this up about him.'

'You saw the pictures in the house. The gravesites.'

'I saw photos of the woods, nothing more. Alan confessed nothing to me. Maybe you want me to kill an innocent man.'

'Can you honestly tell me you think Alan is an innocent man?'

Tommy knew Alan was not innocent. He hadn't recognized his evil immediately, as he had with some killers he'd interviewed over the years. But those were criminals Tommy already knew were guilty. Alan was just a deputy sheriff he'd met. No reason to suspect him of anything other than intense loneliness. But in Stykes's house, in his bedroom, with Stykes blocking the door as Tommy had looked at those photos of the woods, Tommy had seen it. Once he'd recognized the look of a murderer in Alan Stykes's cold stare, he was stunned he hadn't recognized it right away.

'So *you* kill him, then,' Tommy said.

'That's not the point. You need to do this. Once you do, your book will have an authenticity that the readers will feel. I know it, Tommy. After you kill him and write about it . . .' She smiled as she thought about it. 'Your book will come *alive.*'

'My life will be over. Either way. Don't you see that? How can I live with myself after murdering someone?'

She placed her right foot closer to his. 'I think you want to do it.'

'Fuck you,' he said. 'How the hell can you even say that?'

'What father wouldn't want to kill a child murderer?'

'It's not like that.'

'It's not complicated, Tommy. Decisions are easy. It's thinking about them that makes them complicated.'

He squeezed the back of his neck and spit out in frustration. 'Why am I even here? Why come all the way out here to have this conversation? What the hell's the point?'

She leaned closer still, then grabbed his arm and ran her thumb along the scar she had given him thirty years ago. 'Because we're family, Tommy. Families need to be together.'

She was close enough to kiss. She was close enough to kill.

The attitude crept back over him. He wondered if he actually had it in him to kill her. Just finish everything, right here, right now. Could he do it? As superhuman as she wanted him to think she was, Elizabeth was flesh and bone. She used his own paranoia to make herself seem all-powerful, but Tommy had to remember that she was a murderer, not a demon. She hadn't killed Mark. Nor had Mark been in the alley that night. It was too much to orchestrate, even for her capabilities. But she was happy to let Tommy believe all these things, and from them sprouted a fear of her as a god-like figure. So the question remained. Knowing she was just human, could he kill her?

'I don't know what you're thinking, Tommy, but you look pretty damn serious.'

Without another word, Tommy turned and walked back toward the steps. In the distance, high above the jagged sandstone, a hawk circled over the amphitheatre, searching for food.

PART III

PART 5

FORTY-ONE

Portland, Oregon
Four days later

For the second time in just a week, Tommy found himself inside the Portland airport. The luggage carousel squeaked and shuddered as it came to life. He stood before it and watched the faded metal fins stretch and contract. Other passengers from his flight slowly gathered around it and waited with varying degrees of patience to grab their bags and get on with life.

Tommy never checked bags. He only had this time because he was in no hurry to get where he was going. A part of him actually wanted his luggage not to show up.

The e-mail had come within hours of seeing Elizabeth at Red Rocks. It contained detailed instructions on when he was to arrive in Oregon and how he was to proceed after he did. It also said that, were he not on the designated flight, that would be taken as an unalterable sign of disobedience.

Disobedience.

Tommy had had a few days to make up his mind. Days of silence from Becky and the children. A few days to update his book, hoping the words would somehow guide him to the right choice. A few days of complete and utter aloneness.

Yesterday, the day he had finally made a decision, the only decision he could make, he had written five letters, leaving them on his desk. One to Becky. A very long one to the kids, not to be read until they were older. One to Sofia. One to his editor and agent. And a general letter for everyone else in his life. In case he didn't return home, those letters might provide some comfort, or at least some explanation, for what he had done.

His bag was the first to appear on the carousel. That had never happened in his entire life. He grabbed it and walked over to the Starbucks near the exit. He wasn't there for coffee. He was there to meet his driver.

He stood alone scanning the crowd, and after twenty seconds a man approached him from his right.

'Mr Devereaux?'

Tommy turned. The man before him was impeccably dressed in the way a *consigliere* would be. Shiny gray suit. Crisp, cream shirt. Black tie with a gleaming silver tie pin. His tanned face had many more wrinkles around the eyes than Tommy's, though Tommy guessed they were close in age. The wrinkles could be from either too much smiling or too much squinting. Tommy didn't think they were from smiling.

'Yes?' Tommy said.

'I'm your driver.'

'OK.'

The man reached for Tommy's bag.

'It's OK,' Tommy said. 'I got it.'

The man nodded.

'Follow me, please.'

Tommy followed him outside to a black Lincoln Town Car parked impossibly close to the airport. But there was no ticket on the window or cop yelling at him to move the car. The man opened the back door for Tommy. Tommy glanced into the dark interior, feeling that he was looking down the throat of a shark.

'What's your name?' Tommy asked.

'Antoine,' the man said.

'I've never known an Antoine.'

'First for everything.'

Tommy glanced down at the car again.

'Where are you taking me, Antoine?'

'I'm sorry, Mr Devereaux. I'm not supposed to tell you that.'

'Can you tell me how long the trip will be?'

'About an hour. Give or take.'

'And what happens when we get there?'

Antoine seemed genuinely stumped by the question.

'Then my job is done.'

Tommy accepted the answer, having expected nothing more revealing. He took a deep breath and got in the car, keeping his bag with him.

The window tint seemed dark enough to block a nuclear bomb flash. Interior lights revealed a variety of newspapers and a fully stocked bar. Tommy was tempted and didn't really care that it was only two in the afternoon, but he had to stay sharp.

Antoine pulled the car away from the curb. As he did, the doors locked. Tommy half-expected to see the interior door handles missing, but they were there.

Calm down, he told himself. What's the point of coming all this way just to escape now? You've committed yourself by your actions.

Tommy knew he'd end up in Lind Falls, because he was certain that was where the killing would take place. It was where Stykes lived, and it seemed fitting. He didn't know why Elizabeth wanted him to have a driver, but he guessed in large part it was due to her not wanting Tommy to have his own car. Moreover, she wanted Tommy to obey her. Follow her orders.

Tommy closed his eyes, listened to the hum of the motor, and visualized Elizabeth's last e-mail to him.

Bring a printed copy of your manuscript, along with some extra pages. You'll want to take notes. You finally get to write your ending, Tommy.

Tommy reached over, unzipped his bag, and removed the heavy block of pages. He turned on the interior dome light and scanned through the pages, still marveling at how much he'd written in such a short amount of time. And it wasn't just the quantity. The words were good. They were *right*. Tommy had a healthy ego but secretly he'd never thought himself a literary giant, and he had no lack of critics reminding him of that. His sales were strong enough for his pride occasionally to get the better of him, which was why he had a large wooden sign made that he proudly displayed above his office desk. The words kept him humble and reminded himself of his own limitations:

Drinks like Hemingway. Writes like Koontz.

But this book would change that. Maybe it wasn't literary, but it was more raw than anything he'd ever done. There was a pureness and truth to it, even if that truth was an ugly one.

Tommy shoved the manuscript back in the bag and turned off the light. He wanted to talk to Antoine, but he knew the conversation would be one-sided. Antoine was paid to drive, not to talk.

Tommy removed his cell phone from his bag and checked for messages. None. He dialed Becky and left her one more message, which he figured would be the last one for a while.

'Hey, it's me. Just . . . well, I just hope you listen to this. I'm not home. I'm on the road. I've made a decision about things. I don't know if it's the right decision, but I feel like it's the only thing I can do. Maybe this is the last time you'll hear my voice. Maybe we still have an amazing life together ahead. I know I've made mistakes. Terrible mistakes. But I need you, and I'm doing this for all of us. To keep what we have. It's for us, Becky. It's for all of us.' He closed his eyes and pressed the phone harder against his ear. 'I won't tell you to call me back, because you're not going to. So, I'll just call you again . . . later, when things are done. Please tell the kids I love them very much. And I love you. *I love you.*'

He disconnected the call and put the phone back in his bag.

Seconds later he took it back out and dialed Sofia. Again, it went to voicemail. This time Tommy didn't leave a message. He wasn't really sure what he wanted to say to Sofia anyway. Maybe he just wanted to hear her voice. He wanted someone to tell him what he was doing was right.

He could call more people, he could check his e-mail, he could read the newspapers surrounding him. There were a dozen things Tommy could do to distract himself during the ride, but he didn't do any of them.

Despite the stress, or perhaps because of it, Tommy closed his eyes and fell asleep.

FORTY-TWO

'We're here,' the voice said.

Tommy opened his eyes. He'd been sleeping either ten minutes or twelve hours. He looked forward and saw the back of Antoine's head, remembering where he was. He sat up and stared out the tinted windows, trying to focus.

The Town Car pulled into a gas station. The pumps were from another lifetime, when credit cards were only accepted inside at the cashier. A weathered plastic sign told Tommy this station was the property of someone named Nelson. Nelson somehow managed to keep his independent shop open despite, or perhaps because of, being in the middle of fucking nowhere.

This wasn't Lind Falls. It might not be too far away, but Tommy didn't recognize anything. 'Where is this place?'

'This is where we get out.'

'And do what?'

'I don't know, Mr Devereaux. I'm just doing what I've been paid to do.' The car locks popped open. 'Get out please.'

Tommy opened the door. The fresh air was heavy on his face, as if rain was imminent. He took his bag and got out of the car, scoping the area around him. There was only one other car in the cracked and faded parking lot. It was a brown Subaru wagon that looked older than the gas station. Tommy guessed it belonged to Nelson.

Antoine got out of the driver's side and walked up to Tommy. Tommy instinctively put his right foot back and shifted his weight, not knowing what exactly Antoine was going to do next.

'Relax, Mr Devereaux.'

Tommy took a step back. 'I don't think I remember how to relax anymore.'

'I'm not going to hurt you,' Antoine said. He held up his hands in the universal but meaningless gesture of peace. 'But I do need to check your bag.'

'Check it for what?'

Antoine ignored the question. He grabbed Tommy's suitcase, then walked over and placed it on the trunk of the Town Car. He seemed to keep one eye on Tommy while he rifled though the bag. When he was done, he zipped it back up and placed it on the ground. He turned to Tommy.

'One more thing. I need to pat you down.' Antoine walked up to him and stood just a foot away. Tommy noticed a small scar on his left cheek, one that had probably been there for decades. 'Please raise your hands, Mr Devereaux.'

Tommy did as he was told.

Antoine patted him down quickly and professionally, and Tommy guessed he had done it hundreds of times before. He removed Tommy's phone.

'Why do you need that?' Tommy asked.

'I don't,' Antoine said. Then he slammed Tommy's cell phone

on the asphalt, and Tommy watched it shatter into three visible chunks and probably countless microscopic ones. 'I just need to make sure you can't use it.'

'Motherfucker,' Tommy said.

'No need for names.'

Tommy stared down at the pieces of his phone. 'You could just have taken it.'

'I have my instructions.'

Tommy looked at him and realized Antoine was probably very good at obeying instructions.

Then Antoine reached around and grabbed Tommy's wallet from his back pocket. He removed the cash and handed the bills back to Tommy before sliding the wallet into his own jacket pocket.

'Seriously? How the hell am I going to fly home without a license?'

'Like I said. Instructions.'

Tommy felt his muscles tense and willed himself to stay calm. Maybe he wasn't going to be flying home at all.

'So now what?' Tommy asked.

'Now I leave.'

'And what happens to me?'

Antoine shrugged. 'I have no idea, Mr Devereaux.'

Tommy watched Antoine walk back to the car, feeling both anxious and relieved to know he was leaving. Before he got into the car, Antoine turned around.

'*The Blood of the Willing*. That was my favorite book of yours. I liked that there was a cat in the story. You should use cats more often. Made me like the guy, you know? Anyone who would stick his neck out for a dumb cat, ya gotta like him.'

Tommy couldn't seem to do anything but stare at him. By the time he managed a feeble 'thank you' Antoine was already pulling away in the Town Car. Tommy watched it until it disappeared over a distant rise.

Seconds later, a phone rang.

Tommy looked behind him and saw the ancient pay phone. The once-black handset was faded gray from years of exposure, and a large crack ran down the back of the earpiece. Tommy couldn't remember the last time he'd even seen a pay phone, much less used one.

The phone kept ringing. No, it wasn't ringing. It was screaming. Tommy knew who was calling.

He lifted the phone off its receiver and held it up to his ear. The warm plastic handset felt reassuringly heavy. Weapon-like.

'Hi, Elizabeth.'

'Hi, Tommy.' Her voice was so clear he thought for a second she was standing behind him. He couldn't help but glance over his shoulder.

'Welcome back to Oregon.'

'Antoine broke my phone.'

'You're a multi-millionaire. You can afford a new one.'

'I was hoping to hear from my children,' he said.

'That would only be a distraction, Tommy. I need you all to myself for now. I need you to focus.'

Tommy looked down at his bag. 'Why all the cloak and dagger?' he asked. 'Why not just let me rent a car?'

'Because I need to make sure you're completely alone,' she said. 'I'm sure you've been thinking about calling the police. Leading them to me. I'd be thinking the same thing if I were you. So I need to be in control of how you move and how you communicate. It's the only way I can be assured you're going to do what you're here to do.'

'So what now?'

'Now you walk.'

'Walk?'

'Yes, Tommy. Walk. Your fancy little suitcase has wheels, doesn't it?'

Tommy didn't answer. His muscles tightened again.

'Antoine left you some cash. You can stop in the store and buy a Ring Ding if you want to. You might get hungry.'

'Where am I walking to?'

'West. Take the road right in front of you and head west. You're going to go just over two miles and you'll get to an abandoned farm house with an American flag painted on the barn. When you get there, go inside the barn.'

'That doesn't sound promising.'

'Are you questioning me?'

'I haven't stopped questioning you. I'm might be doing what you want me to, but contrary to what you think I'm not stupid. Walking blindly inside some barn sounds pretty stupid.'

'What do you think is going to happen, Tommy? You think I'm going to kill you? Get you all the way here to do that?'

'So what happens in the barn then?' he asked.

'Whatever I want to happen. Remember? You do what I say. That's how this all works.'

Tommy hung up the phone. If she had anything else to say, she'd call back. She didn't.

Tommy knelt and picked up the pieces of his phone. Instead of throwing them away, he put them in the bag, hoping that at least the SIM card could be salvaged.

He considered going inside the small store to buy something. To see another human, at least. Then he decided it would do no good. It wouldn't make a difference.

So Tommy rolled his bag over the loose gravel on the asphalt and headed west.

FORTY-THREE

Walking two miles wouldn't take long, but he wanted to make it last. The fall day was gray and growing long. A small breeze goosed his skin.

The country road stretched straight and long, rising up to a peak where he'd last seen Antoine in the black shiny Town Car. Spruce trees lined the south side of the road, and every now and then a bird would call out from within one of them, warning others ahead that a stranger was approaching.

No other cars came. The road seemed too worn and in too much disrepair for the little use it likely received. The smoothest part of the road was in the middle, right on the faded striped yellow line, so Tommy walked there, knowing that if a car did come he'd hear it from far away. He walked up the small rise, the rolling of the plastic wheels constant and assuring. His body ached for exercise. He wanted to run. To burst down the road at full speed, feeling his body itch with the first small beads of sweat, then his shirt soak through as his heart rate reached its peak.

Tommy finally reached the top of the rise. From there, he could see the farm house in the distance. It was about a half-mile away, and it gave him something to focus on as he walked. Even from a distance he could tell the farm house was abandoned.

As he got closer he saw that all the windows of the main house were broken. The wood siding was faded and worn, appearing layered in elephant skin. Shingles on the roof were sporadic, revealing faded tar that had surely long since lost its tack.

The barn was just on the far side of the house. Sure enough, the side of the barn was painted with a massive American flag, but it was so weather-worn that it appeared more as an after-image, a fading ghost on a cooling TV screen. It was both picturesque and depressing at the same time. At some point, years ago, someone had spent a lot of time painting that flag, and when the artist was done, the family who had lived in that house gathered around and stared at it, thinking it the best thing they'd ever seen.

Now they were all gone, the house rotted into the ground, and the flag disappeared a little more each day.

Tommy could feel himself being watched as he approached.

He sucked in a breath. Today was the day. However it turned out, he had made his decision. The hard part would be making sure he committed to it. A moment of indecision could be the difference between a future of happiness and none at all.

Can you do it, Tommy? Can you do what you need to do?

He finally passed the house. The weeds alongside the foundation reached higher than his waist. Two of the four steps leading up to the front porch no longer existed. The front door once had a window in it, and an ancient cotton veneer wisped in front of the gaping hole like an abandoned spider web.

He continued past the house and made his way to the barn. The weeds became difficult to navigate with his suitcase so he left it behind, figuring it wasn't going to be stolen by anyone.

Fresh tire tracks cut swaths in the weeds that led directly to the massive barn door. It was closed.

Tommy went up to the door and stood in front of it. The wooden arm that would lock any livestock inside was down, and all Tommy had to do was pull on the rusty metal handle to swing the door open.

Tommy looked behind him. Nothing but the road. The smell of dirt and damp weeds filled the air.

He pulled on the handle and the barn door creaked. It opened with almost no effort, and a shaft of light from outside spotlighted the front of a vehicle parked inside. White van, dusted gray by dirt.

Tommy walked inside the barn, his steps short and cautious, his shoes crunching on scatterings of hay.

The van belonged to Elizabeth, he knew. Had to be. And she had gone to the effort to back it into the barn, making it easier for her to drive out quickly.

He stood a few feet inside the barn and stared at the van, waiting for something to happen. The barn seemed impossibly cavernous on the inside, but maybe that was because most of it hid in the darkness, though some cracks in the wood allowed for jagged scars of light. The smell changed to mold and ancient cow shit.

Tommy took another step and waited.

Nothing.

Of course, he thought.

He knew that he was meant to go around to the back of the van. Whatever was waiting for him would be there. Elizabeth liked to create a scene, and she was certainly painting a beautifully creepy one now.

Tommy passed the passenger side and looked into the window, seeing nothing. The rear of the van was windowless. He reached the back of the van, turned, and faced the entrance by which he'd come in. The vehicle was silhouetted by the light streaming in from the open barn door, and Tommy could barely make out any of the features of the back of the vehicle. He reached forward and felt for the cargo door handle, and his fingers quickly found the cool, metal latch.

The darkness of the barn began to suffocate him, like a python beginning to coil around his legs and slowly making its way around his waist. And then chest. And then face.

Tommy pulled the latch and the cargo door opened.

The smell of vinyl and perfume washed over him.

From the even deeper blackness inside the cargo area, her voice.

'Hello, Tommy.'

FORTY-FOUR

'**G**et in and shut the door,' she said.

Tommy could see her outline, but nothing more. He'd gone this far, he'd go further. He stepped into the cargo area of the van, reached behind him, and pulled the van door closed.

Blackness cloaked them. The air in the van was easily twenty degrees warmer than outside. The smell of her overpowered all other scents.

It was *the* perfume. He remembered it. The smell was distinct, and it washed over him with a mix of horror and sensuality. She'd worn it the day she smashed a rock into Rade's head. The smell of excitement and anticipation. No one would have believed him if he'd said that he recognized a smell he'd only known for an hour thirty years ago, but Tommy knew it was true. In the darkness of that van, Tommy briefly wondered what the odds were the same perfume would even still exist thirty years later. She probably has the same bottle, he thought. Saved it for an occasion just like this.

A small noise. The van rocked slightly. Then, directly in his ear:

'Can you, Tommy?' Her hot breath flowed over his ear. 'Can you follow instructions? Will you do everything I say?'

He felt the flicker of her tongue on his earlobe.

Her essence surrounded him. He saw her as she was, back then. He saw her perfect skin as she removed her shirt. Her puffy, *almost-a-junior* nipples. He saw her broad shoulders sloping to a narrow perfect waist as she straddled Rade.

The tongue went in his ear. Tommy reached out and pushed her away.

'That's why,' he said. 'The darkness. The perfume. It's the only way you can bring me back to that day. Fully.'

'You think you don't want to remember,' she said. 'But I think you do.'

He spoke into the darkness. 'Why would I want to remember any of that?'

'You need to be in that day, because today will be just like it. Only this time, you get to be me.'

'I'm nothing like you.'

'You need to be. At least for a while.'

A shaft of light exploded in the back of the van, startling Tommy. Elizabeth held a flashlight, pointing the beam up toward her face, the way a kid would when telling a ghost story to his friends at a sleepover.

Her lips were a deep red. 'It's time,' she said. Then she swung the flashlight down and the beam swept across the floor of the van.

There was a body in there with them.

Bound. Duct tape covering his mouth. A man, motionless, lying on the floor, as lifeless as a rolled-up carpet.

Alan Stykes.

'Jesus,' Tommy said. 'You killed him?'

'Oh no,' Elizabeth grinned. 'What would the point of *that* be? He's very much alive. Just a little sleepy at the moment.'

Alan Stykes did not move. Elizabeth must have drugged him and then loaded him in the van, Tommy thought. Tommy leaned over and could hear a faint wheeze come from Stykes's nostrils every few seconds, confirming the man was very much alive.

Tommy looked at her. 'We're going to the woods, aren't we?'

'Of course we are.'

'How did you get his body into the van?' Tommy asked. 'You're strong but you're not that strong.'

'You're concerned there's someone else helping me,' she said, nodding her head in professional concern. 'And maybe that person is also a threat to you.'

'Everything's a threat to me.'

'There's no one else,' she said.

'Well, I'm glad I can just take you at your word.'

Her hand grabbed his wrist. 'Tommy, you're not going to die today. Unless you try to do something very stupid.'

Tommy only heard the word *today*.

'Besides,' she said, 'how do you know he didn't come into the van willingly and I drugged him in here?'

Tommy looked around, absorbing only what the single flashlight beam allowed. There was nothing he could see that would entice anyone to come in here, he thought.

'You stay in the back,' she said. 'I'll take your suitcase up front with me. You brought your manuscript?'

'I did. In the suitcase.'

'Good.'

With that, Elizabeth opened the back of the van and stepped out, taking the flashlight with her. She closed the door and Tommy disappeared back into blackness. The wheezing from Stykes continued. Growing louder.

Sssssssssss

He heard a click and knew she'd locked him in.

The van rumbled to life and moved for a few seconds before stopping. The driver door opened once again.

Closing the barn door, Tommy thought.

The seams along the back doors of the van allowed tiny shafts of light inside, but not enough to feel any sense of orientation. Already seated on the metal floor, Tommy crossed his legs and bent forward, leaning over his thighs. He closed his eyes and tried to escape within himself. Find some degree of calm.

The van started up again and Tommy lurched as it turned on to the paved road. There would be calm, he knew. It would be hard enough just to keep his balance.

Now he could smell Stykes. Sweat. Dirt.

Tommy's foot made contact with Stykes in the dark. The man's leg felt like a tree trunk. Tommy poked at it with his sneaker. Once. Twice.

More wheezing from the floor.

The van slowed and came to a stop. The motor grumbled as it accelerated once again.

Tommy reached out this time with his hand. Slowly. His fingers poked the blackness until they found Stykes's torso. Solid, but soft at the same time, like an out-of-shape fighter.

Tommy pulled back before reaching out again. This time he touched Stykes's bare arm, feeling the warm skin through thick hair. Tommy wondered how many little boys' final memory was of Stykes's hirsute arms.

Tommy thought of Chance. Thought of this monster killing his own little boy. The thought didn't just make him angry. No, the feeling of anger was almost intangible. Angry was what you got when you read about a child killer in the news. But when you were actually touching the naked arm of the monster himself and thought about what that monster had done, you didn't get angry.

You became irrational.

Think, Tommy. Think of the unspeakable things this person did to little boys, boys just like Chance. Think of the cruelty, the unbelievable fucking cruelty and horror. The terror. And the complete confusion going through the mind of those little boys. The moment of *Why are you doing this to me?* That final jagged thought before the darkness.

Just like Rade.

Tommy squeezed his eyes shut in the darkness as his fingers burrowed into the meaty arm of the man on the van floor. His fingers plunged deeper into the flesh. Harder. Clawing. He wanted his fingertips to burst down past the surface so he might grab hold of all his skin at once and tear it right off.

He hadn't intended to do this, but once he made contact with Stykes, he wanted to kill him. Wanted him to suffer, wanted him to feel the pain and the fear and the sense of ending that all his victims had surely felt. How easy it would be to kill him now, here, in the van. His mouth was already covered in duct tape; all Tommy had to do was squeeze Stykes's nostrils shut and in minutes the world would be free of at least a few ounces of evil.

Tommy felt his hands lift from Stykes's skin and move toward his nostrils. But before he completed the act, Tommy pulled back, telling himself it wasn't the time. He needed to adhere to the decision he had made a day ago, the decision he had explained in detail in those five letters he had written. Stick with the plan.

Tommy sucked in a breath, wiped a bead of sweat off his forehead with the back of his hand, and leaned back against the wall of the van.

Then Alan Stykes woke.

FORTY-FIVE

tykes wasn't just a little awake. He was fully awake, as if someone had just passed a massive current of electricity through him. Tommy could hear and feel the concussive thumps of the restrained body flopping on the floor of the van.

'*Mmmmppphhhh . . .*'

Over and over the gagged screams throttled against the duct tape covering Stykes's mouth, the horror of it accentuated by the dark. Tommy desperately wanted out of the van.

Stykes suddenly stopped flopping, and Tommy hoped that he'd slipped back into the drug-induced coma he'd been in.

But he hadn't passed out again, Tommy realized. Stykes was strategizing.

Stykes suddenly began swinging his bound legs out, back and forth. Tommy realized this when the legs slammed into his own left shin. Tommy lost his balance and fell on top of Stykes's chest. Stykes tried to attack, but his efforts were fruitless. Legs tied together. Hands bound behind his back. Mouth covered in duct tape. Stykes heaved against Tommy but could not seriously harm him. Tommy pushed himself off and stood, keeping his balance as the van continued on.

Tommy wanted to give him a warning. *Stay still, you fuck.* He lifted his right foot off the floor of the van, steadied himself, then slammed the heel of his shoe down. A good stomp in the chest would calm him down.

But it took only the moment of impact for Tommy to realize his foot hadn't landed on Stykes's chest, but rather on his face. He felt nose cartilage crumple under the force, like stomping on a hard-boiled egg.

Stykes howled into the tape. Tommy jumped back and steadied himself against the side of the van, but that lasted only until the van veered hard to the right and shuddered to a violent stop. Tommy went flying and landed again on Stykes, who kept screaming like a pig being repeatedly speared.

Tommy felt the slimy glaze of sweat on the man's skin as the body thrashed beneath him.

Before he could push himself off, Tommy heard the driver's door open. Seconds later, the back door opened.

Sunlight stabbed Tommy's eyes. He could only see Elizabeth's silhouette against the hazy sky. Her voice was sharp and deep.

'What the fuck is going on back here?'

Tommy pushed himself off Stykes.

'He's awake,' he said.

Elizabeth started into the back of the van. Then her eyes widened.

'What did you do?' She jumped into the back of the van as Tommy freed himself of the space and sucked in the fresh outside air.

'I kicked him in the face,' he said, turning. 'I kicked him in the goddamn face. I was just trying to calm him down. He was trying to attack me.'

'You kicked him in the face to calm him down? Nice thinking, Tommy.' Elizabeth stared at Stykes, whose face was streaked with gushing blood. He shook his head as if trying to rid himself of the pain, and thick ropes of blood followed the motion of his head, splattering Elizabeth.

'You broke his nose, goddamnit,' she said. 'We can't leave the tape on his mouth. He'll choke to death. This is *not* how it's supposed to happen.'

She reached up to Stykes's face and grabbed a corner of the tape, then ripped it off in one fast burst.

Stykes screamed as he vomited blood.

FORTY-SIX

They entered the woods.

Elizabeth drove them down a path farthest away from the sleepy subdivision bordering the eastern edge, the one where Tommy grew up, and the one where Rade's father sat out on his porch at night, staring out to the trees, waiting for his little boy to come home.

She maneuvered the van down a small access road, guiding them deep into the woods, away from the streets and the houses and into an area where they could be alone. Tommy knew that someone could come out for a jog or to walk their dog, but he guessed Elizabeth had spent time finding a spot of reliable solitude for the day's events. It was a quiet place.

Stykes's screams, however, would travel far once the van's doors were open.

Elizabeth turned the engine off and looked at Tommy, who had relocated to the passenger seat. Blood spray from Stykes's screams and curses had transformed her blouse into a macabre Rorschach test.

She had Tased Stykes to get him to calm down, though it had simply enraged him more. He had thrashed about in the back of the van like a crocodile drowning its prey. Elizabeth seemed resigned to this, as the only other alternative was to tape his mouth again and risk Stykes choking to death on his own blood.

Tommy looked over and locked eyes with her. The trauma of everything he had seen and done, and what he needed to do, left him almost detached. There was a problem to be solved, and there were specific steps that needed to be taken to solve it. If he followed the steps precisely, the desired outcome would be achieved.

'It's time,' she said.

Tommy studied her. 'How long do you have?' he asked.

'We can't take too long,' she said. 'We need to move fast.'

'No. How long do *you* have? Your cancer.'

She blinked. 'Why?'

'Because one of my greatest friends died from cancer seven years ago, and she had all the treatment in the world. She didn't last more than six months from diagnosis. You say you aren't doing any treatment at all, and here you are looking like you could pass for a twenty-five-year-old.'

Her answer was immediate. 'Uncertain, but less than eight months from what I've been able to discern. I stopped going to doctors, so I don't know for sure.'

'How do you feel?'

'I feel like we need to move forward now and stop with the questions.'

'Maybe you don't have cancer,' he said. 'Maybe that's all part of your game.'

Elizabeth then opened her door and simply told Tommy: 'Come.'

After it was clear she would not answer his accusation, they moved to the back of the van and Elizabeth opened the doors to the cargo area.

Stykes immediately spat out blood in her direction.

'You fucking whore!' he shouted, though it came out *fuggin hor* through his shattered nose. His eyes were the only things not painted red on his face, and they shone through like pieces of smoldering coal.

Elizabeth calmly leaned forward, pushed the Taser into his neck, and pumped him with electricity. Stykes screamed and temporarily flopped silent, at which point she produced a leather glove and shoved it forcefully in his mouth. Stykes began gagging almost immediately.

Her voice was still as lake water. 'Slow down, Alan. Breathe. Focus. There should be enough space to breathe around the glove. You just need to calm down and focus.'

Tommy watched the scene and was quickly losing his sense of detachment. The man was choking to death.

'It's not working,' he said. 'He can't breathe.'

'He *can* breathe,' she corrected. 'He's just not listening to me.'

Stykes began thrashing about more, screaming into the black leather glove filling his mouth. When he spun and looked at Tommy, his eyes bulged from the sockets.

Tommy took a step back, as if he could physically remove himself from the suffering.

Elizabeth watched Stykes for a few more moments, tilting her head twice, analyzing the problem in front of her. Finally, she stepped forward.

'Fuck.' She said it with the annoyance of having just broken the heel of her shoe. She reached forward and grabbed on to the small bit of glove protruding from his mouth. 'Open,' she said. As Stykes did, she yanked the glove free.

Stykes sucked in the air around him, wheezing and struggling to fill his lungs.

'I could drug him,' she said to Tommy, 'but I don't want to. That would knock him out for too long.'

She reached back in and grabbed a fistful of Stykes's hair. 'I'm not going to bullshit you, fuckface. You know you're here to die. So just take it like a man and don't scream. Understand?'

'*Fuck you*,' he mumbled through his pain. *Fug you.*

Elizabeth pulled her arm back and smashed the side of his face with her fist. The motion was so quick Tommy almost couldn't process what had happened.

Stykes hung his head down and was indeed silent for a moment.

'You know what I can do,' she told him. 'You've seen what I'm capable of. If you don't scream, then our friend Tommy here will kill you. I'm sure it will be sloppy, but he's going to want to do it fast. He's not like us, Alan. He won't take pleasure in it. But if you *do* scream, then I'll make sure I get to spend some time with you first.'

This seemed to soak in to Stykes. He nodded.

'Good,' Elizabeth said.

Tommy looked at Stykes, who was secured by multiple loops of duct tape and had blood still seeping from his face. He looked like some kind of mummy–zombie hybrid.

'Where are we taking him?' Tommy asked.

Elizabeth nodded past the trees. 'In there.'

'How?'

'That's your first job,' she said. 'Transport your victim.'

'I can't carry that much weight. At least not that far.'

'Then it's a good thing I think of these things for you. In the van, mounted to the side panel. There's a dolly.'

Tommy remembered. He'd almost smashed his head into it when the van had lurched.

'Bring it out here and stand our friend here on it. You can wheel him forward, Hannibal Lecter-style.'

It's just another task, Tommy told himself. Break everything down into a series of small, manageable tasks. *Grab the dolly, stand it on the ground, swing Stykes's legs off the van, stand him in the dolly . . .*

Three minutes later the small tasks were complete and Tommy stood behind Stykes, who was secured to the dolly with a belt around his hips and his chest.

Elizabeth went to the passenger side of the van, reached in, and pulled out a small leather bag, the design of which reminded Tommy of a doctor's bag from the nineteenth century. He pictured it filled with various elixirs and intricate scalpels. She also grabbed a shovel, which Tommy knew was for burying Stykes's body.

'I'm going to walk ahead of you,' she said. 'Let me get out fifty paces ahead and then follow me.'

Elizabeth walked into the woods, the medicine bag in one hand and the shovel in the other, her feet making small crunching noises in the dirt and rock of the narrow pathway that threaded the towering trees. Tommy watched her, and he had a fleeting desire to wait until she was far enough away and then just jump in the van and drive away. But he knew he couldn't. First, he didn't have the keys. But more importantly, running away wouldn't put an end to everything. However this was going to end, it wouldn't be with him running away.

Stykes was still going to be difficult to move, even in the dolly. Tommy tilted the man back and took the weight on his front shoulders. He couldn't lean him too far back or the weight would overwhelm him. Tommy could lean him back about fifteen degrees and then manage to push him forward on the wheels of the dolly.

It was slow going and Tommy didn't like having Stykes's bloodied face so close to his own. Stykes closed his eyes and wheezed, and small bubbles of blood popped as they grew from his nose. Tommy could smell the man, a rank, sweet smell, the smell of an unclean animal. Rot.

As Tommy slowly made his way down the path with his burden, Stykes began to speak.

FORTY-SEVEN

'Think you can kill a man?' He spoke slowly, calmly, trying to make his words clear despite the broken nose. *Think* still came out as *thig*.

Tommy said nothing.

'Stuff happens when you kill someone,' Stykes continued. 'Chemical reactions in the brain. Changes you.'

Tommy grunted with effort as he wheeled Stykes over a small bed of rocks.

'Most people don't have it in 'em,' he said. 'Think they do. Think they can unleash violence like a wild animal if they have to, but most can't. And those who can, usually it's because of those same chemicals in the body.' His speech was painfully slow and at times

Stykes struggled to speak at all, pausing when he needed to work through the pain and fatigue, but Tommy knew the man wouldn't shut up until he was dead. He was pleading for his life, after all. 'Someone's attacking you, your instinct is to run. If you can't run, you have to fight or die. Those instances, the chemicals let you fight. Take the pain away. Give you amazing focus. You can hear *anything*. But for most folks, that's only when they have no choice.' Stykes turned his head to try to look at Tommy, but Tommy leaned his head back. 'You have a choice. You got me helpless, and she's gonna ask you to end my life. With your own hand. *I* don't think you can do it.' He spit a glob of blood into the dirt. 'Takes someone like me to do it, and we are different folk, you and me.'

Tommy looked up the path and saw Elizabeth at least fifty yards ahead.

'Where did you bury the children?' Tommy asked.

Stykes grunted a laugh. 'What children?' *Chidden.*

Tommy heaved Stykes over a half-buried tree root. 'The photos in your bedroom. That's where they are, aren't they?'

'Don't know what you're talking about.'

'It's one good thing you can do,' Tommy said. 'Give some closure to the families. Tell me where they're buried, so I can tell the police.'

Stykes said nothing.

Tommy thought for a moment. 'You're the one who moved Rade, aren't you? She asked you to.'

Stykes wheezed. 'I did. About a month ago. Nothin' left but bones.'

'Is he still here?'

Again, Stykes did not answer, and Tommy knew he wouldn't. He stood Stykes upright in the dolly, relieving the strain on Tommy's arms and back. He looked up the path toward Elizabeth as he spoke in Stykes's ear.

'So you've been talking to her. All this time.'

Stykes nodded. 'We keep in touch. Ours is a special relationship.'

'And you never thought she'd try to kill you? Get rid of the loose ends?'

'Not until now. Didn't think she had it in her.'

'Had it in her? That's some fierce denial, Alan. She killed Jason, or at least drove him to kill himself. Then Mark . . .'

Stykes spit out another glob of blood, most of which landed on his own shirt. 'Hell, son, she really is in your brain, isn't she? She didn't kill Mark. Not sure what happened to him – man was probably drunk. But she ain't the bogeyman. Maybe you think she's invincible. But she's just a scared little girl, just doing what nature is telling her to do. Simple as that. Doesn't mean I feel sorry for her. 'Sides, if there's any real loose end here, it sure as hell is you.'

Tommy saw Elizabeth waiting for them. She stood next to a tree, the most distinguishing feature of which was it was taller than the dozens of others in the same area. Like the others, it was gnarled and old, its skin around the base dark from the lack of sunlight.

'There,' Stykes said. 'That's where it'll happen. Take it in, Tommy. Take it all in.'

Tommy moved his gaze from the tree back to Elizabeth, who suddenly seemed no different from the sixteen-year-old he'd first met in these same woods. She looked upon him like a ghost gazing in from an outside existence. She motioned to him to come.

Come to my world.

The afternoon was growing old, and Tommy could see the darkness ahead, the shadows from the trees, spread along the dirt and scrub like a cold, stiff sheet. Tommy sucked in a deep breath and leaned Stykes back on his shoulder, pressing him forward in the dolly, which moved slowly, the rubber wheels digging into the dirt, an inch at a time, as it rolled toward the clearing.

FORTY-EIGHT

'What's in the bag?' Tommy nodded at the medical bag she had placed on the ground. His heart was still pounding from transporting Stykes the distance from the van, though he doubted his pulse would have been slow and steady otherwise.

Elizabeth reached down and opened the bag, pulling from it Tommy's printed manuscript along with the extra pages in the back. She walked over to Tommy and dropped it at his feet.

'You're not used to handwriting these things, are you?'

'No, I'm not.'

She went back into the bag and pulled out a pen, which she similarly tossed to the ground near him.

'Hope your hand doesn't cramp up. You'll have some good things to write down soon.'

Tommy didn't bother to pick up either the manuscript or the pen. There would be no writing. Besides, he wanted to know what else was in the bag.

He didn't have to wait more than a few seconds to find out. He and Stykes followed Elizabeth's movements as she reached back into the bag again, this time extracting from it a black hand towel. She unfolded the towel and spread it out neatly on the dirt.

Then she pulled a knife from the bag. Eight-inch chef's knife, cherry-red handle, full tang. As she placed it on the towel, Tommy briefly saw her distorted reflection in the blade. To him, in that instant, he saw the face of a clown, pulled in all directions, smiling and frowning at the same time. Laughing and crying.

'Option number one,' she said. 'Messy, but if you do it right, relatively painless. Over in seconds. But doing it right requires full commitment. You have to really stab, and stab hard. Can you do that, Tommy? Can you look at him and push this blade into his chest?'

Stykes coughed up more blood. 'Cunt,' he said.

Elizabeth reached in the bag again.

Tommy recognized the object immediately. He had one at home.

A jump rope.

'Option number two, if you prefer to strangle. Not messy, but again, requires commitment. Takes a bit longer, and you'll be tempted to let go, but if you release too early you'll just have to start all over again. You're strong, Tommy. Big muscles. But it's not so much the strength you need with this. It's the will.' She placed the jump rope on the towel. 'By the way, don't get your hopes up for a gun, Tommy.'

Into the bag she went again, dipping into it like a child searching for her favorite candy from her Halloween-night plunder.

Tommy looked up as she pulled out a small aluminum-brushed canister. It had a red nozzle on top, and the thing looked like a small unlabeled can of aerosol deodorant. She pulled out two sets of rubber gloves and face masks.

'Hydrogen cyanide,' she said. 'Not easy to make, I can assure you. I've never used this but I was inspired by one of your books. I have an attachment, and all you have to do is spray it in his face. But—'

'Apnea, coma, cardiac arrest within minutes,' Tommy said. His female villain Adrienne had used hydrogen cyanide in *The Blood of the Willing*. 'I'm familiar with it. Horrible agony.'

Stykes began to shake. 'You can't do this to me.'

'That's right,' Elizabeth said, talking to Tommy and ignoring Stykes. 'Not so much dirty work for you – just a quick spray in his face. But you'd have to watch him suffering. Hear the screams. If you choose this method, I have masks and gloves for the two of us.' She turned the canister over in her fingers as she studied it. 'Wouldn't want to breathe any of this lovely stuff in accidentally. In my bag I also have a Cyanokit IV bag, just in case. Can never be too careful.'

She set the canister on the towel.

'So those are my options?' Tommy asked.

'Not quite. One left.'

Stykes's eyes followed as he watched her go back into the bag one last time.

The final item she extracted was a rock. It was about the size of a softball and its surface looked to have been smoothed over the years by water. River rock, Tommy thought.

'Option four,' she said. 'Rock to the skull, just like Rade. Relatively painless for him if you do it with the right amount of force. Very, very primitive. Brutal.' She placed the rock on the towel next to the other items. 'You can use one of the four items here before you to kill this man.' She turned her head and flashed her blue eyes at Tommy. 'So what's it going to be, Tommy?'

Tommy stared at the items on the towel and tried to picture himself using any of them. Could he really kill?

'Don't do it, Tommy.' It was Stykes, whose face had lost all color.

Elizabeth turned to him. 'Would you rather me do it, Alan? Because if it's up to me, it's not going to be quick.'

'Monster.' The blood seemed to have stopped clogging Stykes's nose so much, though the word still sounded like *monstug*.

With a sudden move of her arms, Elizabeth pushed Stykes over.

Unable to brace himself, Stykes crashed to the ground on the dolly, the impact knocking the wind out of him.

He laid on his back, gasping for air through a wide mouth, fish-like. Elizabeth stood over him, looking down.

'I'm a monster? *I'm* a monster?'

He spit up at her, and more blood sprayed on her pants. 'You *are* a monster, Elizabeth. You weren't supposed to be this way.'

Way? Tommy wondered what that meant.

Then Elizabeth kicked him in the ribs. It was a child's kick. An angry, tantrum-throwing child who can't reason, so resorts to aggression instead. Tommy had never seen her lash out like this; even in the killing of the homeless man in Charleston she seemed controlled, scripted. But this was anger. Real anger.

She leaned over him. 'How the hell was I supposed to turn out?' she yelled. 'Tell me! How was I supposed to turn out? Normal? Normal like you?'

Another kick, this time to the face. Stykes's face swung to the side.

What the hell is going on?

Stykes grimaced before looking back at her. 'That's right, Lizzie. *That's right.* Take it out on me. It's what you've always wanted, isn't it? You ungrateful bitch. After all I've done for you.'

Tommy felt himself stepping back. One step. Two. Three.

'*Done for me?*' She dropped on top of him, straddling his waist. His hands remained firmly pinned against his sides by the rope and he was defenseless to absorb her blows, which she alternated between her right and left fists, each one landing with equal strength and precision on each side of his face. One. Two. Three. Stykes's head twisted back and forth like a speed bag under the punishment of well-trained knuckles.

She paused after the sixth or seventh blow, gasping with exhaustion and anger. Stykes's face began to swell, and blood oozed from the corner of his left eye.

'*Done for me?*' She raised her arm and smashed her elbow into his already broken nose, caving it deeper into his face. Tommy heard a smashing sound so sickening he almost thought he imagined it.

He took another step back, uncertain of what he was witnessing. Elizabeth had snapped, of that much he was certain. What he didn't know was why, but Stykes did. Stykes knew exactly what he was doing, and Tommy could only assume he was provoking her in hopes of a quick death.

She leaned over Stykes, who seemed barely conscious, and spat in his face.

Tommy held still, straining to hear what she said to Stykes as she leaned closer to him.

'You made me,' she said, panting. 'I *am* you.'

He wheezed his words out slowly through a swollen mouth. 'You were born this way, Lizzie.' Stykes's eyes were now closed from the swelling and his lids puffed with blood. He faced Elizabeth's voice but did not see her. 'Even as a little girl. Remember? Remember the cat? That was you. That was *all you.*'

'I'm this way because of you.'

He shook his head slowly. 'The only thing you have of mine is blood,' he said. His speech was slow, his voice raspy. 'And if killing is in my blood, then that's why it's in yours. But you could have done something different. You *wanted* me to teach you. You *begged* me to teach you.'

'I *wanted* a normal life,' she said.

'There is no normal.' His breathing slowed. 'There's only what we know.'

Elizabeth, still straddling him, leaned to the side to the towel on the ground. She picked up the rock.

She held it high above her head with both hands, and Tommy suddenly saw her and Rade, thirty years ago.

She was going to kill him.

'You tell me,' she said, her words growled through tight teeth. 'You *tell* me why you killed her.'

'You know why I killed her.'

'Tell me,' she repeated, hoisting the rock even higher.

'Because I had to,' Stykes said. 'She found out what I was. I had to.'

'*She was my mother!*'

Tommy blinked. Elizabeth screamed.

Stykes turned his head and waited for the end.

FORTY-NINE

The rock came down, but not on to Stykes's skull. Elizabeth's long, muscular arms squeezed the rock above her head for a few more seconds, and then, as if someone pulled a plug from her, her body simply began to crumple, bending down, her arms collapsing, the rock falling uneventfully to the ground. She put her bloodied and swelling hands on Stykes's chest, supporting herself.

Tommy watched from a distance, detached, as if watching everything unfold on his living room flat screen. None of it seemed real.

Stykes said nothing, and he kept his head turned to the side, expecting, perhaps hoping, that she would kill him at any second. But she didn't. Instead, she slowly lifted herself off him and stood, turning toward the weak sunlight and closing her eyes, then running her fingers through her hair and putting herself back in place. She ran her hands over her blood-stained pants, smoothing them. She stood straight, her posture perfect, her breasts round and large, pushing up tight against her blouse. She kept her eyes closed a few seconds longer and Tommy could see her taking deep, slow breaths, composing herself.

She opened her eyes and walked over to Tommy. A small part of him screamed at him to *just run away*, but he knew that would accomplish nothing.

Tommy stared in her eyes, the deep denim softness, and for the first time he saw the resemblance. It wasn't strong, and he wasn't surprised he hadn't seen it before, but it was there.

'He's your father.'

Elizabeth nodded.

'Why didn't you tell me before?'

'It's irrelevant,' she said.

'No, it's not.'

'Your job is unchanged and unaffected by this,' she said.

'Your name is Elizabeth Stykes.'

'I haven't used that last name in a long time.'

'He molested you. You said you were molested as a child.'

'No, you asked if I was abused, and I said you can't call it abuse if you like it.'

'He killed your mother. How old were you?'

'That information isn't relevant either.'

But it *was* relevant, Tommy knew. Elizabeth the monster had always been just that. A monster with no context around who she was. Yes, she had given Tommy some idea about why she was who she was, but only in a controlled, staged interview back in the Oregon motel room. This was the barest he had ever seen her. The most vulnerable. She was stripped down to her core, and if Tommy could use this moment to really understand her nature, then maybe he could do something with that information.

Tommy nodded to the manuscript on the ground. 'You might not think it's relevant, but I'm the writer, not you. I need this information for the story. This is the last scene, isn't it? How can I write this scene without understanding your relationship with . . . with the victim?'

'Tommy, we can't waste time here. We've already been too loud. Someone could come along any moment.'

'They won't. You picked this location. You must have scouted it for some time. You would make sure we had plenty of alone time here. Elizabeth, you want this to be a bestseller, don't you? I need to know these details.'

She flicked her gaze away for just a second.

'Quickly.'

FIFTY

'He molested you,' Tommy said.

'Yes.'

'How old were you?'

'It started when I was five.'

'When did it end?'

'Who said it ended?'

'What do you mean by that?'

'How do you think I got him into the van?'

Tommy shuddered.

'What about your mother?'

She blinked and tried to look defiant, but to Tommy she looked scared.

'Back in the motel, you suggested she had abused you as well.'

'She . . . she wasn't like him. She was just too scared to do anything about it.'

'So she never laid a hand on you?'

Elizabeth shook her head.

'But she knew?'

Stykes's wheezing breaths became the soundtrack for the conversation. Tommy tried to ignore them.

'She knew.'

'For how long?'

She took a moment to answer. 'Years.'

Tommy sensed she wanted to talk more, so he remained silent.

Finally she spoke. 'If you must know, we tried to run away once. I was seven. It was just my mother and me. I don't have any other siblings. My mother was so fucking scared but she finally came in my room when he was at work and said, "We're leaving." I remember . . . I remember putting everything I loved in one suitcase. That was all she said I could take. One suitcase. I put some clothes in it, but mostly pictures. Polaroids. I had taken all these pictures of my stuffed animals. I had spent hours arranging them, pretending they were holding parties, and had taken so many pictures of them. I don't know why, but I loved those pictures. The expression on the animals' faces never changed. They were always happy. They were the only faces they had, and those faces always smiled. And I remember filling up the suitcase with the photos and my clothes.'

Polaroids. The same Polaroids Tommy saw in the picture frame in Stykes's home. Stykes kept them as a souvenir, Tommy thought.

'You only took the pictures with you? You didn't take any of the animals?'

'No,' she said. 'Why would I do that?'

Tommy then saw how detached she was. She didn't care about the things themselves. She only cared about how she could arrange them. How she could set the scene just the way she wanted. Her control was all that mattered, and she cared nothing for the thing she was controlling.

'Where did you go?' he asked.

'At the time, we were in Portland. We didn't have much money, so we just went to a cheap motel.'

Stykes now turned his head and watched her as she spoke. Tommy realized it was probably the first time the man had ever heard this story told.

'But *Daddy* was a cop,' Elizabeth continued, looking at her father. 'And it wasn't too hard for him to find us. And then he brought us home.'

At that moment Tommy heard a soft crackling in the distance, the sound of weight on fallen leaves. He turned his head and saw a small deer about a hundred feet away. It had just made its way into a small clearing and was pushing its nose into a pile of leaves, foraging. It brought its head up once and looked over in their direction but seemed to care little for the humans. Behind the deer another soon emerged, and then a third, the last one the largest of all. They cautiously walked forward, fanning out in formation, like soldiers on patrol in high grass.

'And then he killed her in front of me.'

Tommy snapped his head back around to Elizabeth, who seemed to care as little for the deer as they did for her.

'In front of you?'

'He beat her to death with a golf club in the basement. Funny thing is, he didn't even play golf. I don't even know why he had the club.'

Stykes finally spoke, his voice weak. 'It was a gift.'

Tommy remembered the ancient-looking golf club sitting in the corner of the man's living room. That was the club he beat his wife to death with, and he just kept it in plain view for all the years after he did it.

She ignored him. 'He made me watch, and when it was over he told me the same thing would happen to me if I ever tried to leave again.'

'Bitch had it coming,' Stykes mumbled.

Elizabeth walked over and kicked him in the head, the point of her shoe slamming into his left temple.

She walked back to Tommy as if nothing had happened. 'It was horrible. And I was scared. Traumatized, of course. What little girl wouldn't be?' She moved her hair out of her face. 'But there was a part of me that looked at my mother's body and was simply fascinated by it. The blood. The damage. The life that had simply . . . vanished. And the power that was associated with that, you know?' Elizabeth began to pace back and forth, looking at the ground as she spoke. 'Here was this woman I had known for all my existence, and she was simply and suddenly no more. I didn't feel so much a sense of loss as I did a wonderment at the vulnerability of life. How easily it can go away. I think even then I knew that wasn't a normal feeling to have.'

'He *did* create you,' Tommy muttered. He did the math and realized Stykes must have become a father at a young age, maybe twenty.

She nodded. 'If you got me on a psychiatrist's couch, they would probably tell you my mother's murder and the repeated sexual abuse at the hands of her killer made me what I am today. But I think I was already wired for the kind of life I was destined to lead. My experiences just made sure I didn't have a chance for something normal.'

She kept pacing, a panther in a city zoo. She no longer seemed to care about the time, the urgency of what they were all there to accomplish. Elizabeth had probably never said any of this out loud before, Tommy realized, and now that she'd started it was difficult to stop.

'So he buried her God-knows-where,' she said. 'Probably under the basement floor or something macabre like that.'

Stykes looked up at her but said nothing.

'And then we quickly got out of Portland. I think the fact that he was . . . *is* . . . a police officer is the only reason he was never really investigated. You know, blue code of silence and all that cop bullshit. We moved around a lot in those next few years, always staying in Oregon. Each time we moved, it was always suddenly and without any kind of warning. I got used to it. Later I discovered our departures always coincided with a young boy going missing.'

'He was already killing,' Tommy said.

'Oh, goodness yes,' she replied. 'Though I didn't know that until later. Until he decided I needed some training.'

'Training,' Tommy said, nodding, seeing where this was headed. 'You never wanted to leave him, did you?'

She laughed, and it was such a soft, gentle laugh. But Tommy had quickly learned nothing about Elizabeth was either soft or gentle.

'Leave him? Tommy, I wanted to *be* him.'

And the moment Elizabeth killed a boy, her father switched to boys as well, Tommy realized. Did Stykes molest them as he had his own daughter? Or was he simply trying to recapture what he had experienced as a Watcher in the woods?

'And then you moved to Lind Falls and got your chance.'

'Yes.'

'Alan had just started work with the police department. It was summer, so no one knew you from school yet.'

'That's right.'

'But after the killing, you disappeared. He stayed.'

'I ran away. I was scared of getting caught, so I left. I'm sure Dad told anyone who asked that he shipped me off to boarding school for a few years, but I never came back to Lind Falls until now. Dad finally stayed put. Guess the town grew on him.'

'Where have you been all these years?'

'Everywhere.'

'How did you live? The story . . . about your parents and the car crash and the insurance money. That was all bullshit. So how did you survive?'

'Tommy, you're stalling.'

'I've been thinking about you for thirty years. Humor me for two more minutes.'

'This is pointless.'

'Right here, Elizabeth. This is the arc of the story. The readers won't feel any connection to you if they don't understand who you are.'

He could see in her face that his words made an impact. She wanted to be understood. She needed to be in control of the story. It was her weakness.

Tommy just wanted to keep her talking.

FIFTY-ONE

Elizabeth looked down at her father, who alternated between staring at her and squeezing his eyes shut, as if trying to will himself to another part of the earth. He did not speak.

'I drifted, mostly,' she said. 'It's not too hard to have a decent life if you're good-looking and manipulative. Men came into my life.' She shrugged. 'I would fuck them and then take their things. Some of them I would kill. Most I didn't. Most would wake simply to find me gone. On to the next city. Next state.'

'Did you ever come back to Oregon?'

'No. I stayed mostly on the East Coast. Better quality stock.'

'Did you follow stories about your killings? Ever get an idea if you were close to being caught?'

'Tommy, when you're like me, you're always close to being caught. That's why you have to keep moving. Keep planning ahead.'

Tommy knew this was true. He also knew serial killers rarely, if ever, had the kind of career Elizabeth claimed to have. For a killer to be active over a fifteen-year period was rare. To be active for double that, and not have been caught, was almost unprecedented.

'You've had help,' Tommy said.

'Help?'

'You must have. An accomplice. Someone you trusted for at least some time.'

'You don't think I can take care of myself?'

'I think there are things you seem to be capable of that would be far easier done with help. You haven't lived your life as an escort. In New York, you said you were an escort. But you couldn't have sustained that kind of life. You've been much more comfortable than that. You've needed to rely on others, haven't you?'

'I've found that relying on others only leads to heartbreak.'

'Heartbreak? How would you even know what that meant? You're a sociopath. You're incapable of caring about anyone but yourself.'

Her eyes flared for the briefest of moments, a rare tell of emotion. 'Spoken like someone who spends his time researching and not participating. You cannot understand me, Tommy, if you continue to see me for only my acts.'

'Tell me who broke your heart. Let me understand. Have you ever loved someone, Elizabeth?'

Again she looked at her father, whose eyes were closed.

'I have loved two men, Tommy. The first one never loved me back. The second one did, or at least he was obsessed with me.'

'What happened to them?'

She let out a long breath, as if the words coming out of her took along with them some of her life. 'They both killed themselves.'

Tommy took a step back and studied her face. There *was* pain there, and if it wasn't real then she was a great actress.

'Jason?'

She nodded.

'How could you love him? He detested you.'

'He was the first boy I ever had sex with. At least when I wasn't being forced.' She spat at her father. 'That did something to me. I loved him for years without ever knowing where he was. Then I tracked him down in New York. I thought maybe . . . I don't know what I thought, actually.'

'You wanted to find someone like you.'

'Don't we all?'

'But Jason wasn't like you at all. You forced him to be a Watcher and then he killed himself.'

Another shrug, but this time she seemed to use it to help hide a deep sadness.

'Who was the second?'

She looked up at him and her eyes were genuinely glistening.

'He was a rising politician.'

FIFTY-TWO

'**M**ark?'

She nodded.

'How is that possible? He was married.'

'I was the mistress. We didn't see each other often. Once a year at the most.'

'For how long?'

'The past twelve years.'

'Bullshit. He wanted you dead.'

'I don't doubt that. He was taking risks with me. I remained deep in the shadows, but if I had come out with what I knew about him, his life would have been over. But he couldn't live without me. Back at Red Rocks, you were right in what you said. Mark was a lot more like me than he was like you. He had the darkness, and I was the only person he could share that with. I was his god, Tommy, but I was also his demon. When you have things like that battling inside you for too long, you have to give up at some point. Mark killed himself over it. You have a little of it in you too, Tommy. The struggle.'

Tommy wanted to deny it but couldn't.

'So he was there that night in Charleston. He was a Watcher when you killed that man.'

'No, Tommy. Mark hadn't done anything like that in a long time. It would have been too risky. But he did make time to fuck me earlier that day. Politicians never see that as too risky.'

She walked up to him, as she had so many times before in the last two weeks, and put her mouth close to his ear. A lover's secret, hot breath inside his head. Her fingers found the buttons on his shirt, and she flicked the top one open without seeming to try.

'Are you going to remember all of this, Tommy? After what's going to happen here today, are you going to be able to write all this down?'

And as he had before, Tommy felt compelled by her. *Enticed* by her. Despite the violence around them, or perhaps even because of it, Tommy was coaxed by her voice. Her smell, the scent of excitement and anticipation. *Her power.*

He looked at his manuscript on the ground. 'I don't think that's going to be a problem,' he said. He turned his head to her, their noses almost touching. 'You said he trained you. What does that mean?'

Instead of answering, Elizabeth went over to her father and straddled him once again, her pelvis aligned with his, her small hands resting casually on Stykes's bulging gut.

'Training is all about control, Tommy.' She leaned over and peered into Stykes's rage-filled eyes. 'That feel good, Daddy?' she said to him, slowly beginning to grind on him. 'You like me like this? I'm on top, a position of power. You're not used to that, are you?' She leaned down and whispered something in his ear. Stykes immediately tried to bite her but she pulled her head away and laughed. He spat at her, but even that missed.

'I thought I wanted to be you,' she said to him. 'But I realized I'm my own person. My own desires, not yours. And in a way, you being alive has always stopped me from forming fully. But today you're going to die, so at least I'll have a little time to enjoy truly being my own person. I will die a happy daughter.'

Stykes looked like a cobra ready to spit again but he held back. 'The hell you talking about? You're not the one going to die.'

'Oh, but you're wrong. I have cancer, and I've decided not to treat it. I doubt I have a year left in me.'

Tommy watched Stykes study her. How would he react to this news, this man whose daughter faced a painful death, yet was the architect of his? He looked at her deeply, intimately. And then Stykes began to laugh.

A hearty laugh, interrupted only by wheezes of pain and clogged nasal passages.

'You don't have *cancer*,' he said.

Elizabeth stood and moved away from him. 'You don't know anything about me,' she said.

'Lizzie, you think I'm just a monster, and maybe I am. But I *do* know my own child, despite what you think. One thing I could always tell was when you were lying and when you weren't. And you sure as hell are lying right now.' He chuckled some more, but it quickly faded into silence. 'There isn't an ounce of sickness in you.'

Tommy looked over and studied her face. She brought her gaze to his and he could tell she was struggling to keep eye contact. But she did, and those blue eyes didn't blink.

'He's a fool,' she said. Elizabeth walked over to the weapons on the ground and stood over them.

'Choose,' she said, turning back to Tommy.

Stykes warily eyed the weapons from his position on the ground.

'Convince me you're sick,' Tommy said.

'Choose . . . your . . . weapon.'

Tommy looked down at the killing tools on the towel. The time was soon. Minutes away. Maybe seconds. He felt the greasy sweat on his palms as he dug his fingers inward. He had to kill before the day was over. He wanted to feel the rage he thought he would need to do it, but more than anything he just felt scared. Could he do it? Could he pick up a weapon on the ground and attack with it? Tommy knew it would have to be the knife. The knife was the only thing on the ground that he could use quickly and with any degree of confidence. The cyanide would also be effective, assuming that *was* what was inside there. But Tommy wanted nothing to do with that canister. Way too unpredictable.

'Tommy.' Her voice was that of a school teacher correcting an errant student. 'Tommy. Darling. I'm going to tell you again. There is only one thing you need to believe, and that is what's going to happen if you don't kill this man. I will ruin your life, and I will do it with so much commitment and dedication you might even get more prison time than me. You will lose everything, just because you refused to dispatch a child killer. Is that what you want?'

'I'm thinking. Jesus, just . . . just let me think.' Another minute of silence passed. Stykes's groans of pain had softened, or at least had become so regular Tommy barely noticed them.

'Tommy,' she said, 'You came all the way out here. You came committed. Ready to end all of this. Ready to get your life back. Your only hope of doing that is to kill this man.' Another half-step toward him. 'So I'm going to tell you again: choose a weapon.'

Tommy stared at her in silence, his mind racing. Just choose a weapon, he told himself. Do it now. You can do it. *You can end this.*

She walked up to him and stood only a foot away, her gaze burrowing deep into him. Tommy felt his eyes search for the ground, but Elizabeth put a finger under his chin, lifting it up, demanding that he look at her. She looked at him quizzically, as if trying to solve a math problem written on his forehead. Then her face relaxed, she smiled and dropped her hand. She seemed to have solved the problem.

'I see. Now I understand,' she said. 'You never cease to amuse me, Tommy.'

Tommy blinked. 'Understand what?'

Elizabeth put her hand on Tommy's chest and pushed back lightly with long, blood-red nails. With a graceful pivot she turned from him, walked a few feet, then dropped to one knee next to her father. She reached out to the pile of potential murder weapons on the ground and grabbed the jump rope.

Stykes twisted his head just in time to watch her wrap the jump rope around his throat.

FIFTY-THREE

'**N**o!' Stykes's eyes bulged.
Elizabeth slowly raised herself, holding one handle from the rope in both her hands, and standing on the other handle on the ground. As she lifted her body, the rope grew taut around Stykes's throat.

'No,' Stykes said again, the word becoming a choke this time.

Tommy felt his weight shifting toward them. His mind told him to do *something*. But there was nothing to be done.

'Is this what you want, Tommy?' She lifted more, and Tommy could see the thin veins pulse in her strong arms. Stykes began to thrash, his arms useless bound against his body. Halibut gasping in the throes of death. 'Can you do this?' she asked Tommy. Stykes's eyes now bulged beyond what Tommy would have thought possible. 'This is how you do it, Tommy. The question is: can *you* do it?'

Tommy had no real answer to the question. Was Elizabeth really going to kill her father? If so, what did she see in Tommy's eyes that made her change her perfectly planned afternoon?

He got a quick answer to the first question. Tommy stood still and watched the man on the ground die, choked to death by his daughter. It took a couple more minutes, the sounds of gagging nearly making Tommy vomit. He watched it all happen. It was the third person he saw die at her hands, and Tommy knew whether he lived for only one more day or another fifty years, he would never forget the sight of Alan Stykes being strangled on the floor of the woods.

Tommy had finally become Elizabeth's Watcher, just as Jason and Mark had been before him, and Alan Stykes before that, and here she was, completing the cycle. The sight of the death and the ritual transfixed him, and before Tommy could think about his next move, her orgasm ended. Elizabeth's body gave one last shudder, then she dipped her head down and brought her eyes up to his.

'I know you want to kill me, Tommy. It's written all over your face. You're just trying to figure out how to do it. If that's why you really came here today, I suppose it's time to get about it.'

Tommy looked over to the knife on the towel.

FIFTY-FOUR

Tommy's decision to kill Elizabeth and not Stykes had come to him in the days before boarding the plane for Portland, culminating just hours before he left. The realization came from the slow trickles of moral intuition finally breaching the dam walls he'd constructed, thick walls of logic buttressed by ego and fear. Gradually, over the course of that last day, Tommy had been consumed by a profound sense of *what it was all about*.

Elizabeth wasn't sick. Tommy realized that even before Stykes said as much. Elizabeth didn't give a shit about a book written about her. Elizabeth just wanted to control him, and she would never go away until either Tommy destroyed her or she destroyed him.

It took Tommy being alone in his house for the dam to crumble behind the booming silence of his absent family. Alone, in his bedroom, Tommy had closed his eyes and had seen Becky's face. In his mind, she looked at him with the one expression that always tore deep into his belly: crushing disappointment. He saw the lick of crow's feet around her eyes as she looked at him, studying the man who had lied to her, the man who had desperately tried to plead his case, insisting that everything he did he did for *them*. He saw a hesitant love in her, a changed love, the kind that could be redeemed but only with great effort, humility, and selflessness on his part. He'd been able to redeem that love once, but now didn't know if Becky would ever give him the chance to do it again. Then Becky's face fell from his mind and was replaced by an image of his little girl. Evie was smiling at him, the innocence in her face so profound it seemed impossible someone like Elizabeth could ever have emerged from a child. Finally, his eyes still closed,

Tommy saw his boy, Chance, throwing a football toward him, the pass a wobbly spiral, the laces on the dusty brown leather worn from use. Chance wore a crooked grin, cocksure but seeking approval. *Was that a good one, Dad?* Tommy could hear the words as sure as if Chance were right there in front of him. In that moment, alone, on the bed, Tommy knew the truth of everything. It was so simple and so pure and so goddamn obvious. But the truth had eluded him all his life until this moment, lurking just beneath the surface of his own wants and desires. For up until that point, Tommy had always thought he was the good guy. But he wasn't. Not the way he needed to be.

The truth was, it wasn't about Tommy at all. It never had been. The truth was it was about everyone *except* Tommy.

His family needed him, but only the real Tommy. The one who not only knew the right thing to do, but actually did it. Any other Tommy they could do without. They would get by without him. But if they had the Tommy they needed, they stood a chance together. And they would all be stronger, together, because of it.

Tommy had to remind himself that Elizabeth wasn't a person, she was a poison. Tommy wasn't going to kill a woman, he was going to rid his system of a toxin. It was the only way. Any other way, going to the police, or just hoping Elizabeth would disappear again, was just naive and hopeful thinking. She would destroy him, and God only knew what kinds of ways she would get to his family.

No, this wasn't going to be murder. This was war, and Tommy was going to kill an enemy combatant before it was he who was taken out. It was the only way.

'That's number forty for me,' she said, nodding at the body on the ground. 'Tied for second place.'

It took him a moment and then Tommy realized she meant her kill record. He thought back to the night in Charleston. Then she'd told him she had thirty-eight kills. The homeless man was thirty-nine. With the death of her father, Elizabeth was now tied for second place for the most prolific female serial killer in history.

Tommy was two large steps away from the towel on the ground, which still held the small canister of gas and the knife. The jump rope was firmly entrenched around Stykes's neck, dug into his skin. The rock was a foot away from his lifeless head.

'You're not the type to be content with a tie for second place,' he said, shifting his gaze back to her. 'You'll never reach the hundreds that Elizabeth Báthory had, but you want at least one more.'

Elizabeth stood and buttoned the top of her pants. 'And you think you're that one?'

'You drove Jason to suicide after you made him a Watcher,' Tommy said. 'And now. Here. With your father, that cycle is complete.'

She took a small step to the left, and she was now closer to the weapons on the ground than Tommy.

'You were never going to let me live,' he said. Which was why he had already decided to kill her. He was now questioning himself less about *whether* he could do it, and instead more about *how* he could do it.

'Is that what you really believe, or what you're trying to convince yourself of?' He knew she saw him eying the weapons, and she shifted her weight, taking a step closer to the knife. 'There's a big difference between the two, you know. Very different consequences.'

Tommy shifted his weight. 'That so?'

'Of course. If you don't think I'll keep my end of our deal, then of course you'll try to kill me here. In these woods. Bury me along with my father. Kind of poetic, really.' Her fingers twitched, nervous excitement. '*However*, if you're still trying to figure out if I'm going to go away, your resolve is lessened. It takes a lot of resolve to kill, Tommy. Unless you really feel directly threatened, you won't kill me. I know it.'

Tommy felt the woods around him still, as if a large door had just been closed, sealing them in a small room. His vision sharpened as he looked again at the knife on the ground. He could read the writing engraved on the blade. Adrenaline coursed through him, and his hands shook as they dangled by his side.

'I'm through with you thinking you know me,' Tommy said.

'Oh, but Tommy, I *do* know you.'

'Then you should know I made my decision before I even came here.'

They caught each other's eyes. The moment lasted seconds or an hour.

Elizabeth lunged for the weapons.

Tommy pounced.

FIFTY-FIVE

Tommy had never been in a real fight before in his life. He'd boxed for years and sparred several dozen times, and though there was a reality to being hit in the face, there was always safety behind every move. Headgear. Mouth guards. A referee making sure no one was getting dangerously hurt. But most of all, there was humanity. The ability to stop and everything would be fine.

This was life or death. Tommy was strong and fast, but Elizabeth was a killer. She knew how to move, and Tommy couldn't deny the fact that she simply might be a better fighter than him. If he lost, he would die. Existence would simply end, Tommy would die in the woods, and his family would never know what happened to him. He would either miss every single part of his children's lives from this point on, or he wouldn't. It all came down to the next several seconds.

All these thoughts somehow found time to rush through his head as he flew toward the ground. Mid-air, he could already see Elizabeth would reach the weapons first. The best he could hope for was to tackle her before she could use one of them.

Tommy landed on top of her, his jaw smashing into the back of her skull. He bit hard down on his lip and felt a sharp pain. Then he tasted the salt of his blood.

Her hands seemed to move in slow motion, but not as slowly as his. He lifted his head from her hair to unblock his vision, seeing the wet patch of red his bleeding mouth had left behind. It was too late to go for the weapons because he couldn't see them, so he went for her arms instead.

Tommy focused on the right arm, assuming it was her strong one. He grabbed under her shoulder and wrenched it back, but it did little good. She held firm, face down on the ground, scrambling for either the knife or the gas canister. Maybe both.

My God, she is strong.

Elizabeth grunted as Tommy slid his right arm back under her, this time trying to lock the crook of his elbow beneath her throat. She pressed her head down, digging her chin into his arm, but he managed to secure a hold. He pulled back as hard as he could, using his left hand to help. She reared up backwards, and once she did Tommy locked his arm around her neck even tighter.

She began to choke as her hands frantically searched the ground for something to use against him.

'You . . . don't do . . . this, Tommy.'

He squeezed tighter, knowing he would kill her. It was no longer a question of whether he could do it. He *had* to do it. It was either her or him, and he wasn't going to let his kids grow up without him. He wasn't going to make Becky a widow. It couldn't happen.

In an instant her right hand found the knife. Tommy saw her fingers grab around the handle like a snake squeezing a mouse. She was still facing the ground with Tommy behind her, so she didn't have an easy arc to swing the blade at him. He could release his grip and go for her hand, but that might free her up enough to stab him with more force. And he knew Elizabeth could use a knife.

No, he thought. *Keep choking her.*

He pulled harder and tried to twist her neck at the same time, and the gurgled sounds coming from her throat told him he was slowly succeeding in killing her. Tommy looked down again at her hand and it seemed as if her grip on the knife was loosening.

He was wrong.

She swung her right arm in a backwards arc, using a flexibility Tommy imagined only yoga instructors capable of. In that instant, Tommy knew he had miscalculated. His mind processed the sight of the silver blade racing toward his body. He was calm about it. *I'm about to be stabbed*, he thought. *I can try moving, but I'm too close and there's not enough time. The best I can hope for is a flesh wound. Just try not to let go. Finish the job.*

He shifted his torso the best he could and he managed to move a couple of inches before the knife entered him.

It pierced though his pants and entered his right thigh. She didn't have enough momentum to bury the blade fully into his flesh, but at least two inches of the knife disappeared beneath his skin.

Tommy howled. In his endless research for his novels he had always read that, in a fight, adrenaline significantly dulled the pain of any wounds, at least temporarily. *Bullshit.* Pain seared though his body and he could not hold on to her.

He let go.

Elizabeth twisted beneath him, pulling the knife out of his leg. Pain shot through him as she pushed him off. He lost his balance and fell hard on his back. Elizabeth scrambled to be on top of him, where she could deliver a lethal blow.

Tommy saw the trees above him. He saw the spiny hands of the barren top branches in such detail he wondered if he could reach up and touch them, though they were fifty feet above his head.

Those trees are the last thing I'm going to see.

Elizabeth came into view. She now straddled him, just as she had straddled her father. Just as she had straddled Rade.

Her throat was red and swollen, but she paid it no attention. Both hands were now wrapped around the blade of the knife, which she raised high above her head.

Her blue-jean eyes were wide, and there wasn't a trace of rage in them. There was only excitement. The excitement of a kill. A special kill.

'This doesn't make you win,' Tommy said. It was all he could think of to say. Appeal to her ego. Tell her what she won't get if she kills him.

'Tommy,' she rasped. She cracked a crooked grin, the smile of a young girl, a girl with perfect skin and long red hair that spilled down her back like water. 'I *always* win.'

She stretched the knife higher until it seemed lost in the spiny branches of the distant tree limbs.

In the final seconds, Tommy noticed the tree-filtered sunlight making its way to his face.

He could almost feel its warmth.

Almost.

FIFTY-SIX

He reached his hands out. His only hope was to throw her off balance as she brought the knife down. The blade would surely slice easily through his hands, but maybe he could keep from going into shock long enough to overpower her.

He no longer felt the wound in his leg. Guess that bit about the adrenaline was true, after all.

Tommy brought his left hand up to stop the knife as he swiped his right hand along the ground. His fingers ran along the small towel before touching something else. Cool and smooth. Metal.

The small canister. The one with the hydrogen cyanide.

Elizabeth brought the knife down.

His left forearm partially blocked her strike, and instead of the top of the blade puncturing his chest it buried itself in his left shoulder. Tommy screamed in agony as she twisted the blade, an effort not simply to cause more damage but also to extract it for another blow. A fatal blow.

He grabbed the canister and turned it in his hand. It was small, no larger than a travel-size shampoo bottle, the top of it containing an aerosol-style spray head.

There were so many things wrong with his only chance of survival. First, the canister could be empty for all he knew, or contain nothing more than water. And if it did contain some kind of lethal gas, Tommy was just as exposed as Elizabeth was. He would be spraying it up at her, and gravity could simply bring it back down on his face. Finally, Tommy couldn't see which direction the spray nozzle was pointed. He could press down on it and the gas could shoot out to the side or right back on his own face.

But it no longer mattered. He didn't have a choice. He had to try something, or his two stab wounds would be accompanied by countless more.

Elizabeth finally pulled the knife out of his shoulder and Tommy's stomach lurched with nausea from the pain. She held it up, dagger style, both hands around the handle. Tommy tried to raise his left arm for another block but his shoulder was too damaged, the muscle torn.

Then he raised his right hand.

Elizabeth saw the metal canister as she brought the knife down.

Tommy yelled as he pressed down on the nozzle.

FIFTY-SEVEN

At first he didn't know what had happened. In fact, he thought nothing at all had happened. He thought he felt the nozzle of the canister press down, but maybe that was just his imagination. He heard nothing. He saw nothing except for Elizabeth bearing down on him. As Tommy sprayed he rolled as hard as he could to his left, over his damaged shoulder.

Elizabeth thrashed as Tommy felt her weight shift. She collapsed on the ground, the knife burying into the dirt just inches from Tommy's torso.

As he pushed her off him, Tommy realized he was no longer holding the canister. He looked at the ground and didn't see it, and then guessed it was underneath her.

Then the screaming began.

FIFTY-EIGHT

It lasted only seconds.

Then the screams were consumed by a series of frantic gasps, of futile breaths. Elizabeth twisted on the ground and flipped on her back, her mouth widening to suck in oxygen to no avail.

Tommy rolled away and then looked over at her in horror. Elizabeth tried to stand, as if by doing so maybe she could breathe, but her body spasmed and she collapsed to the ground, inches from the body of her dead father.

The seizures began seconds later.

The woman whose physical movements had always been so planned and graceful, sexual even, now shook as if in the jaws of an invisible monster. Tommy heard her voice try to escape through the convulsions but all that came out was a series of horrible stutters, violent death rattles.

Tommy, on his back, blood seeping from his shoulder and thigh, watched her die, wanting to do something to help her, wanting to run away, and wanting to do nothing at all. It seemed to take an hour, though probably less than three minutes passed until the shaking stopped, her body stilled, and Elizabeth's head lolled to the left, staring with blood-filled eyes into the distance, staring in the same direction her father stared, and together they looked at something that was no longer there.

They stared vacantly into the woods where ageless children slept beneath chilling layers of dirt and time.

FIFTY-NINE

Tommy stood. At first it was a struggle, the muscle surrounding the wound in his thigh threatening to collapse. But he fought through the pain and stood, because he knew if he couldn't stand he couldn't walk, and if he couldn't walk then he would likely bleed to death and join the two other corpses on the dusty and dead floor of the woods.

There was so much to process, but he knew well enough to let his survival instincts take over.

The thigh wound was the most concerning. He forced himself to pull apart the torn fabric of his pants and check the gash. It was deep, the pain excruciating, but the blood flow from it didn't seem severe. *Must have missed the femoral artery*, he thought. *Lucky.* He hobbled over to Stykes's body, reached down, and slowly unwrapped the jump rope from around his neck. The body wheezed its last stored bit of oxygen the moment the rope came free, and Tommy, even knowing it was a corpse, nearly fell over as he jumped away from the dead man.

Tommy looped the rope twice around his upper thigh and knotted it tight, slowing the blood flow to the open wound. The harder he pulled on the rope the more his shoulder blazed in fiery pain, and he next turned his attention to that wound.

Slowly and with delicate motion, he unbuttoned his shirt and pulled the fabric down, exposing his bare shoulder. Blood oozed from the wound and covered his chest and stomach.

A chill washed over him and wouldn't leave.

Tommy worried about passing out from blood loss, and was tempted to cut some fabric off with the knife and stuff it in the hole in his skin, but he decided against it. The effort and sight might make him pass out, and then he'd be in serious trouble. Again, he felt sudden iciness and he slipped the blood-wet shirt back over his arm, which brought him no comfort.

He then looked at Elizabeth and thought about the cyanide. She had mentioned an emergency IV kit in her bag.

If I had inhaled enough cyanide to be a problem, I'd already be dead, Tommy thought.

His attention then turned to the shovel leaning against the tree. It was meant for Stykes, but now there were two bodies that needed burying. Afternoon sunlight lit upon the spade, highlighting it against the moth-gray bark of the tree it leaned against. It stood out like some kind of amulet, some representation of hope. A way out.

Tommy limped over to the tree and touched the cool metal handle of the shovel. He wrapped his fingers around it, feeling its energy. He remembered two other times in the woods when he had to dig. The first was when he was fourteen and burying a little boy. The second was just in his recent past, when he went to go find those same bones and instead found only a doll.

Can't dig two holes, he thought. *Not in this condition. My body would give up long before the first hole was even dug.*

He pulled the shovel away from the tree and used it as a crutch, supporting his throbbing leg.

But I could go into town, get medical help, and maybe get back here before anyone finds the bodies. It's a bit of a long shot, but it could work.

He looked down at Elizabeth. A long, slender spider scurried across her cheek and seemed to float along her disheveled hair.

If Tommy buried the bodies and got rid of all evidence, there was a chance of normalcy. He'd have explaining to do for damn sure – the two wounds the most complicated things to create a story for. But he *could* create a story, couldn't he? That was his job, after all. He was Tommy Devereaux, storyteller. Create a story, answer a lot of questions, and then hopefully get on with his life. There was no one left alive who knew the real truth anyway. Just him.

Yet it had stopped being about him. Tommy wasn't sure when that had happened because, as much as he didn't want to admit it to himself, for a long time it had always been about *him*. But not anymore.

There was still a chance at getting his life back. But it wouldn't be through more lies.

Tommy let the shovel fall on the ground, and then he bent over and picked up his manuscript, which was still sitting in the dirt where Elizabeth had dropped it. There was no title for the story yet but Tommy was pretty sure what it would be. It was the subject line from Elizabeth's first e-mail to him:

THE BOY IN THE WOODS

Elizabeth had told him to come with extra blank pages so he could write the proper ending, after it had happened. He'd brought them, but he wouldn't need them. Tommy already had an ending he'd written the day before, and while it didn't include him being wounded, at least in his version he was still triumphant. It was the only part of the story he'd written in anticipation of the events themselves, and overall he'd been mostly right. Right enough in that he was alive and she wasn't.

The book was done.

Tommy clutched the papers in his right hand, his left being too weak to hold anything. Then he began to walk.

SIXTY

The afternoon was drawing old, and the chill on Tommy's skin was slowly being matched by the dropping temperature of the air. Tommy didn't see those deer again as he hobbled out of the woods, but he looked for them. He didn't know why, but he wanted to see them one more time.

Walking the relatively short distance from the woods seemed like hiking the Appalachian Trail with his injuries. The pain had settled into a dull throb and the blood loss had abated enough for him not to think he was going to pass out, but the torn muscle in his leg threatened to hobble him at any moment.

He forged ahead along the same direction from which they'd come – north, if he was correct. North would lead him through the old clearing where he had spent so many days as a teenager. North would take him back toward his old house, the one some stranger had long since bought and would only put up shitty decorations at Halloween.

His instinct served him well, and a lifetime later Tommy limped past the last row of trees and into a clearing, a place where the dirt path ended and a cracked sidewalk began. The sidewalk forked and Tommy turned left, away from his old house and toward a row of six houses that looked pretty much the same now as they had thirty years ago, save a few coats of paint and much taller trees.

He walked up to the third house down, the one that seemed a little more run-down than the others. His leg screamed a few choice words at him during his climb up the four steps of the front porch. But he climbed them, paused a moment at the top, and went up to the front door.

Tommy rang the bell.

There was a funereal silence on that front porch. Not even the wind seemed to care, and Tommy soon thought no one was home. Finally there was a shuffling inside, a slow drag, as if answering the door was going to be the major accomplishment for the day.

The door unlatched. Two locks.

Charles Baristow opened the door. He looked at Tommy, the fading sunlight warming over the old man's milky cataracts.

'Goddamn,' Charles said, looking over the man on the porch. 'Tommy Devereaux. What the hell happened to you?'

Tommy held out his manuscript, which was now streaked with blood and tearing at the edges. A thick rubber band hugged the middle of the pages.

Charles took the manuscript as if he had no choice. He looked at it for a second and then looked back up at Tommy.

There was only one thing for Tommy to say.

'I know what happened to your boy.'

AFTERWORD

*I*t was 1981 and we were twenty minutes away from the rest of
our lives. Time and direction, wrapped around each other and
wielded like a club, smashed all of us that day. Rade Baristow
died before he even knew what it was like to drive a car or kiss a
girl in the back of a movie theater. Jason's life ended a decade later,
a rope around the neck the only thing that let him escape what he
had seen. Mark made it to his forties before that summer afternoon
finally caught up with him. Elizabeth and Alan Stykes died two years
ago today, violently and with great suffering, only a few dozen yards
from where Rade's body would eventually be discovered.

I still wonder why she came back. Why then? If she wasn't really
sick, why at that moment, after thirty years, did Elizabeth decide to
torpedo my world? Maybe it was because she saw my teaser chapter
and felt threatened by possible exposure. That makes the most sense,
though sense had a very loose relationship with Elizabeth Stykes. My
guess? I think she was desperately lonely and insecure. I think she
read my chapter and liked the attention and wanted more. Moreover,
I think she hoped I had turned out like her. She wanted a partner,
someone to share a very singular existence with. Mark was too
conflicted with his religion and career ever to be a true partner for
her. She had told me that night in the alley that she had come back
not for her, but for me. She wanted to teach me 'the game'. I think
she wanted me to kill, with the hope I would feed on it as she did. I
was her next hope. But even though I have killed, I'm nothing like
her.

So here I am. The only remaining witness to what happened that
day in the woods, and I can't say for sure there haven't been moments
in the last two years where I envied those already dead. You can
call that self-pitying if you want and you'd be right, but that doesn't
make it less true.

There's nothing so powerful as the urge to forget, except maybe
the force that makes us remember.

Charles Baristow took one look at me that day on his porch and *called nine-one-one. It wasn't lost on me Alan Stykes himself would normally have been one of the responders, but he was too busy being dead. Paramedics came and did something with me, but I don't much remember. All I do remember is waking up in a Portland hospital and still breathing. In my life I had never appreciated that simple act as much as in that moment.*

If you're reading this book, you probably already know the rest of the story. Pretty much hard not to; press has been up my ass and through my mouth for two straight years. You probably know about my wounds, my permanent limp. You know about the attention I got in the hospital, and then my arrest, which just about broke my children's hearts. You might have been one of the five million people who watched my two-hour interview with Piers Morgan, where I told the story as best I could, even though my lawyer advised against it. Fuck it. I was tired of lying; besides, I'd written it all down anyway. What would happen, would happen.

You have likely read Mark's suicide note, which his wife finally released to the press. He called himself tormented, though there was no mention of Elizabeth or anything that actually tormented him. But I know the truth. Mark was tormented because he was more like Elizabeth than he was like the person he presented to the world. He had the darkness, Elizabeth said. I think that's just about the perfect way to put it. Did he really have an affair with her? I don't know for sure, but I do believe Elizabeth was right when she said she was for Mark both god and demon. I believed he killed himself because he didn't know how to live with both of those things inside him. Mark was the one who decided to crash his car that night, but in the end it was Elizabeth who killed him.

You probably saw the breaking news the day Rade's body was finally discovered. You might even have watched as each additional body was eventually unearthed, although it seemed that by the time the final body was pulled from the earth the media slacked a little in its coverage, kind of like the third moon landing. No one even seemed to care about all the other unsolved killings in Oregon, all the missing boys from the towns where Stykes and his family lived for brief moments before uprooting once again.

Maybe you know about my fund for the victims of childhood abuse. I would urge you to donate at www.forgottenonesfund.com. *Even a little bit helps.*

Did you watch my trial? A lot of people did. What a fucking circus that was. Some people decided to hate me and that was that. Most people didn't. Most supported me, and some of the letters I received touched me more than I could ever describe. Maybe you watched the verdict. Maybe you were happy when the words 'not guilty' stumbled from the foreman's mouth. Maybe not.

This book was more than a little past its original deadline. Two years and some change. But I've been a bit preoccupied, not to mention I didn't know if my publishers were going to jettison me like some kind of cruise-ship waste. They didn't. (Thank you for that, by the way.) Two years late but hopefully worth it, though that's for you to decide.

My kids are my soul and continue to grow with me, even as they've been put through more than any child should have to bear. All my worst fears about what they would be exposed to have pretty much come true. They've endured hateful things said by kids in their school. Sometimes even by those kids' parents. One teacher told Evie her daddy deserved to go to prison. One of the few happy moments over the past two years was when I got that teacher fired.

But, thankfully, my kids are in my life, and I share their time with Becky. Fifty–fifty, as they say. Funny: I always think of fifty–fifty as being a term about survival chances. I guess in some ways the term applies here. I need my family to survive. Right now I'm at fifty–fifty. A year ago, I'd have put my odds at thirty–seventy against. So I'm chipping away, day after day, just trying to increase those percentages. Just trying to survive.

I don't live with Becky, as you've probably gathered. We're not divorced, but we're separated, which is just divorce with a thin glaze of hope spread on top. I had left my completed manuscript along with my letter for her before I set off that day for Oregon, so even if this hadn't come out she would eventually have read that the one-night-stand-with-a-stranger I had confessed to her was actually an affair with Sofia. Now she (and anyone who bought this book) knows everything, the manuscript laying bare my life for all to see, the tidbits of good and the mounds of the bad. I do think Becky believes me when I tell her nothing has happened between Sofia and me in the years since our affair, but that doesn't make it any easier for my wife. It just keeps it from being more awful, which is little consolation to someone already hurt.

Sofia and I agreed to part our ways professionally. She moved to New York and is dating a chef, which is perfect since she can't cook for shit. I don't hear from her much, but when I do, she seems happy. Her first novel is coming out next year, and I couldn't be more proud and excited for her. She's a fine, fine writer and I encourage everyone to pick up her book when it comes out. I don't know the finalized name of the book yet, but the working title was The Last Time I Saw You. *It'll rip your heart out.*

I see Becky as often as I can, which isn't enough but probably more than I deserve. I can't say she's forgiven me, but she hasn't cut me from her life, and that alone shows the depth of her character. There was a fundamental shift in our relationship, and she doesn't quite know how to get her footing back, at least not enough to make her want to keep standing next to me for the moment. Losing her, even if not yet entirely, is like waking up every day and forgetting who I am. She is how I define myself, and without her there's just empty space and an unwrinkled side of the bed.

We have a date tonight. Our first one since she even agreed to begin speaking to me again, in fact. I decided to finish this book today because of this. I like the idea of today being the last chapter of one thing and the beginning of another.

I'm taking her to Beatrice & Woodsley, a little restaurant here in Denver. It's modern enough to be hip but cozy enough to be romantic. Funny how I'm over-thinking every detail about tonight, just like I did when I was a much younger man. If all goes well, she'll say yes to another date, and perhaps one after that. I don't have any illusions about our future, but I'm not giving up on it either. All I can do is try, because I need her, simple as that.

Baby steps. Survival skills.

Maybe after tonight, we'll be at fifty-one–forty-nine in favor.

Tommy Devereaux
Denver, Colorado

Acknowledgements

First off, this book would never have sold without the tireless efforts and critical feedback of my wonderful agent, Pam Ahearn. Pam, I owe you a margarita. Or two. And thanks to Edwin Buckhalter, Kate Lyall Grant, Joe Pittman, Anna Telfer and all the other fine folks at Severn House for taking this book on and making it better.

All authors need a critique group to keep them honest, and the people in mine have done more to sharpen my writing than anyone else. Ed Bryant, Sean Eads, Dirk and Linda Anderson: *salut.*

Ili and Sawyer, to whom this book is dedicated: I keep promising someday I will write something *age-appropriate* for you, but by the time I get around to it you'll be old enough to read my scary stuff. At least I keep my nighttime stories tame.

To Jessica, thank you for your love and support, as always. You're always the first one to read the finished product. I like that.

Mom, thanks for reading this and not thinking something went terribly awry with my upbringing. Sole, thanks for being a great parent and wonderful friend. We've done a good job.

Dad, I miss you. More than anyone, you taught me how to appreciate a good story. *Just listen.*